A Town In A Home

by
Terry deFranco Martino

Pittsburgh, PA

ISBN 1-56315-192-8

Paperback Fiction
© Copyright 1999 Terry deFranco Martino
All rights reserved
First Printing—1999
Library of Congress #98-60366

Request for information should be addressed to:

SterlingHouse Publisher, Inc.
The Sterling Building
440 Friday Road
Department T-101
Pittsburgh, PA 15209

Cover design & typesetting: Drawing Board Studios

This is a work of fiction. Names, characters, places, and incidents either are the
product of the author's imagination or are used fictitiously. Any resemblance
to actual events or persons, living or dead is entirely coincidental.

Printed in Canada

Chapter 1

Early in the day, as the mid-morning sun rose high above towering evergreens, Paul drove into town and was greeted by a wooden sign: *WELCOME FROM 62 OF THE FRIENDLIEST PEOPLE IN THE ADIRONDACKS PLUS A COUPLE OF SOREHEADS*. The road's long stretch of flatness bordered surrounding mountains. Paul laughed and drove slowly away from the wooden directive: *Hold All Objects, Gravity Free Zone*. Past a curve marked with yellow arrows, a cluster of buildings came into view.

He parked in front of the *STORE GENERAL* and walked toward *THE INTERNATIONAL AIRPORT* sign that was stuck in a stretch of spring grass. The little wings of a wooden plane turned round and round in the wind. The *GROUP TOURS AVAILABLE* plaque beckoned him to stand on a four-foot cement strip and view the surrounding vista. What a funny place, Paul thought. There were three small cabins behind the airstrip. To the right of the store, a dirt road led into the woods.

Not much commerce going on here, Paul realized and looked at the store's entrance. The building was about sixty-feet in length with wooden shingles for siding.

A *UNITED STATES POST OFFICE* seal was situated in the window. The postal office had a separate doorway.

Inside the store he saw a range of items on sale: bread, Coleman fuel, wicks, candles, and a variety of American beer. A metal rack showcased a wide assortment of postcards. He quickly examined a card with a large bear that said "miss you beary much." The windows and pine walls were covered with posters of bikinied women advertising a variety of cigarettes. *HOW KOOL DO YOU LIKE IT?* One poster questioned.

In a darkened corner, surrounded by wooden crates and beat-up chairs, a white-haired man sat carving a loon. The man looked up, said hello, and came to the counter. He wore leather trapping boots, partially laced, a denim shirt, and blue jeans.

"Is there anything I can help you with?" he asked. His calloused hands drummed the edge of the countertop.

"Uh," Paul hesitated, "I'd just like a loaf of bread. Italian would be great," he said, suddenly feeling out of place and hot in his starched shirt and khaki pants.

"None of that type bread here," the man said. "We can't cater to specialty brands here."

Paul felt taken back, but saw that the man was grinning. He noticed a sign on the wall: *JUST KIDDING*, and tried to relax. "What kind of bread do you carry?" he muttered.

"Good old Wonder bread: America's finest," the man said, and pointed to a shelf. He reached out and tugged at a loaf.

"That'll do," Paul said. He decided not to risk asking if the store carried his favorite dijon mustard.

"That'll be a dollar fifty," the man said, handing over the bread.

From a wire cage in the corner a large parrot cackled. "Customer need money. Man need money," the bird squawked. Paul felt unsettled with the bird's comments. "Customer need money, money," the bird repeated. Paul stared at the cage and saw a *BIRDBRAIN FOR LIFE* sign stuck in the cage. He sensed the man peering curiously at him. Looking closer at the bird, he realized that it was artificial, with opaque white beads for eyes, and an assortment of feathers stuck randomly together over a furry body.

"You have a fake bird that talks?" he asked.

"Yup," the storekeeper said, laughing with pride. "Otto keeps everyone honest."

"Oh," Paul said, and handed over a five dollar bill. He didn't bother to try to find out how the bird's voice worked.

"Here's your change," the man said. The drawer of the ornate cash register clanged shut. "You just visiting?"

"For awhile," Paul said, twitching his lower lip. "I'm renting the Carlye camp."

"You up for school?"

"This fall I'm taking some college courses in environmental studies. I'm Paul, Paul Wilson." He extended his hand and noticed the man eyed him strangely. He wondered if his habit of moving his tongue over his bottom teeth appeared like making faces, or worse, throwing kisses.

"Bert Gendron." Bert extended a rough hand. "Nice to meet you. The Carlyle camp, huh? You family or friend?"

"My father works with Mr. Carlye at a bank in Amsterdam. That's where I'm from." Paul's voice was suddenly raspy and his throat felt tight. "My younger twin brothers and sister grew up playing with the Carlye kids." He sneezed.

"Bless you once. Then Carlye told you about our northern spot?" Bert questioned.

"Somewhat," Paul said, sniffling. He was unwilling to say the family never mentioned the signs, or the bird. "Only thing they said is it gets like forty-below zero in the winter."

"No, is that so!" Bert exclaimed. "They told you that? What they'd try to do, make you scared or something?"

"Uh, I was hoping they meant only a few days here and there," Paul said timidly. "All of this is pretty new to me." He nervously tugged at his hair and was surprised to look down and see a number of blond strands. He quickly shoved his hands into his pockets and hoped that Bert hadn't noticed him absentmindedly pulling his hair out. What with the mouth twitching and hair pulling, Paul wondered what Bert could possibly think of him.

"New is good for you," Bert said happily. "You'll get by."

"I hope so." Paul was pleased with Bert's confidence in him.

"If you need tools or materials or something, you let me know."

"Great," Paul said, thrilled with Bert's generosity. He sneezed again.

"You got a cold?"

"I don't know," Paul said, wondering if the excitement of the move affected him physically.

"Maybe it's the dust or you're allergic to Otto," Bert said and laughed heartedly. "Well, I'm glad you have a place. You'll like it here," he said, and pounded the countertop for emphasis. "We folks are pretty friendly. Even our soreheads are harmless, and that bird is mostly quiet. Just shout if you need anything, and be sure to let me know if you need a postal box."

"You own the store and run the post office too, huh?" Paul said, trying to figure out how to keep the conversation going. He reached into a pocket for a handkerchief.

"The store's mine, but I'm retiring from the post office. We're getting us a new postmaster." Bert smiled proudly. "A real government man is due any day now."

"I've never seen a place where the office is part of a store." Paul wiped his nose.

"Well, that's the way we do things here. At least up to now." Bert tapped a pen against the counter.

A real northern entrepreneur, Paul thought, and eyed the tall man, who appeared to be in his sixties. The drumming of the pen made him nervous, and he felt unsettled and somewhat dazed with the onset of the sniffling.

"Sure is pretty up here," Paul said. He poked at the plastic bread bag.

"Yeah, folks always come wanting to get away from who knows what. You know—New York City, Jersey. It's funny but you know what the young ones do, first chance they get? Go swimming naked in the pond down the road. It's some damn baptismal; always the same," Bert muttered and wiped the counter top.

"Is there much water around here?" Paul asked.

"The land of many waters; you name it and we got it." Bert smiled smugly. "Remind me in the future to show you some of my maps I got at the house."

"I will," Paul said, and sneezed. "I'll be around once I'm settled. Thanks again." Paul walked outside. The screen door slammed behind him.

Paul hesitated on the porch and felt his head clear. His bottom lip twitched as he thought about being a newcomer in a small town. How long would it take to get to know everybody? Who were the soreheads?

He was really happy that Bert was so friendly, and was pleased the town looked so different from home three hours south. Memories of suburban traffic and shopping malls receded quickly. Except for the intermittent sound of the bird squawking, "Customer is nice; customer is pretty," Paul was thrilled with the surrounding silence and woodsy smell which permeated the air. He looked at the cluster of buildings and felt giddy.

Both exhilarated and fearful, he remembered a family trip out west at thirteen when high atop a mountain with his father he began to cry at the edge of a glacier field. He had feared the treeless, rocky peaks and the stark sky. His father was angry when Paul screamed to leave the mountain. It was one of many disappointments he gave his father through his junior and high-school years.

After high-school, rather than attending a prestigious college like his folks wanted, he worked temporary jobs driving cab and doing cashier work. A stint at welding school was followed by classes at a local community college. Within a year a college transfer northward was a ticket away from family, especially when his dad was thrilled to fully finance the costs.

Now at twenty-three Paul knew the drastic change in scenery was perfect. He couldn't define success or failure, but was driven to find an answer about what to do with his adult life.

His move northward was a calculated risk to a place where even the name sounded different. "Adirondack," the word rolled over his tongue. "Adirondack," he repeated, and remembered the way his girlfriend, Francine, pronounced it—"A-ron-diacks."

A swarm of bugs surrounded him and Paul thought about how much he liked Francine. Her long dark hair, great smile, and toned body had been real turn ons. Somehow she gave him a passion that he so often felt lacking. He wondered if they had a future together.

Paul walked to his glossy truck and checked his directions: left from the front of the store, down road 50 feet, head along black dirt road 100 feet and up hill to wood frame camp. A wide driveway led toward the building Carlyle said had been built twenty years previous as a summer camp. Paul stopped the truck and wondered—what kind of a residence would it be for fifteen bucks a month?

Paul stood outside his vehicle and was immediately surrounded by swarms of blackflies and mosquitoes. A strange odor mixed with the scent of pine and wood smoke. He wondered what it was and felt exhilarated with finally viewing the new home.

He crunched through leaves and headed up a driveway toward the rustic cabin. He passed a screen frame which lay on the nearby grass. At the porch entrance, Paul nudged the door open, stepped into the kitchen, and looked around. The floor was covered with leaves, twigs, and moss, and Paul felt confused by the disarray. He sneezed and dropped a leather backpack on a chair. There was a noise in the other room. He listened.

Cautiously, he walked into the living room which was in shambles. Two tall brass reading lamps lay disconnected on the floor. Pieces of ripped books and magazines fluttered under his footsteps. Paul heard a loud scratching noise, looked out a dirty window, and saw nothing but towering pine trees.

Paul followed a trail of debris to the bedroom doorway and saw a torn rug piled in a heap with tree limbs. A closet door hung crooked on lopsided hinges. A large jagged hole gaped through a corner wall.

He heard a loud noise, turned around, and saw a large black bear crash through the living room. "Holy shit!" Paul yelled, overwhelmed by the musty odor of the animal. Then he saw a cub peering out of the bedroom closet, and realized the extent of his trouble.

Adrenalin exploded in his cells and he scrambled to one side of the room. The bear rushed and swiped at him. He felt the claws cut into his leg and immediately saw the gush of blood. Struggling toward the kitchen, he escaped out the door and ran down the driveway, heading to the center of town.

"Bert! Bert! Help!" he yelled the name of the only person he knew in town.

He ran fast, tripping over branches. The cabin driveway that had been so inviting now felt like a warzone. Trees pressed in while rocks and puddles made every step impossible. He glanced down and was amazed at the amount of blood that had gushed onto his khakis. His heart pounded and his lungs felt empty of air as the bear raced behind him. Paul prayed: Oh Mary, please help me now? All those Sundays of church, my dues are paid up. Help! He heard the bear growling and lumbering behind him and feared being clawed again. The ground shook from the weight of the running animal.

And what could Bert Gendron now think? Here he was—an urban newcomer being chased by a bear. Holy Mother, Paul thought. He needed help!

Paul stumbled to the ground and heard a loud gunshot; a bullet flew overhead. With a mouthful of sand, he pushed his shoulders up and saw Bert Gendron towering above him with a big grin. In the distance Otto cackled, "Customer is nice; customer is pretty."

Chapter 2

⊱─⊰─◦─⊱─⊰

"Do I dare look?" Paul spoke from where he lay sprawled on the ground. He could feel his clothes and hair were covered with a mixture of mud, twigs and blood.

"Yeah! You're safe now!" Bert exclaimed. "It don't take long for our local habitants to make the newcomers welcome." He chuckled. "Man, you must've upset that bear."

"Upset that bear?" Paul groaned. "What did that bear do to me? Almost killed me, and I was only going to the camp where I'm supposed to live."

"Must be the bear thought the camp was home to her cub. Explains why people have said they've seen sightings." Bert hummed as he reached for Paul. "You look like you're in need of medical attention."

Paul grabbed Bert's outstretched hand and stood.

"Now what do you reckon we do?" Bert asked. "I'll help with anything. Do you want to go to the hospital twenty miles away? Or I can take you to my doctor friend up the road."

Paul pondered his options as Bert helped him toward a park bench situated in front of the store.

"Here, sit down," Bert instructed. "You need a bandage before we go."

Bert left him a moment and returned with a clean apron. "You know, last time I took my wife, Carol, to the hospital it cost close to three hundred bucks for emergency work, and they only did some x-rays and told her to rest." Bert spoke rapidly as his large hands positioned the apron around the cuts. "Here, let me help you toward my truck."

"What about that doctor; is he good?" Paul stammered as Bert helped him into the front seat.

"Good! He's the best," Bert said cheerfully. "Why, I take, Porko, the pig to him for a workup. Jackie, my old beagle, too. And years ago he even saw my daughter, Isabelle, when she was little. He's the best!" Bert winked at Paul and backed the truck onto the road.

Paul remained slumped in the corner. Blood from the large gashes in his left thigh bled onto the apron in streaks.

"Yup! You'll like old Doc Waller, and save money to boot." Bert whistled loudly and gestured toward a pine split in two down the middle. "Why look at that tree!"

Paul moved his head and saw nothing but a green haze around the few white birches next to the road. He felt each bump in the road as the truck sped along.

"Must've been lightning," Bert pondered. "The tree never looked like that before. It had to be wet too, for nothing else to burn, cause that's how fires start here—electricity."

Paul's body jerked to the side as the truck turned into a dirt road.

"Hey, hang in there kid, we're almost there."

Paul felt spasms of pain in his leg as the truck stopped suddenly in front of a rectangular building with a circular tower. Where did he wind up? Paul wondered as Bert waved to an old man in blue coveralls. The man stood in a stooped position near a large pile of stones

"Hey, Doc Waller, what's up? Why are there rocks in your front lawn?" Bert yelled. "Can you steal some time? I got a patient for you."

The doctor put down the shovel, walked toward the truck, and peered in the window "Whoa! What do we have here?" He opened the cab door and moved quickly to keep Paul from falling.

"How you doing?" Paul muttered.

"Can you believe it?" Bert exclaimed and rushed to the passenger side. "This young man arrives into town, buys a loaf of bread from me, and introduces himself. Says he's going to rent the Carlye camp and take some courses. Next thing I know, he's running down the road, screaming my name. And there's a larger than life bear in pursuit."

"Come on, Bert!" the doctor exclaimed. "Quit talking for a change and help me get this kid inside. He's weakening and he's going to need a tetanus shot. What's his name, anyway?"

"Paul," Bert said, moving to help the doctor. "As I was saying, I just grabbed my trusty rifle and aimed between the eyes. I thought of trying to wrestle that bear, but decided I'm getting too old for wrestling. I knew I needed to shoot, and that gun went off just as Paul fell flat on his face. He's one lucky dude. That bear ran off, but I think I got her."

Paul winced. His leg was on fire. The pain burnt through his thigh muscle and traveled the length of his left side. How long were these guys going to keep talking? He sneezed and tried desperately to keep from crying.

"Move it, Bert," the doctor said. "You know I've been listening to your stories for years; a bear chasing this kid? You wrestling it?" The doctor's lined, tanned face expressed disbelief. "I don't believe you," he said emphatically. "Your story's really far out."

"No more far out than when the radio announced my pigs were loose in town and visitors who saw them thought they were wild pigs from down south." Bert spoke quickly. "Doc, you remember the line up of cars in town with windows rolled up? The kids screaming and those pigs running around having the time of their life. Why Doc, you even helped me catch them."

Paul couldn't believe they were talking about pigs. He felt dizzy and too overwhelmed to ask for help. Maybe he'd made the wrong choice of a doctor.

The doctor wheezed. "Look, Bert, you need to pay attention to getting this kid inside." The old man reached into an overall pocket, pulled a bandanna out, and wiped his nose. "Paul's going into shock. You said a cub was involved?"

"That's for certain."

"Why did you kill the mother then?" The doctor rasped.

"Cause that's what we had to do to get him out free." Bert gestured and reached for Paul. "Anyway, that bear ran off. Dead or not, she's no threat."

"What did ya say his name is, again?"

"Paul. Paul Wilson. I'll wager he had something of a new vision after arriving in town."

Paul felt Bert grab under his arm as the fire in his leg exploded in bursts of pain.

Chapter 3

"I'm home." Paul groaned. "Leave me alone." He heard a strange voice. Where was he? he thought, confused and panicked.

"What's that you said?"

The pinchfaced doctor stood above him and steadfastly threaded a needle. It took a minute for Paul to remember the bear.

"You sure got some nasty claw marks." The doctor motioned. "Needs stiches too." Doc Waller bent over and with trembling hands began to slowly hook Paul's flesh together. "Had to use almost a quart of Betadine to clean everything out," he mumbled. "When you blacked out outside and fell sand got in everything." He looked up. "When was the last time you had a tetanus shot?"

"About thirteen years ago." Paul lifted his head off the table and saw long strips of blood across his leg.

"You can't leave without a shot then. These types of wounds can be pretty nasty." The doctor knotted the black thread and snipped the end with surgical scissors. "I'm finished here. Bert come back here now. You keep an eye on him," the doctor said and shuffled from the room.

"Pretty nice introduction to our sleepy little hamlet." Bert gestured toward Paul's blood stained underwear. "Looks like you almost lost your family's crown jewels. Good thing you didn't. We don't need any unicorns in town." Bert doubled over with laughter.

"Come on." Paul grimaced. "Please don't make me laugh. Where'd Doc go anyway?"

"To get one of his potions for tetanus. He'll be back soon enough."

"I should thank you for saving me." Paul spoke slowly.

"Aw, that's not necessary. I'm just glad I didn't need to personally wrestle that bear to the ground." Bert grinned happily. "Proves my aim, hands and eyes are still good. Glad I could be of help."

"It took a while, but I think I finally got it." Doc Waller entered the room. "You ready for this one?" He waved a needle through the air.

Ready? That thing looked like a garden tool, Paul thought.

"Let's move those bloodied shorts over a bit and turn you round. Bert, give me a hand."

Paul looked at the doctor and groaned. "That's a needle?"

"Why, you're familiar with the tools of the trade?" The doctor smiled and showed small, coffee-stained teeth.

"Don't you have those disposables?" Paul asked, looking back over his shoulder.

"No. I have a sterilization unit. I live in the country, and I don't want to deal with questions about disposal. No sirree. Now hush." The doctor plunged the needle quickly into Paul's backside.

"Ouch!" Paul yelped. The needle felt like a drill boring through his skin.

"Well, we're finished up now." The doctor dabbed at Paul with an alcohol swab. "Let me just end with a bandage. By the way," the doctor continued, "you can go or stay, but not for the night. I'm using my observatory tonight to look at the constellations, and hopefully the northern lights." The doctor wheezed. "As I was saying, I need to see you again in a week or so to take the stiches out. Whatever you do don't strain yourself and have lots of rest. You can keep an eye on him, eh Bert?"

"That's certain."

"By the way, Paul, you owe me ten bucks."

"He'll mail it, Doc," Bert said.

Paul was grateful when they helped him back to the truck. As they pulled out, the doctor went back to his stone pile.

"See you soon." Bert waved, backed the truck up, and headed down the road. After turning on the main road, they drove slowly past the split pine.

"We sure were lucky there was no fire," Bert said. "Last time we had a fire acres and acres of woods burned. The fire even jumped the main road. I'll show you the scarred land someday when you're feeling better."

"Sure," Paul said thickly, overcome by the events of the day.

"But for now," Bert continued, "I know what I'm going to do with you. I have a cabin I rent right across from the store. We don't have any renters now. My wife, Carol, will agree that it's a great place for you to recuperate. I'll even bearproof it with bags of mothballs," Bert said with a big grin.

Paul mumbled, "I really appreciate your generosity." He wondered about how hard it would be to go back into the mess of the Carlye's cabin with a stiched up leg. "Sorry to be such a nuisance."

"No problem." Bert smiled. "What are neighbors for? You'll see that we take care of friends and neighbors alike, but all of our friends are not our neighbors, and all the neighbors ain't our friends. I'm certain in time you'll figure it out and find a way to help me out of a jam."

"I hope so."

"Yup," Bert continued, "lots of jams up here. Particularly in winter when there's cold batteries, frozen pipes, and broken furnaces. You know, one of those forty-below days Carlye warned you about in our winter that lasts a whole of seven months."

Seven months of winter? Paul questioned what he got himself into.

Bert slowed down in the center of town and parked the pickup in front of the store. "Wait here. I'm just going to run in and get a key.

Pain set in as Paul thought about his hopes: to go to school, to study environmental science, and to settle in a small community. And what happened? Before he knew it, he had a camp invaded by bears, perfect strangers were merciful, and there were fifteen stitches in his leg. He wondered about how to get the prescriptions filled.

"Okay, Paul. We're set. Here let me help you down." Bert opened the truck door. "Can you make it across the road?"

"Sure, if you can just give me a hand though. I'd like to keep the pressure off. It wouldn't be pretty if this thing opened up."

"No problem." Bert extended his hand. "That happened to my beagle once. I got her from a pound two hours from here. Had her spayed and the stitches weren't put in right. Carol was real mad when we visited the local vet cause Doc Waller was out of town. The dog was spilling her guts."

"Great story, Bert," Paul said despairingly.

"Yeah, it cost me over a hundred bucks to get her stitched. The dog then wandered around with a plastic bucket strapped on her collar to keep her from chewing the stitches." Bert continued, "I don't want that to happen to you." Bert nudged Paul's arm. "So don't go chewing on your stitches," he said and laughed. "I do have some crutches at home if you need them," he offered.

"I think you'll like it here, and you'll be in shouting distance of me at the store," Bert said, helping Paul into the cabin. "Bed, kitchenette, and bath. Now give me those prescriptions. I'm sure I can get someone to have them filled for you in town." Bert paused and then questioned, "What about clothes? You got any?"

"There's a suitcase in my truck."

"Well, I'll bring that here. Hopefully you have some shorts or a bathrobe so you can settle down."

"Hey, how can I thank you?" Paul lowered to the bed.

"There'll be plenty time for that. How long you say you're going to be here?"

"My coursework will be finished in one, two semesters at most. I had a lot of transfer work."

"Well, remember that any of the time you would've spent introducing yourself will be speeded up. Why, you'll feel downright local before you can blink the words out in proper sequence. Your introduction to our sleepy hamlet will be a story in itself," Bert said, and exited the cabin.

Restless and in pain, Paul shifted around uncomfortably on the bed. After an hour of troubled sleep, he heard a knock on the door. Bert peeked in and came in carrying a small bag.

"You still with us? I brought you the medicine," he said, and he walked over to the porcelain sink for a glass of water. "Here take this, it'll help."

"Thank you," Paul said.

"I'm going to leave you rest now. Like I said earlier, you just shout. Hopefully it won't be another bear chasing you down."

After Bert left, silence seeped into the room. Paul felt the soothing effects of the medication. He pulled up a blanket and thought about meeting Bert. What a character. And so friendly. He didn't want to think about the bear. The memory of it made his heart race all over again.

He turned on his side and thought about Francine. She had asked him if after school was over he'd look for a job back in Amsterdam. He had avoided answering, but knew she usually called the shots in their relationship. He stared at the cabin wall and thought about marrying Francine and living in the suburbs forever.

He grimaced and thought of those interminably boring magazines Francine read. He remembered seeing her answers, scrolled in nasty prose, to a magazine questionnaire that asked: "Do you understand and care about your man's moods and complexities?" Her response had been quick and angry: "No. He wants to live in a rural area. Talks constantly about nature—what does that mean? Just don't understand!" Even though they had dated for about a year, Paul was increasingly amazed about Francine's need to control. He wondered where she fit in his life. He wondered what she'd think of his claw marks.

Paul drifted off to sleep. He dreamed of walking alone down a long, dark road. Suddenly a large rectangular transformer blocked the path.

"What do you want?" he screamed as a strong electrical current blasted a fire path that reduced his body to a pile of dust. Paul woke up shaking and looked around the room.

"Bert is that you?" he called into the silence.

Chapter 4

▸┼◀▸━○━◂┼◀

Three miles from town, Sarah Moore stood outside in a vegetable garden and absentmindedly braided her long blond hair. A cobalt sky, painted with clouds, touched the edges of a white shingled cabin where she'd lived for the past two years. Dressed in a t-shirt and running shorts, she bent down and carefully examined the rows of corn, beans and swiss chard. Reassured the plants were okay, in spite of the night frost, she walked over to a rounded plot which bordered the vegetable rows. After a lot of hard work the perennial and herb garden had taken on a life of its own. The softness of the green silver mound contrasted with the spring growth of the lupines and rubbery sepums. Sarah dropped to the ground and touched the newly sprouted leaves of a daisy plant.

Back inside the kitchen, Sarah made peppermint tea, cut pieces of apples into a bowl, and covered the fruit with plain yogurt. She returned outside and sat down on a tree stump.

"Here you go, Jupiter," she called to the small one-eyed, three-legged dog. The chestnut colored animal hopped over, stopped in front of Sarah, and balanced on two left legs.

"Good girl!" Sarah said. "Now say asparagus!"

The dog stood upright on hind legs, lifted its single front leg and growled, "gr, gr, gr."

"Good dog, Jupe! What a groundhog! Here you go." Sarah handed the dog a piece of apple.

The dog grabbed the offering, hopped toward the swiss chard, and lay down.

"Better than Totoland, huh?" Sarah asked. The animal reminded her of Dorothy's dog in the Wizard of Oz. And what a strange yellow road she and Jupe had followed! She had moved north five years ago to take college courses, but had soon dropped out. Desperate for a change she had left on a winter day for a western sojourn and landed in San Francisco. After two years of acupuncture training, she framed the certificate, complete with calligraphy ideograms. She had waved goodbye to the Pacific fog, journeyed back over the Rockies and through the flatness of America's heartland. Settled in a cabin three miles down the road from the STORE GENERAL, she combined part-time work at the local veterinarian's office with occasional treatments of people and any possible temporary work that was available.

How many jobs were needed to get through the winter? she wondered. Two months ago she attended an application session for a position listed in the local newspaper. Along with fifteen other candidates, she was chosen to travel around the county as a census data collector for the United States Government. Silly work to help pay for winter wood, she thought.

During the orientation Supervisor Joe provided detailed instructions about how to travel, identify dwellings and create maps on white paper with number two pencils. Sarah had listened to his careful explanations: each employee would be paid ten cents for individual dwellings; twenty five cents per mile, and a small hourly compensation. And she learned a report had to be submitted verbally during every working day at a scheduled hour.

Joe had told her, "Travel down every road, dirt or paved; remember a dwelling is any physical structure where people can live." He had droned on for three hours... "We are not looking for how many people live in any location; we are not checking address data; most of all we are not checking to see if there are any bathrooms or indoor plumbing capacity."

Overall, Sarah was thrilled with the two-month opportunity to be paid to travel back roads. In the bathroom, Sarah washed, dressed quickly, and fluffed her bangs. "Well, Jupe, we better go."

Sarah remembered that during the training, Joe emphasized government employees must travel alone. "But Joe never said anything about you," Sarah said as the dog jumped into the car and hopped on the front passenger seat.

Sarah started the car, drove north toward the Store General, and moved in a northeast direction away from the hamlet. Five miles later she switched on the left turn signal, slowed, and turned on a rutted path. Pine and spruce trees pressed against the car as it bounced over moguls. Fearful of the increasing isolation, she was relieved when the car finally emerged into a small clearing. She saw a building located diagonal from where she parked.

"You stay here, Jupe," she commanded. A flock of squawking chickens rushed at her. The building, which was only about seven-feet wide with two windows, appeared to be the only dwelling. A sink with an attached hose was set in the corner of the porch. A sudden movement distracted her.

"What the hell you doing here?" an overweight man yelled and flailed a gun in the air.

Sarah jumped back and stared at the man, dressed in a dirty tee-shirt with holes. Green khaki pants hung below his large potbelly. "Uh... uh. I'm just seeing if there are any buildings. I need to know for my map."

"What map?"

"Well, I'm... I'm working on precensus data collection," Sarah stammered.

"The government ain't ever taken any interest in me before. Why are they taking it now? Do you think it really matters how many of us live in these woods to determine how we're represented?" he yelled. "Washington, that city is a joke! Are the homeless there being counted? Or do you just need a building to be part of the government's tracking?"

"I'm just following instructions," Sarah said timidly.

"Yeah, me too, when I jumped off that frogging boat in Laos. I've learned to not just follow directions." The man pointed the gun directly at Sarah. "Now get off my property. I own it and you're trespassing."

Sarah scrambled into the car and drove away. She looked at her shaking hands and knew this was one of her biggest fears: a madman alone in the woods.

The remainder of the morning passed quickly. By early afternoon Sarah parked at the *INTERNATIONAL AIRPORT*, noticed someone had changed *INTERNATIONAL IRRATIONAL*, and began to count dwellings in the hamlet. At one point, she walked along a path and felt a chill. A head in a window without a body? There was a feeling of relief when she saw the head was a wig.

With the day's work completed, she walked inside the store. "Hey, Bert, how are you doing?"

"Sarah, haven't seen you in a while. What have you been up to?" Bert looked up from where he stacked cereal boxes on the shelves.

"Working for the government... top secret mission..." Sarah smiled.

"The government?" Bert wiped his large hands on a chef apron as he walked toward the counter.

"Yeah, precensus data—classified information. It's a two-month gig to get some additional money, with the winter coming and all." Sarah hesitated and scanned the counter. "Do you have any more of the red licorice you were selling a few weeks ago?"

"Oh, yeah, I just moved it to that shelf in the back corner," Bert motioned. "What's precensus data?"

"I'm not really sure," Sarah said and paused, "it sounds like something before man."

"Maybe that's it," Bert said laughing.

"Anyway," Sarah continued, "Jupe and me are highly trained agents and we have to go down every road. I get paid for mileage, hourly work, and the number of dwellings I can place on the map. Real scientific."

"Dwellings?"

"Yeah. But people don't have to live there."

"That's different."

"Yeah, addresses are not needed." Sarah shrugged and reached into a glass container for the long pieces of red licorice.

"With the redistricting and all, maybe there's a reason for what you're doing," Bert said. "One never knows though." Bert towered in height above Sarah and took the money she offered.

"Whatever," Sarah said. "There's money to be made and I have the time to do it."

Sarah stood near the circular check-out display and looked around the store. In the background the bird, Otto, squawked, "Customer need money; customer need money." To the right of the counter, there was a sitting area for customers. Shelves of food products lined the side walls. The amount of merchandise amazed her, especially because the store looked empty from the outside.

"Hey," Sarah continued, "I went down a dirt road about five miles from here. Met a guy with a gun outside a house that looked like a rebuilt chicken coop. Who is he?"

"Overweight, dirty clothes and a mean mouth?"

"You got it."

"That's Henry, Henry Ewing. He's lived back there for years. Don't ever see him much here in town, or anywhere else, for that matter," Bert said shaking his head. "Comes in every now and then to buy potatoes, when he can't go strip the fields nearby. That guy lives on potatoes. Even looks like a potato," Bert laughed loudly. "You know what I mean?"

"A potatohead with a gun?" Sarah questioned.

"More than one gun too," Bert continued. "He's fascinated by anything that shoots."

"So he's one of your soreheads?" Sarah asked laughing.

"Well, you know that's always shifting. But I can tell you that he's obsessed with his guns and has a tendency to shoot anything that moves. We tend to stay away," Bert said. "Sometimes, on warm evenings, we hear gunshots coming from his place and know he's out hunting down garden snakes."

"So, I guess I was lucky to get away? Anything else I should know about?"

"Not much. We had a newcomer yesterday. Name of Paul Wilson, who's renting the Carlye's camp. Like you, he came up for college," Bert said, tapping the countertop. "Anyway, as I was saying, he was attacked by a bear in the first half-hour he was here."

"A bear? Here in town?" Sarah asked. She tried hard to hide her disbelief.

"What do you mean here in town? This twist in the road is smack in the middle of the wilds." Bert gestured wildly for emphasis. "Yeah," he chuckled, "a big bear chased that kid down the road. Paul was all bloodied up when I looked through the side window. I saw him run, stumble and scream my name. All done in a flash."

"And you saved the day?" Sarah exclaimed.

"Well, it took me a few minutes to decide between using my gun or wrestling that bear to the ground myself. But I'm getting old, Sarah, if you haven't noticed." Bert looked suggestively at Sarah and patted his white hair. "So I shot that bear. First shot, aimed to the eyes. Paul went down."

"You hit Paul?" Sarah asked.

"Nah," Bert said. "I told you, I aimed for the bear."

"What about Paul?" Sarah asked nervously, fidgeting with the end of her braid.

"Ah, that kid stumbled from exhaustion and fear," Bert said conclusively. "I helped him up and took him to see old Doc Waller."

"So what happened to Paul?" Sarah asked.

"I have him right across the road now, in one of my cabins. Couldn't send him sick back to the Carlye's camp. As a bear lair, I guess it's mighty smelly. I'm fixing to get someone to clean it up."

"Customer is nice; customer is pretty," Otto squawked.

"Did Paul meet the bird?"

"Of course," Bert said proudly. "Otto meets everybody. Paul seemed a little surprised."

"Who wouldn't be?" Sarah asked. "A stuffed parrot that talks in a place that has two soreheads."

"Ah, Sarah, you be careful talking about our supposed enemies. Anyway," Bert said, looking at the Mickey Mouse clock on the wall. "Three o'clock means I should check on Paul."

"That's not the witching hour?" Sarah asked.

"Nah," Bert said, "we're all friendly. You know that more than anyone."

"Do you want me to go over?" Sarah asked, suddenly interested in the man across the road. "You look busy with that cereal," Sarah said and smiled. "I'd be happy to help out."

"That'd be great," Bert said. He walked toward an industrial-size coffeemaker and poured coffee in a styrofoam cup.

"Anyway mission control is over for the day," Sarah said.

"You be careful with that work." Bert passed the cup to Sarah. "Here's two creamers and sugar. He's in the cabin closest to the edge of the airport," Bert said and smiled. "And remember, he hasn't stirred, is on medicine, and is new to all."

Sarah headed toward the door. "Hey, thanks for talking with me. I'll let you know what's up with him."

"That'll be great," Bert said.

Sarah walked across the road. Careful not to spill the coffee, she knocked on the cabin door and waited.

Chapter 5

Sarah waited in silence. After repeated knocks, she entered the cabin and her eyes quickly adjusted to the darkened room. She peered at the form on the bed. She immediately felt sorry for the young man and remembered her own adjustment to the north had been difficult. And still not complete, she thought wryly. The man's hand thrashed across his face. Sarah routinely scanned his hand for a wedding ring and was relieved to see his hand empty of jewelry.

"No, no," he moaned. "Let me be. I'm not going. Not ..."

"Are you okay?" Sarah asked softly. "Paul, I'm Sarah. Sarah Moore," she said, leaning toward the bed. "I told Bert I'd come check on you."

Paul pushed his head up, slowly turned and stared at Sarah. He pushed strands of hair away from his face.

"Paul? Hello again, I'm Sarah. Do you know where you are?" She was surprised at how red his face appeared. "You seem to be feverish," she said, reaching out to touch his forehead.

Paul instinctively lunged at her arm.

Sarah jumped back. "Man, you're real touchy. I don't mean to offend you. Uh, I just have a coffee here. I told Bert I'd see if you're okay."

Paul shook his head, wiped his face and sat up. His eyes were bloodshot and glassy. "Sarah?"

"Remember you came to town yesterday and were attacked by a bear? Bert Gendron helped you out and took you to Doc Wallers for medical treatment. Have you been taking your medicine?" Sarah picked up the vials of medication. "There appears to be a lot of pills gone."

"What?" Paul mumbled. "I took the medicine when I thought it was time," Paul said and looked around. "I'm going to stand up now."

Sarah watched as Paul threw the covers aside and attempted to get off the bed. She saw his bandaged leg. "Are you sure you're okay to stand?" she asked. Paul pulled himself upright, reached toward Sarah, and fell to the floor.

"Oh no! Here let me help you up," Sarah said frantically.

In a crouched position, Paul seemed disoriented. His head moved back and forth. "Why are you here?" he demanded.

"To check on you. You seem, uh, I'm not really sure. I think I'll leave this coffee," Sarah said.

"Leave?" Paul screeched. "Leave me to this? Don't go!" He lunged at Sarah and grabbed her left ankle. Sarah pulled frantically away. Her leg hurt where he had grabbed her.

"I feel sick," he said.

Sarah looked down at his crouched position and watched as he vomited a pool of pink bile at her feet. Ug, Sarah thought, sickened by the smell.

"I'm sorry. Sorry," Paul mumbled and collapsed.

Sarah panicked and reached down to help him. "It's okay. You're definitely sick," she said. "Too much medication."

Paul hung on Sarah as she helped him to the bed. He fell in a heap on the sheets.

"I'm going to get some stuff to clean up in here. I'll be right back," Sarah said, overwhelmed by the encounter.

Sarah rushed out of the cabin and ran toward the store. "Bert! Bert!" she called. "Can you help? Paul vomited and is real disoriented."

"Man! This guy is getting to be a real bird!" Bert exclaimed. He walked toward a shelf and grabbed a can of Lysol and paper towels. He followed Sarah back to the cabin.

"Well, lookee here!" Bert said entering the cabin. "You've been mighty busy keeping yourself active. Phew, let me just clean this yuk up." Bert leaned over and wiped the floor. "Giving Sarah a hard time, too?" Bert questioned.

"Sorry," Paul moaned.

"We'll forgive you." Bert stuffed the dirty towels into a plastic bag. "Now don't worry. You'll be good as new real soon. I'll be back sometime later to check on you."

Paul grimaced and repositioned himself under the sheets. "Thanks again," he said, looking at the ceiling. "I owe you both one."

"We're not counting, but this is certainly one mighty introduction to friendship." Bert laughed and pressed his hands together. "Let's go, Sarah."

Sarah followed Bert. "Do you think he'll make it?" she questioned, stopping in front of her car.

"Yeah," Bert said. "That leg will heal within the week."

"But can he live here after such an introduction.?"

"Why not?" Bert questioned, shrugging as if the attack and illness were all par for the course.

"But remember how that first year I had to leave," Sarah said, twirling her braid. "And since being back it often feels like a struggle just to get by."

"But you're making it," Bert said reassuringly.

"I guess you're right," Sarah said doubtfully, getting into her car. She waved goodbye to Bert and drove home thinking about Paul. Because Paul was such a mess she worried that maybe he couldn't make it. She found herself intrigued by his vulnerability.

Chapter 6

⊢•⊶•◦•⊷•⊣

In a Virginia suburb of the nation's capital, Charlie waited impatiently and peered out a bay window as a moving truck crept down the street. He ran to the front door, opened it, and stumbled down the brick stairs. He jumped in place on the lawn, waving his arms to motion the driver to stop.

"Hey, it's about time you guys showed!" he yelled. "I arranged to have the truck here at nine this morning." Charlie poked his thumbs through the beltloops of his trousers and tried to look menacing.

"Ah, we got tied up and couldn't call," the driver said and jumped out of the truck. "My name's Specko." Charlie immediately noticed the stocky man was dressed in dirty blue jeans and hightop sneakers.

"And this here is Oleo." Specko motioned to his wiry, dark-haired partner. "We're behind schedule on everything today. Yelling don't help."

"Well, you never called or anything!" Charlie paced and tried to understand how he could get the two movers to understand the urgency of his situation. "Look," he spoke suddenly, "I'm Charles DeWitt, but call me Charlie, everyone else does."

"So nice to meet you," Specko said and spit a chunk of tobacco on the lawn. "By the way it's your phone which was off. That's the reason we couldn't call."

"But it's half-past twelve!" Charlie tried one more time to be assertive. "Let's get moving," he said, pushing his glasses up on the bridge of his nose.

"Look, I told you we hadda problem. Whaddaya want done now?" Specko questioned.

"Follow me inside and I'll show you belongings that need to be transported to the storage company at Bay Street. I have the paperwork," Charlie said, "but you'll need to finalize the location of the building when you arrive."

"Hope that don't take a lot of time," Specko said. "Like I said, we're behind schedule, and don't want to be messin' none with no storage people."

"Hey! Pretty schmoozy place you got here," Oleo whistled, entering the condo. "Would you just look at these glossy floors? Specko, I'll bet you could see your ugly mug in them!"

Charlie ignored the movers' reaction to his domicile. "Now most of the boxes are piled here in the living room." Charlie pointed with satisfaction. "Each box has been carefully taped and coded with colored magic markers." Charlie spoke precisely. "Everything that is coded with a red marker goes to storage, but I want you to be careful about the second code. I've made it so that each second code must be piled together in the storage room: green with green; blue with blue; purple with purple. Do you understand?"

"We get it." Specko yawned. "But you better be hopin' there's room for your neat little division. Those storage spaces can be mighty tight. Right Oleo? Why you puttin' this stuff in storage anyway?"

"I'm moving north to some hick town; I've been relocated."

"Relocated?" Oleo asked as he counted the boxes. "Whaddaya mean? Ain't you too old?"

"It means I used to work at the House Post Office and I'm reassigned." Charlie shifted uncomfortably and thought, after all, he was only in his mid-fifties.

"You mean you work at the United States House Post Office used by all of those high flalutens in Congress?" Specko laughed. "You mean the post office on the news caught in launderin' dollars and drug trafficking?"

"You obviously know something more than I do," Charlie said defensively. "And you shouldn't confuse the bank situation with the post office," Charlie said in his best authoritarian tone.

"I don't care what you say," Specko said. "You ain't goin' to be here when any of it happens."

"Come on Specko," Oleo motioned. "It looks like there are seventy odd boxes lined up here. In addition there's a couch, three tables, one television and a rug. Any other furniture or boxes?"

"Yeah, there's some other stuff throughout the rooms," Charlie spoke quickly. "Come on. I'll show you the rest of the place." Charlie walked down the hallway and entered the kitchen.

"Table set and umbrella?" Oleo pointed to the outside deck furniture visible through the sliding door.

"No, they stay."

"Whaddaya want done with the 'frigerator and stove?" Oleo asked.

"They stay along with everything upstairs."

"Seems like we have enough here to keep us busy for awhile," Specko said. "Now, you're sure about nothing being upstairs?"

"Of course I'm sure," Charlie said, suddenly paranoid. "I'm the one in charge of my move. Those cartons upstairs go with me. Is that clear?"

"Sure it's clear." Oleo glanced questioningly at Specko.

As Specko and Oleo walked out of the kitchen, Charlie feared they were suspicious of him. He imagined their interest in the cartons and was certain they would check the boxes in his absence. "Hey, before I go, can you help me pack those boxes that are upstairs in my car?"

"Sounds okay to us. Right Specko? You're the one payin' the bill." The men followed Charlie upstairs.

"Hey, Specko, check out this room." Oleo pointed toward the ceiling. "Skylights and all."

"Come on guys stick to the move."

"Yeah, " Specko said, "but since you're leaving, maybe you can tell us why we have a bunch of those lawmakers using a special bank to bounce checks." Specko looked questioningly at Charlie and pushed greasy black hair away from his eyes.

"I told you, I don't know what you are talking about," Charlie said, feeling red faced and angry. He resisted the urge to tell the mover to not touch his belongings if he was going to keep running his hand through that oily hair. "I'm moving and you men are here to help me with that mission. Now let's move these boxes in my car."

Charlie supervised as Specko and Oleo carried the boxes outside and stacked them in the trunk of the sedan. Charlie was pleased that Specko had finally stopped the tirade about government. "Now is everything clear about my instructions?" Charlie fidgeted with a black flight bag wrapped around his shoulder.

"Piece of cake. Just give me your slip about the storage company," Oleo said. "We'll get everything there for you."

"Okay. Well if there are any problems and if anything is out of line I will be certain to contact the company."

"You do that. Goodbye!" Oleo exclaimed and headed back toward the house.

Boy how rude can you be? Charlie wondered and walked quickly to the Buick parked curbside. He lovingly touched the car's slick white exterior for the thousandth time, opened the door, and slowly sat down on a red bucket seat. The seat pressed to the floor as it absorbed his weight. The car's computer screen showed it was eighty five degrees outside and three o'clock in the afternoon. Just in time to meet some traffic, Charlie thought, and headed toward the stop sign.

Within minutes, Charlie was stuck in the suburban sidestreets that connected to the beltway which led into the city. He hummed and played with the tuner on the radio until an announcer's low voice provided an afternoon update:

"Investigation continues into what has become another large scandal by the United States Congress. Mismanagement of the House Post Office and charges of embezzlement and drug trafficking are currently under investigation by the Capital police. Presently the concern is that the police investigation can be stopped by house counsel for constitutional reasons. Turning to the afternoon weather now," the announcer continued, as Charlie flicked the tuner to a country station.

Damn, Charlie thought, and broke into a sweat as traffic began to move more quickly. Comforted that in a couple of hours he would be headed out of the city for good, he was pleased when he found an *AU-THORIZED PERSONNEL ONLY* parking space close to the capitol building. Charlie parked and locked the car. He lumbered, hot and sweaty, past the manicured grass and containers of petunias.

Always like this—people, people, he chanted. Frustrated by the crowds at the entrance, he moved quickly to a private door. Once inside the building, he walked rapidly over tiled floors and past statues. He scooted heavily through a tunnel passage and came out in front of the post office entrance.

The shine of the counters, slick mahogany covered in marble, always impressed him. He was particularly thrilled with how the office was only open to the congressional representatives and closed to the public. After a fifteen year career path in postal service, Charlie knew he was in the final minutes of his five year career at the Washington office.

"Hey, Booker, you still here?" Charlie called to a colleague.

"Yeah, I'm here." The tall, stringy man scrambled out from behind a number of boxes. "Whatta you up to?"

Charlie looked at Booker's face that was pitted from years of uncontrolled acne. How could Booker still wear that shiny skin ointment? Charlie wondered. With those rotted teeth, gummy smile and straw colored hair, he reminded Charlie of a scarecrow. Charlie always expected to see him pull some hay from his pocket and chew on it. Years back Charlie learned to stop asking Booker about the farm and finally accepted that Booker really was from the Bronx.

"Thought I'd stop by to say goodbye. I'm headed out soon." Charlie tugged a handkerchief from a back pocket and wiped sweat from his face. "The moving men are out at the condo now. Most of my stuff will go into storage."

"You keepin' the important stuff?" Booker asked as his left eye twitched uncontrollably.

"Of course. I'll be in touch once I get settled in that God only knows where northern office." Charlie grunted unhappily.

"Don't complain. At least you've got a job. I don't know what's gonna happen here with the rumblin's of an investigation an' all." Booker sighed. "Day in an' day out. Won't be easy, donja agree?"

"Yeah, I agree, but remember we both don't know anything. Now help me carry these few storage boxes to the car." Charlie spoke precisely, careful not to mimic Booker's abuses of the English language.

With his arms filled with boxes and files, Charlie followed Booker out of the office. "Move directly to my car," Charlie cautioned.

"There it is! Must be!" A woman, dressed in lycra shorts and a cropped shirt, pointed excitedly.

Within seconds Charlie and Booker were surrounded by a crowd of young people. In his confusion, Charlie dropped his boxes all over the floor.

"What are you people doing here?" Charlie huffed loudly. He scrambled to pick up the boxes. "Look what you did now!"

"But we only wanted to see the post office. History, you know?" The woman defiantly tossed her head.

Charlie was disturbed by the crowd's loud chants of "History, history!" He glanced at Booker and saw Booker's blue watery eyes twitch in that way he had when he was mad.

"History ain't happenin' here," Booker yelled. "Go look at some statues or paintin's. Scat! Get movin'!"

Charlie felt like swatting at the teenagers but instead decided to concentrate on picking up the boxes. After the disturbance, he was grateful to finally make it outside to his car. Just in time, he thought, and heard the woman's voice again.

"Just remember," she yelled, "to smile." She quickly snapped a picture of Charlie and Booker near the white car surrounded by boxes. "We got the history picture," she cheered. "We can go now." The crowd of teenagers clapped.

"Damn kids," Charlie muttered and unlocked the car. He resisted the urge to run after the woman and snatch the camera away.

Chapter 7

Paul was not sure how many days had passed and couldn't figure if it was morning or afternoon. He fumbled with the blankets, glanced out the window, and guessed it was early in the day. He looked at the blood stained bandage on his leg and decided it was time to leave the cabin. What the hell, he thought; the leg seemed to be healing nicely. He pulled a fleece sweatshirt and running pants from his suitcase and dressed slowly, careful to move the material over the bandage.

"Hey, Paul, you up yet?" Bert yelled from outside.

"Yeah," Paul said, excited about his decision to leave the cabin.

Bert's large body filled the entrance and blocked the light. "How are you today?"

"Better all the time," Paul said enthusiastically. "I'm ready to head out of here today." Paul rotated his leg. "The leg looks good."

"That's great! Yes sirree," Bert said happily. "And your cabin is mostly straightened out. I hired Isabelle Green from down the road to help. Did a pretty good job, but she probably never rinsed the mop except for a swishing here and there in the toilet." Bert mimed, moving his hand around in a circular fashion, as if cleaning a toilet bowl.

"Sounds wonderful," Paul said, trying to hide his disgust.

Bert tapped his forehead, as if remembering something. "Imagine the bear smell is almost completely gone," he said. "Reckon today is as good as any to leave."

"It's time," Paul said and walked down the cabin stairs. Paul was amazed by the brightness of the day. A teal blue sky bordered forest green trees and the landscaped grass of the *INTERNATIONAL AIRPORT*. The wooden bird was still in the morning calm. Did the sign for *BERT'S TOURS* describe his experience? he wondered.

"Here, let me help you into the truck." Bert opened the door and Paul climbed into the front seat. "You comfortable?"

"Better than I've been lately." Paul smiled.

"Well, it will help to drive you over. You probably remember this strip real clear in your mind."

"I sure do," Paul said and grimaced. "What happened to the bear?"

"Gone. Saw some trackings down a ways, but no bear."

"What about the cub?" Paul questioned.

"No sightings as of yet." Bert parked the truck and helped Paul out. "You're okay to walk up?"

"I'm fine," Paul said. The bad smell was gone.

"As good as new this cabin," Bert said. "I even fixed the door." He grabbed the wooden frame and swung it back and forth. "See, and it closes right proper now. I filled in the hole in the wall and can say for a fact there's no more bears inside. Look for yourself."

Paul followed Bert into the cabin and stopped. It was a new place entirely. The kitchen had clean appliances.

"Pretty good job, Bert," Paul said and sneezed.

"You still got that allergy?" Bert asked, motioning toward the living room. "Take a look at the other rooms. Does everything meet your requirements?"

"Requirements, Bert? I don't think I'm in the position to have any," Paul said and sneezed again. He tugged a handkerchief from his pocket and walked into the living room. He saw bookshelves lined with a variety of books and loon decoys. A green checkered couch, pine table, and a twig end table were the only furniture. Paul entered the bedroom and was surprised by the room's tranquility. The torn mattress had been replaced, and the bed was covered with a red blanket. Sunlight shone through the window. In the bathroom, he saw a small stand-up shower, sink and toilet. So much for a lair, Paul thought, and realized the cabin really had the potential to be home.

"Everything okay?" Bert called.

"Picture perfect," Paul said and returned to the small kitchen.

"Well, I'm going to head out now," Bert said. "Most of your belongings are here, and you certainly know where I'll be. If you need anything, just holler." Bert walked toward the door. "Hopefully your hollering won't mean there's another bear. And remember, in two days I'll take you back to Doc Waller's for those stitches and a bandage change."

"Okay, but how can I thank you?" Paul asked, somewhat embarrassed that maybe he had taken advantage of his new friend.

"We've tread over this ground before," Bert said, somewhat bored. "You'll find a way and a time. Especially if you stay past one semester of that schooling. Later, for now."

Alone in the silence, Paul was excited with finally being home. Scratch off a bad week and a bad experience, he thought, still optimistic about the future.

As the morning passed, he sat and flipped through old magazines and lost track of time. In mid-afternoon, he ventured outside and viewed the flat, wooded property. Except for the sound of a tapping woodpecker, there was silence. He saw rocks mingled with ground cover and moss, and walked slowly down a path which led to a river channel. Spruce and pine towered above the sides of the water, which flowed eastward into a lake visible in the distance. Paul kicked at stones and wooden debris as he looked around. The flatness of the river and nearby lake made it easy for him to forget he was in mountain country.

As Paul walked back up the path, he noticed animal tracks in the soft dirt. He heard a noise and felt a sense of foreboding, similar to the first visit in the cabin. Can there be two mother bears in the same area? he questioned. As he approached the cabin, the noise became louder.

Paul turned a corner and froze in place. He saw a black cub scratching at his cabin door. The bear turned, snarled and bounded off into the woods. After seeing the second uncaged bear in his entire lifetime, Paul was immobilized. His heart beat frantically and his leg suddenly ached. But the bear seemed quite young. Did it belong to the bear that attacked him? he wondered.

Memories flooded back of the visits at Gramps' chicken farm where he spent countless hours on patrol with his cousins in search of the dead, hurt and motherless animals. Wild rabbits, and even a fox on one occasion, were found and carefully housed in shoeboxes. Gramps once had to convince Paul to release the limp rabbits, with the hope they would survive. Paul could still remember his grandfather saying: "The only way they'll have a chance now of living is if you set them free."

Paul remembered how patrol consisted primarily of long walks and bicycle rides. Graveyard ceremonies took place with crosses made from popsicle sticks. Paul often had been the preacher. "These animals are of your kingdom, from dust to dust..." he would speak somberly in a high pitched eleven-year old voice. Paul had soon become bored with the carnage, broken feathers, and quantity of destruction found in the landscape. He had easily convinced his cousins to return to ball games and hide-and-go seek.

Memories of his grandfather blended with thoughts about his girlfriend, Francine. He was suddenly desperate to hear her voice.

Paul walked down the dirt road in the direction of the store. He saw the pay phone and decided to call Francine. He soon heard the phone ring on the other end.

"Hello Francine," Paul said slowly.

"Hello," Francine answered. "Paul? Is that you? I'm so glad to hear from you. Where are you?"

"Too far away from you," Paul said and smiled. "I'm at home, up north."

"Home? Why did it take so long to hear from you?"

"Well, I had a unique encounter," Paul said, shuffling uncomfortably in the small booth.

"An encounter?" Francine asked fearfully.

"Well, I met a bear," Paul said, somewhat embarrassed by the story.

"A bear?" Francine exclaimed. "There are bears up there? Are you okay?"

"I guess so," Paul laughed. "Anyway I needed some medical attention and spent the last number of days in a cabin of this guy who owns a store here. I'm fine now."

"Paul, is there anything I can do. Should you come home? Do you belong up there?" Francine said, sounding somewhat desperate.

"It's okay. I'm fine and thought I'd call to say hi," Paul said, surprised by Francine's concern. "I'll still be starting those classes shortly and my cabin is now fixed up just great." Paul talked quickly. "Please write to me. I miss you and unfortunately have to go now. There's another guy here who needs to use the phone. Be in touch," Paul said. He blew a kiss through the phone, hung up and walked outside the booth.

"Hi," he said to stranger. Paul waved hello to Bert who was visible through the store's window, and headed slowly back toward the cabin.

Paul limped toward home and thought about how his experience at Gramps' really made him appreciate a rural area. "It's like a schizophrenia," he had confided to Francine at a lobster restaurant they visited the week previous. The wine he had sipped helped him talk easily. "Urban or rural, I'm caught somewhere in between," he had revealed.

"Schizophrenia?" Francine asked, looking at him intently. "Is that a good description of you, Paul?" she questioned and speared bits of lobster.

"Well, maybe you don't understand because you've always lived in the city," Paul said.

"But I've been on picnics!" Francine exclaimed.

"Right, and you don't like flys and ants," Paul said and caressed her leg under the table. "Do you remember complaining when we picnicked at that historic fort?" Paul questioned.

"Me complain?" Francine said and ripped the lobster's shell in half to expose white meat. "And watch where you put your hand," she said, jabbing Paul's free hand with the small fork.

"Ouch," he said. "Keep that up and maybe I'll be too wounded to stop by before heading north."

"You're leaving on Wednesday, right?" Francine asked. "I'll have the morning off so plan to stop by."

"Only if you don't jab me with that fork again," Paul cautioned.

On that last morning, Paul had driven over, found a space on the street and parked. He buzzed the doorbell repeatedly and was pleased when Francine finally opened the door. He was immediately intrigued by her mini skirt and cropped shirt.

"Hello," she exclaimed breathlessly and leaned over and kissed him. "Come on in."

During the breakfast, Paul had been uncomfortable with the silence between them, and questioned if the move was the right thing. The coffee had made him feel jittery.

"Remember, Paul, I'll still be here when you're done with your stint in those Arondiacks," Francine said.

"Adirondacks!" he had said, moving his lips across her mouth. "I have to go, but I'll be in touch soon," Paul had said, and pulled away from her entwined arms and legs. He left her apartment frustrated by his need to leave his family and equally frustrated about how the move would affect the relationship with Francine.

Paul looked at the dusty road that led to the cabin and remembered how Francine had pressed against him, wrapping her red fingernails around his neck during that last visit. He was glad she was home when he called.

He walked slowly toward the cabin and again saw the cub. He watched as the cub sniffed at the cabin stairs. How could he possibly befriend the cub of a bear which had seriously wounded him? he wondered. The bear appeared to be quite young, but Paul couldn't figure its age. A couple of months? Other than being attacked by a bear, he knew nothing about them. Was it a black bear? A grizzly? Nah, Paul thought grizzlys are only out west. The bear had the cutest facial expression when it turned toward Paul. The cub hesitated, swung its head back and forth, and scrambled back into the woods.

Inside the cabin, Paul looked through the kitchen cabinets and was happy to find a box of corn meal and a jar of honey. He quickly mixed the cornmeal together with the honey in a bowl. A meal for a cub, Paul thought. He smiled and walked outside and placed the mixture on the ground.

Chapter 8

"**A** piece of history, my ass!" Charlie muttered angrily. "This is more than history—it's my life!" Should he run after the girl and rip the camera off her neck? To think! The nerve of some people!

Alone after Booker's quick departure, Charlie shoved boxes into the sedan. Curious onlookers stood idly by and watched.

"What are you looking at?" Charlie demanded, furious with Washington visitors who used anything for a tourist attraction. "Can't you find anything more important to do than watch me load a car?"

"Sir, the contrast of you and the car is quite extraordinary. If I must say so myself." A skinny man in shorts, with a flowered shirt and British accent, stepped forward. "Mind if I take a picture, sir?"

"You must be kidding!" Charlie snarled. Then he whined, suddenly subdued. "I'd like to stand here and let you take my photograph, but I'm really busy. Why don't you check out the senate hearing rooms where there's much more interesting photos?"

From the rear of the crowd, a camcorder zoomed in on Charlie's face. With enough sense to stay calm, Charlie realized he desperately needed to get out of the city. He rushed to complete the packing and ran inside with the hand cart. After a quick goodbye with Booker, he stumbled back to the car and drove away. In the rear view mirror, the reflected crowd of tourists smiled and waved.

With the accelerator pedal pinned down, Charlie was downright gleeful as the car zoomed in with the main stream of traffic. Past the Smithsonian's buildings, he braked quickly to avoid smashing into a line of vehicles stopped at a light. Concentrate, concentrate, Charlie thought. He opened the power window halfway and ignored a man with large plastic bags who rushed toward the car.

"Hey, you got twenty cents?" the man asked, stretching out an empty hand.

Focusing straight ahead, Charlie rapidly pushed a button and the glass slid up. A push of the electric door lock turned the car into a fortress. When the light turned green, he accelerated and began to maneuver through traffic. Bums, he thought; if no one else cared for the ever-increasing number of loafers and bag people on the streets, why should he?

Happy to get away from the capital, Charlie headed northwest through Virginia. Within what seemed like a short drive, he was surprised to cross the Pennsylvania border. Over the years, after his successful organization of the House post office management, Charlie had turned his interests to the

Revolutionary War. The eastern battles lured him as he jockeyed in and out of heavy traffic.

The map he picked up at the border crossing in Pennsylvania showed he was getting closer to Valley Forge. "Getting close, getting close," he hummed out loud.

With the radio off, he listened to his own mental chatter. Charlie proved again and again to himself that he was a warrior—a success without question, and without peers. He ignored the fact that he was close to fifty pounds overweight.

As he sped along a highway bordered with newly-mowed grass, he knew his superior organization was important. Why, just getting out of Washington proved his exceptional skills. Charlie felt confident he would settle into the northern town, keep his enemies to a minimum, and continue a comfortable life.

Charlie exited the highway. He was greeted with a development strip of carpet stores, car dealers, supermarkets, gas stations and fast-food outlets that populated the area. Charlie pulled in a McDonald's lot and parked. Sweaty and thirsty, he entered a restaurant that was crowded with a juke box, pink Pontiac, metal tables, and vinyl chairs. Ah, the fifties, Charlie thought happily, and fondly remembered a ride in a car exactly like the one on display.

"Those days are gone forever," he exclaimed to the young man who took Charlie's order. Charlie paid for the food and asked, "Hey, do I go up a few more miles before there's a turn into Valley Forge?"

"Right. In five miles or so you'll see the turnoff." The man handed Charlie the change.

"Well, that's great." Charlie whistled and left the restaurant.

With the hamburger in one hand, Charlie pulled out onto the highway. Thrilled by the beauty and convenience of the interstate system, Charlie picked at the french fries. Look at these roads, he thought. Now, this is real progress! And in just a little more than two hundred years since Washington marched his troops through the area!

Within minutes he saw a sign for Valley Forge. Charlie was quickly fascinated by the manicured landscape of the historic grounds. He viewed the steel, cement and glass tower hotels across the road from the park. At least there was a place to stay for the night. He whipped through the park's entrance, parked and walked toward the main building.

"Is there a charge to get in?" he asked the uniformed man seated at the desk.

"No there isn't. Here's a map. There will be a movie starting in the theatre in fifteen minutes." The man pointed to his right, "Up the stairs. One of the troop's tents is displayed in our lobby over that way."

Charlie turned and saw a large, canvas tent set in the center of the main room. "Hey, you know?" Charlie asked, laughing loudly, "I'm sure Washington and his troops would've been a lot happier housed in one of those Sheratons across the street rather than staying in that tent. Could you imagine if he would have known the level of progress? Looks good, looks good!" Charlie exclaimed.

Thrilled by the portrayal of history, Charlie toured the main lobby and then watched the movie in the upstairs theatre. He admired the fortitude of the troops during the harsh winter in the forge. They were fighters like me, he thought.

A map of a driving tour through the valley motivated Charlie to leave the building. Comfortable in the Buick, Charlie drove easily through acres of sloped roads. He passed wooden barracks and a large cathedral monument that he knew was in honor of Washington and the troops. Charlie parked within walking distance of the General's headquarters, inspected the stone building, and entered the small hallway.

After a long discussion with a park ranger, Charlie was dismayed with the ranger's interpretation of the war and the ranger's inability to answer Charlie's well thought out questions.

"Look," the ranger finally interrupted, "why don't you go read a book?"

"I've read lots of books," Charlie said huffily. He stomped outside and headed toward the small log structures that were used as sleeping quarters. Wooden bunk beds, covered with leaves, beckoned Charlie. Inside the bunkhouse, Charlie lay down to get the full experience of being in the continental army. Even for just a few minutes! Images of a movie scene of the troops whipped into shape over the long winter, and marching out bright and new in the spring of 1778 to take up the war again, washed before Charlie's eyes. He sat up and decided his fellow compatriots were a bit small for his liking.

Progress is a magical thing, Charlie thought and walked back toward the car. He drove out of the park, crossed the road, stopped at the Sheraton, and booked a room for the night.

Early the next morning, Charlie headed northeast. He soon drove parallel with the Delaware River toward a crossing at the New York border. North of Easton, a patchwork of farms, homes, and commercial properties lined the road. Animal farms with reptile shows competed with flea markets and country diners. The uncontrolled development thrilled Charlie. Moving along at a high speed, he was surprised when traffic suddenly slowed and he was forced to skid to an abrupt stop behind a truck.

A row of honking cars, RV's and tourist buses crowded the road and moved slowly. Charlie realized that unless things rapidly speeded up, he was not going to reach the border before early afternoon. He stopped the car completely, put it in neutral, and walked toward a traffic cop who substituted for a traffic light.

Charlie lumbered forward and demanded, "What's happening here? Why can't I move? This is a forty-mile hour zone."

"Ain't nothing we can do," the cop muttered. "All these people came in response to our preacher's claims that the Virgin Mary will appear soon after midnight tonight at our church."

"I'm headed north to start a new job, and now I'm stuck in a line of traffic looking for a vision?" Charlie yelled at the cop. "How long will this thing take?"

"I don't know. You have to get back to your car." The officer motioned to Charlie's sedan. "You're holding up traffic. We don't have roads for this type of crowd or any real hotels or motels either. Just a lot of campground space."

Charlie walked angrily back to his car and slumped behind the steering wheel. "Stuck again in a congested crowd," he muttered and slowly inched the car forward. He passed the cop and hollered, "Hey! How long does the traffic jam go for?"

The cop stood with his right hand fixed in the air in a ninety degree pose as flies buzzed overhead. "Seems to extend for miles in both directions. Doesn't look like it will break for hours, probably late, late night. Consider camping in the grass field to the right, three blocks up. We're opening up that space."

Charlie shut the window and screamed, "Just what I need! To camp in a field. I don't have a tent! No sleeping bag! Nothing! I don't want to be here in a line-up of people waiting for a revelation!"

Chapter 9

In spite of the warmer weather, Sarah stayed bundled under a pile of blankets, and listened to the loud buzzing of a chainsaw across from her cabin. She groaned with the thought of doing another day of census work, and felt dreadful about having to get up and call Joe with the result of the previous day's work. How could she tell him there were only five dwellings in a small mobile-home park on a mostly deserted road? What about the fact that she drove into a ditch while turning around. And how about going back to the trailer nearest the road, talking with the woman, while the toddler screamed in the background. Or the man who came, half drunk, with a chain and truck to pull the car out. Sarah's thoughts were jumbled, and she knew Joe would not believe her.

"Jupe, we're having some mighty interesting happenings," she said and stumbled out of bed. A mirrored reflection of puffy eyes and blotched skin made her grimace and remember that in just a few days the map-making work would be over. After breakfast, she called Joe exactly at 9:30.

He responded in a routine manner: "Why so few dwellings? You did what? Got stuck?" he demanded.

As he talked, Sarah patiently remembered how fixated Joe was on being organized. She knew he saw himself as masterminding a work of extreme importance. "Talk to you tomorrow," she said, relieved to finally hang up.

Dressed and ready for a new day of solo wandering, Sarah grabbed a roll and walked outside. "You know, Jupe, this is just a job. Let's go." Sarah sat in the car, turned the radio on, and immediately tuned to the day's weather forecast. "Yeah gods! A prediction of a hurricane with violent winds and rains. Come on, Jupe." She looked at the grey, overcast sky which wiped out the surrounding mountains. "I promise to be a good driver."

The morning passed quickly as Sarah marked dwellings on a quickly constructed map. Early in the afternoon, hungry and exhausted, she drove onto a road that had a number of buildings, situated one after another. This looks great, she thought excitedly. She stopped near a red barn and began to scribble.

"Well, Jupiter," she shoved the papers in a backpack and peered at a sky blotted with clouds, "I think we're done for the day." She started the car, turned into a driveway, looked over her left shoulder, and backed up. The wind blew as thunder rumbled in the distance. "Let's get out of here before this storm hits," she said, as the car suddenly stopped. Sarah pressed the gas pedal. The engine revved. Why would the car not move? she wondered. The wind blew violently as she stepped outside the car and saw it stuck atop a large boulder. "Oh no!" she groaned. "This can't be!" Rain began to fall in a torrential downpour.

"Come on Jupe, we've got to see if we can get a ride home." The dog scrambled behind her. "Maybe somebody is at that barn." Together they ran down the street. Leaves and rain blew against the building as Sarah clanged the brass doorknocker. Rain poured off the roof, drenching her. "Damn! There's no one here."

Sarah knocked at the next house and listened to loud moans from inside the building. Poised to leave, she was surprised when the door was opened by a middle aged man.

"And what can I do for you?" he asked crossly and tugged at his zippered fly.

Sarah was surprised to see that the man appeared to have climbed out of bed, even though it was past mid-afternoon. "Uh, I'm sorry to bother you, but I've been doing census work and got my car stuck. I need a ride into town. Can you help me?" Sarah pushed wet strands of hair off her face.

"Sorry, can't help." The man spoke gruffly, blinked rapidly, and slammed the door.

Well, let's see? Sarah thought as the rain poured. We have a good record now, so why not try another house? Sarah ran across the street to a blue house and knocked. A tall, white haired woman answered.

Sarah hesitated momentarily and expected to see another door slam in her face. "Uh, I'm sorry to bother you like this, but my car is stuck. Is it possible for me to use your phone?

"Of course." The woman opened the door and smiled warmly. "It's okay, the little dog can come in too. Let him rest near the rug at the door." Sarah noticed the house smelled of freshly baked bread as the woman motioned toward the phone at the counter. Sarah dripped on the floor and made a call to the vet's office to tell them not to expect her that night.

"If you need a ride to town, I can give you one now," the woman said, as she wiped the counter with a dishcloth.

"Oh, thank you," Sarah said, feeling wet and uncomfortable. "I'm sorry to bother you in this condition. The first house I went to no one was home; then at the second one the man slammed the door in my face."

"Well, we're not all like that," the woman said. "You must have met Mr. Hoofer. He can be quite rude. By the way, my name is Bertha Myers."

"Hello. I'm Sarah Moore," she said.

Within seconds, Bertha went to the closet and returned dressed in a vinyl rain coat and a plastic rain cap.

"If you'd like, it is okay if we wait out the extreme rain." Sarah sighed. "I'm already off schedule."

"No, that's okay. I don't usually get a chance to drive in the rain. I now have an excuse even my daughter can't question." Bertha winked at Sarah.

Sarah followed Bertha outside. She easily sunk into Bertha's car and coaxed Jupe to sit on the floor. The storm raged as Bertha slowly maneuvered the car through the deep puddles.

"Did you say you live on this road?"

"I live past the store, in the other direction. If you drop me off at Bert Gendron's store, I think I could possibly get some help there." Sarah knew only Bert could possibly help her in such a situation. She wondered what type of story he would make up about her driving skills. Sarah could just imagine his comments: "Lucky it's a small car, and that you weren't driving a bus to get stuck on that boulder. No sirree, this girl don't need a bus license," he would say. By the time the hamlet came into view, Sarah saw that the rain began to clear.

"Can I give you some gas money?" Sarah asked as the car came to a stop.

"Certainly not," Bertha said. "I was happy to be of help. Tell Bert I said hello. And you stop by and visit me again sometime when you're drier." Bertha waved goodbye and drove slowly away.

Sarah walked past the beer bottles that were stacked in cartons at the left of the store's entrance. Once inside the store, Sarah headed through a right door that opened into a small post office. She decided to check her mailbox.

"Well, well. Lookee here at what the proverbial wind has just blown in to greet us," Bert said as he looked up from the corner where he stood packing cartons. "Looks like those dark clouds have shifted away from you Paul. You remember Sarah, don't you?"

"Sure do," Paul grinned sheepishly at Sarah. "But don't let me off too easy. I do clearly remember our first encounter. What happened to you, Sarah?"

"Stuck," Sarah moaned as she opened her box and peered inside to see it was empty. She felt like a lost fool seeing Paul for the second time. She was surprised at how attractive he was with mid-length blond hair, green eyes, high cheekbones and full lips. Sarah was disgusted that she must appear like a drowned cat. "Uh, I deposited my car on a stack of boulders, then was refused a ride into town by a man who slammed his door in my face," Sarah stammered. "And then Bertha Myers, who I've never met before in my life, stopped baking and gave me and Jupe a ride here." Sarah shifted uncomfortably in wet clothes that hugged her body. Suddenly conscious of the long mass of blond wet hair around her face she faltered, "I uh, I thought I'd stop here and maybe you'd help me get my car. It's stuck at the Wheelers."

"Why, sure we can help," Bert offered.

"Sarah, I have some dry clothes if you're interested," Paul suggested.

"Really?" Sarah questioned. "That would be great."

"Okay then, it seems to have let up outside, so you two go get ready," Bert said, and shooed them out of the store.

Sarah and Paul walked outside and entered Paul's truck. Sarah sat quietly and looked out the window for the few minutes it took to reach his cabin. She felt strangely disturbed to be so close to him. What a flip of circumstances, she mused. During their first encounter he was out of it and now it was her turn.

"That Bert is really something," Paul said. "In my few weeks here, I've realized he both owns and controls everything that happens here in town." Paul left the truck and Sarah followed.

"You got that one right. Not too much gets by him," Sarah said, stumbling over slippery branches that covered the walkway to the cabin. "Did you know his family has lived here for close to one hundred years and they had been some of the early settlers who arrived on stagecoaches?"

"You're kidding?"

"No, it's true. By the way, what were you guys packing when I arrived?" Sarah asked and followed Paul into the cabin.

"Bert's giving up the post office responsibilities. Says the paperwork is becoming too much. Hey, come here for a minute," Paul said and gestured toward a bedroom. Sarah stood in the doorway and watched as he searched through a dresser drawer.

"You seem really quite small, but I think these running pants and t-shirt will help," Paul said, handing the clothes to Sarah.

"Great, and the shirt is perfect," Sarah said. She read the words on the front out loud—*"TOTO, IT'S TRUE, WE REALLY ARE NOT IN KANSAS ANYMORE*— yup, this describes my day."

"I'll wait for you. The bathroom's there." Paul pointed around the corner. "Do you need a hairdryer?"

"Maybe just for a bit, thank you."

"Here you go then," he said.

Sarah changed quickly, rolled her wet clothes into a ball, and dried her hair. "Ready to head back?" she asked. She felt better now that she was no longer soaking wet in Paul's presence.

"Sure," Paul said.

The dog jumped up excitedly and hopped around in circles when Sarah re-entered the store. "You're not closing the store down too are you Bert?" Sarah asked.

"Nah, won't do that. Just the post office. Paul has helped me pack up some stuff. The new postmaster is due in town shortly." Bert paused. "It won't affect your box though."

Sarah peered at Bert as he motioned toward an FBI picture posted below the counter. "Look at this, Sarah. Says this guy is wanted for United States postal fraud. Can you imagine the lengths people will go to for a crime? It's the white-collar crime and the paperwork that's making me get out of this business."

"Boy, that's tough," Sarah said.

"Yeah, anyway, what can we do about your car?" Bert questioned. "I was thinking we'd get it now. I got a tow chain and we can use my truck. It's usually slow now too, so I'll just shut the store down."

"Are you sure Bert? I wouldn't want to inconvenience you."

"Ah, we need to get away from the post office stuff anyway. I'm sure Paul agrees."

Sarah and the dog followed the two men outside. She sat next to Paul in the truck and was surprised to see the clouds had lifted. The scent of freshly wet balsam thrilled her.

"Now, Sarah, how much longer do you have at this job?" Bert asked as he spit a chunk of tobacco out of the window.

"Just another week or so," Sarah groaned. "This is the second time I got stuck, and I'm getting more and more fearful of doing something like this miles and miles into the woods."

"It'd be harder to hear from you in that case." Bert laughed. "Paul do you know that like me Sarah has also been an employee of the ol' U. S. of A's government?"

"Oh really, doing what?" Paul inquired.

"Tracking down buildings on an important mission for the Census Bureau. Not very exciting, except for getting stuck in major rainstorms," Sarah sighed.

"Yup, and we're both going to be finished with that ol' government real soon," Bert said.

"When is the new postmaster actually due into town?" Paul asked.

"Ain't certain. Heard he's a Dimwitt, I mean DeWitt. He'll be situated at the old trailer on the road coming into town. They're fixing that he'll live in the back and make the office in the front extension. I can't wait to give him my boxes. Hey," Bert pointed to the right of the truck, "look there's that tree again. The one split by lightning. Doesn't look like she suffered much more damage in this storm."

Sarah sat in the front seat and thought about her friendship with Bert for the past year or so. She was comfortable with the fatherly guidance and also appreciated Bert's blunt, honest reactions to situations. The young man, Paul, posed a different concern. For one thing, when he was not medicated and grasping on to her leg for dear life, and puking at her feet, he was awfully attractive. Over six feet tall with a mesomorphic built, Sarah thought Paul had to be in his early twenties. She wondered if he was single? She again saw that his hands were free of jewelry.

"How's your leg, Paul?"

"Much better, thanks. I think it'll hold for school and early winter." Paul grinned and sneezed.

"Bless you for one," Bert said. "Sarah, Paul needs your medicine fixing cause he seems to have a cold since arriving."

"Oh, Bert, I'm fine," Paul said. "Just ignore him," he said, turning toward Sarah.

"Well, my treatments are a bit different, but if you're ever interested in acupuncture or homeopathy, call me."

"Those words are too big for any of us to remember," Bert said. "If you need help, Paul, just call her and ask for the medicine. That'll have to do."

Sarah sat and thought about how it would be to treat Paul. She remembered her first winter in the area the year before and the isolation of living in a cabin with a small dog. She sensed Paul's vulnerability and wondered about his survival instincts after such a unique introduction to the town. She wondered if her attraction to him was based on her interest in helping him.

"Sarah, you said the Wheelers?" Bert's voice sounded through Sarah's revery. "If I reckon correct, their house is down to the left?"

"Yeah, about a mile," Sarah said. "You'll see the car at the end of the driveway."

"I ain't surprised that Mr. Jim Hoofer, Jimbo, didn't help you," Bert said. "I can't figure that guy." Bert turned into the driveway and parked near the volkswagon. "Jimbo always gives me a feeling of someone who has something going. You know what I mean?"

Sarah shrugged and realized she wasn't quite sure of Bert's insinuations. "In spite of the rain, I could hear all sort of moaning coming from inside his house when I knocked."

"Was he dressed when he opened that door?" Bert demanded.

"Yeah, but he was sure mighty rude," Sarah said. "Looked like he just climbed out of bed."

"That's our Jimbo!" Bert exclaimed.

Sarah watched how within minutes Bert and Paul hooked the volkswagon to a large chain and pulled it off the rock.

Bert looked under the car. "There's no oil or anything," he said. "You were lucky again, Sarah. Let's go say a quick hello to Bertha. Haven't seen her in awhile."

The trio tramped over to the house. Bertha answered the knock and happily let the three guests inside.

"Bert Gendron! It's been ages," Bertha sighed. She leaned toward Bert and hugged him.

"Yeah, Bertha, and here's another newcomer, Paul Wilson. We became friends after I wrestled a bear for him." Paul groaned as Bert proceeded to tell the story Bert had entitled "Paul's Arrival and Vision Story."

"Would anyone like a slice of freshly baked zucchini bread?" Bertha asked.

"Now there's an idea," Bert said. "Did Sarah tell you about Hoofer's refusal to help her in a raging storm?" Bert asked and wiped butter on the steaming bread.

"Doesn't surprise me," Bertha said. "I've watched him for two years and that man is one of the rudest individuals. Hardly ever says hello and always seems to be in that barn of his at all times of the day and night. Constant deliveries too. Do you know what he does for a living, Bert?"

"I've told you before, Bertha. I have no control over things outside our little hamlet down the road. The problem is I don't even get to know those people either. That's why I rely on you as part of my network." Bert smiled in a flirting manner. "Now, just what do you think he's up to?"

"I'm not sure," Bertha said. Her leathery skin stretched into a smile. "Maybe he's part of the witness protection program."

"Nah," Bert said, "him being protected? Why we need to be protected from him."

"You could be right," Sarah said, remembering her fear when he came to the door.

"Well, Bertha, you keep a keen eye on him cause we need to know." Bert stood and wiped his mouth with the back of his hand. "Hey, you guys, we better be going now." He winked at Bertha. "And you come visit sometime and let us know about Hoofer. It's not good to have you out here all alone."

"Sure," Bertha laughed. "I'd fit right in—a white haired, wrinkled grandmother sitting around with you all drinking your Old Swill. Say hello to Carol for me. Sarah, Paul, you stop by again."

Sarah and the men waved goodbye and walked past the Hoofer residence which was surrounded with overgrown grass and weeds.

"Sarah are you coming back to the store? Paul still hasn't told you about the bear yet."

"Another bear?" Sarah asked. She peered at Paul and wondered what he could possibly do with a bear.

"Yeah," Bert said, "the cub of the mother that we wrestled down."

"Wrestled?" Sarah questioned. "I thought a gun was involved. Anyway, I wish I had time, but I really have to get home and finish up work. Can I take a raincheck?"

"Sure," Paul said, "but come by real soon."

"Thanks again." Sarah waved from inside the car. She felt warmed by Paul's invitation, but couldn't imagine going to visit him. She could hardly talk to Paul, let alone visit, she thought, feeling both fascinated and confused by her attraction to him.

Chapter 10

"I can't afford to be here in a line of traffic," Charlie huffed and walked back to the car. It was easy for him to recognize that the town's belated rush into the late twentieth century resulted in a strip of take-out food buildings: the McDonald's, the Stewarts, the Nice and Easy. How can any place be empty of a Hilton, or the Sheraton? he wondered. How can a department store's expansive parking lot be the main attraction? Charlie quickly noticed the lot, already crowded with various sized RV's and trucks, was packed with people seated in lawn chairs outside campers strung with plastic lanterns.

"What's going on here?" Charlie approached a grey haired woman seated in a Rubbermaid chair. "When is Jesus due to arrive?"

The woman looked up and said indignantly, "It's not Jesus who's coming. It's his sweet Mama, Mary."

"Mary? You mean we're not going directly to the source himself?" Charlie asked.

The woman smoked a cigarette, peered suspiciously at Charlie, and said, "Jesus needed a Mama, ya' know. She was a Virgin."

"Hey, Carla!" A man yelled from inside the camper. "You better get in here now to help with dinner or we're not getting to see nobody."

"Yeah," Carla said, "I'm coming. I'm coming. Remember, Mary is due at midnight," she said in a drunken voice and stumbled up the stairs.

They're really going to stay and wait till midnight? Charlie wondered, and walked back to the car. He realized it was pretty obvious that nothing had ever happened in the town, so now the people set their sights on the Virgin Mary. Strange circumstances, he sighed, and realized the campground was probably a good idea.

Seated in the car, Charlie followed a column of vehicles that led off the main street toward the park. He passed town cops who stood at a newly barricaded entrance and waved passenger vehicles straight ahead in a grassy field. Charlie parked, locked up and headed to the cops.

"What's going on here?" he asked casually.

A young cop looked at Charlie and responded stiffly. "We're setting to fix everyone up here for the night. Tents are going up yonder. You can stay in one if you like but you're on your own for food. There are restaurants in town; try to use their facilities cause we only have a few port-o-johns here."

More people drilled the cops with questions as Charlie decided to walk toward town. He was immediately stuck in a crowd with people who clutched rosaries. Charlie watched as heads swiveled expectantly. What vision did they really expect? he wondered. Totally bored by the situation,

Charlie thought the people were like little rats in a maze—fearful of the potential of the next electric shock. He walked through the Liberty diner's entrance and a door slammed as he sat down at the one remaining counter
stool.

A young waitress approached and asked for his order. "You ready now?
We've got michigans with fries for the special."

"A michigan? What's that?"

"A hotdog with a tomato and hamburger sauce. It's real good."

"I don't think so. How about the hot turkey?"

"Oh, you'll like that. We use real turkey."

"I'll take that with coffee," Charlie said. "You ever seen crowds like this
before?"

The waitress reached below the counter, poured a coffee and placed it
in front of Charlie. "No, crowds like this are new to me. We get some summer visitors, but this is a real surprise."

Charlie smirked and thought of the area's commercial possibilities—en-
trepreneurs could market Jesus and his family as the town's main attraction—a boon for tourists!

Within minutes the waitress returned with the meal. She talked excitedly as Charlie stuffed the turkey into his mouth.

"I'm a parishioner in our church, so I'll get to be inside."

"What do you mean?" Charlie wiped his mouth with a paper napkin
and peered at the attractive young woman. "The church will be closed off
to all of these people?"

"Oh yes," she said emphatically, "our parish is quite small. Even
though it's a new building, it can only accommodate less than a hundred.
Other people will just have to gather outside." She shrugged her shoulders
in a manner which defined her as the chosen for a midnight destiny encounter. Charlie stared at her shapely legs as she scurried off.

Charlie pointed to his coffee for a refill when the waitress returned.
"Well I ain't from around here," he said, "and I think it's very interesting
even if I am stuck for the night." Charlie almost slipped and said the whole
thing was a crock and that the town was the missing hole in the donut, but
restrained himself and patiently asked for the check. "Why do you think the
Virgin Mary picked your church?"

"Well," the waitress said, "our new building really creates a community
of God-loving people. I imagine it was pretty obvious to her that we are
the faithful."

"Really?" Charlie remembered the last time someone told him about a
newly built church that had a community feel. He knew better when he had
visited the church and had seen that its interior looked like his old high
school gymnasium. "Is your building cement block inside?"

"Why, yes! Did you go inside already?"

"Nah, I was just wondering," Charlie said, realizing that the same architect had probably designed churches throughout the country. "Can I have my check now?"

The waitress smiled broadly, hurried off, and returned with the check. "Thank you," she said. "Hope you feel the Lord."

Charlie placed a large tip on the counter and winked at the waitress. He left the diner and thought it was a real waste of good flesh to let her go to God.

On the outside street, Charlie was caught in a crowd of laughing people who rushed in all directions. With no idea about what to do to pass the time, Charlie walked back to the tent-town. He immediately saw that a large bonfire sparkled in the park. People stood and sat in a circle around the fire. A middle aged man at the edge of the group offered Charlie a beer.

"Sure, sounds like a good idea." Charlie took the beer from the man's outstretched hand. "Mighty interesting day here. Did you travel here specifically for the revelation?"

"Sure did. Name's Mike Platter, from North Carolina. Wouldn't miss this for the world."

"I'm Charlie DeWitt and I'm stuck. I was just passing through and realized the traffic was too much so I thought I'd better settle in for the night." Charlie extended his right hand and shook Mike's free hand.

Mike took a swig of beer and said, "Mighty good you did. This is going to be one occurence. I'm fixing to get me a spot on the road so I can look straight at the church's stained glass front." Mike peered quizzically at Charlie. "You going over?"

"Not sure. Do you know what they did with the tents?"

"Tents?" Mike asked. "They were totally unprepared for this, but they did get some tents. I hear there's a limited amount though. So if you need room, you can use a space in mine."

"That's very generous of you," Charlie said. "Who came with you?"

"My wife, Janet, over there with the yellow hair, my two kids, Mike and Joey, and Jan's Mom, Ethel." Mike pointed to the back of the crowd. "We're all mighty excited."

"Really? How did you hear about this event?"

"Oh, word travels fast about these happenings. We heard verbally through old Miller in our home town. He's got a cousin who lives up here. Last time we went to a revelation we heard about it on the radio. It was months ago and God came down on a cloud. Very nice and all, except for being so dark, we couldn't see nothing. Everyone could feel the spirit, though, if you know what I mean?"

"Yeah, I think I do." Charlie yawned.

"So, as I was sayin', about the tent. We've got room. Sleeping bags too. You fixin' to stay with us?"

"Sounds too good to pass up," Charlie said and realized his options were limited. He thought of sleeping in one of the larger tents and imagined the sounds of background tap music and the high notes of a tin flute while colonial brigades marched in formation on the horizon. Forget it, he thought, this isn't wartime. Nope it's peace with God. So forget the revolution, Charlie chided himself, and kept an eye on Mike.

Charlie was amazed at the number of people who stood around the campfire laughing and talking loudly. Parents appeared to have lost control of their children. A young man approached Charlie, looked him up and down, then plopped on the ground at his feet.

The man pulled at Charlie's polyester pant legs and whined, "You look like someone who can help me. I've been away for a while and lost forty thousand minutes of my life. I want it restored. You're a lawyer right?" the man pleaded. "Can you help me with my claim? All's I want is my oneness restored."

"What are you talking about?" Charlie demanded and pulled his leg away. "I'm no lawyer."

"Not a lawyer? Then what are you?"

"What business is it to you?" Charlie huffed.

"Then you're a lawyer." The man pushed greasy hair out of his eyes. "You just don't want to admit it."

"No, I am not!" Charlie exclaimed.

"Then what are you?" The man persisted.

"A postmaster."

"A postmaster?" the man questioned, his voice tinged with disbelief. "How can you help me restore my life? This is a court case."

"Listen," Charlie bent over. "Listen carefully. You want oneness? I was figuring you'd get that by being here. You're just going to have to wait," Charlie spoke reassuringly.

The man looked at Charlie with a beatific grin. Charlie watched as the man stood up and stumbled away.

"Thank you, thank you," the man muttered repeatedly.

This can't possibly take much longer, Charlie thought and continued to drink beer.

As the evening grew darker, Charlie saw Mike approach. "The family and me are headed over. You innerested in joinin' us?"

Charlie responded slowly, "I guess so. Then can I follow you back to the tent later?"

"Sure, like I said. We have room."

Charlie followed the group toward the main road. Mike's kids ran ahead and Janet held on to her mother's elbow. Ethel babbled on about the excitement of the upcoming event. "This is an actual spiritual happening," she said. "You'll look back one day and be mighty happy and proud you were here." She limped slowly. "I wonder where it will take place? Do you think inside or out of the building?"

Charlie listened to the old woman as the group finally reached the road where a crowd was already assembled. Most of the parishioners arrived at the church by foot. With a full moon, straight above in the sky, an eery brightness dominated. Charlie saw the church's stained glass reflected the images of surrounding trees. He could feel the crowd's restlessness. As time passed, he was surprised the crowd became quiet and subdued. The sky darkened to pitch blackness as storm clouds hid the moon.

At twenty to midnight, Charlie sensed a palpable anxiousness in the crowd. Various "oohs," and "aahs" floated in the night air. He jumped at the sound of distant thunder. At exactly five to midnight, a man stumbled into him and knocked Charlie's beer bottle on the ground. The bottle hit with a loud crash of broken glass.

"Now, look what you did," Charlie said, angrily. The man wandered away as Charlie looked at his watch. He saw it was midnight and felt the wind whip through his crew cut. As the church bells rang, rain began to pour.

Chapter 11

P aul was surprised at how easily a large block of wood split. He stuck the metal wedge in the center of the log, stood, swung the maul, and brought it down in a direct hit. The wood broke into two uneven halves. Overhead the sky was a clear blue and the distant mountains appeared purple.

During a recent phone conversation Francine had asked him, "Are the mountains really purple?"

"Yeah, I guess you could say that," he had said, at a loss to describe the different colors. He still wondered why Francine asked such a question. It was so unlike her to be interested in anything about the outdoors.

Paul continued to work and had the sudden, prickling sensation of being observed. His hands gripped the maul's wooden handle. He turned and saw the cub seated nearby, staring at him.

"Come here, bear, come here." He reached down and moved his fingers together. The cub watched unblinking as Paul stood and walked slowly into the house. He came back with two unwrapped granola bars in an outstretched hand. "Here you go." He reached out slowly. "You'll like this."

The bear shifted restlessly from one paw to another, darted quickly forward, grabbed the bar, jumped back and began to eat. Wow! Paul thought and stayed in place with the second offering. The cub chewed, looked up and snatched the other bar.

"There, that wasn't too bad was it?" Paul slowly reached out to pet the bear. The shaggy fur felt dry, matted and coarse. Paul's fingers searched through the fur and felt the bulk of the animal's body. For the life of him, he could not figure out the bear's age. His hand approached the animal's head and he was fascinated by the brown eyes and smooth wet nose. For the first time touching a bear, Paul felt surprisingly fearless, as if liberated from his previous nagging fears about being bit again, catching rabies, or being made a fool a second time. He watched the bear move toward the brush that surrounded the cabin and was fascinated with how it ambled with its head close to the ground.

Paul felt his skin begin to itch. He looked down at his hands and saw the beginning of red welts and couldn't remember a time when he had had so many allergic reactions. He itched his hands and thought about having a domesticated bear. He followed the animal to the edge of the clearing.

"You be careful playing with that bear. Your track record ain't that good," Bert said, walking up the dirt driveway. Dressed in a pair of leather, pointed cowboy boots, he appeared even taller than usual.

Paul scrambled upright as the animal moved into the woods. After evenings spent socializing at the store, Paul was pleased that Bert decided to stop by. He reached out and shook Bert's hand.

"Hey, you know," Bert said reminiscing, "there has only been one case of a domesticated bear here many years ago. When I was young, my Daddy used to take me to see it. The adults would give it beer and watch it get drunk."

Paul sneezed and looked doubtfully at Bert. "I hope this bear won't have a life as a boozer." Paul had been feeling guilty about the disappearance of the cub's mother.

"Well, don't you go having any ideas," Bert responded. "Hey, changing subjects, can you lend a hand moving the rest of my stuff out of the post office? I'm still waiting for the new postmaster, and I want to be ready."

"Sure thing," Paul said, appreciative of any opportunity to help Bert.

Twenty minutes later Paul stood in the middle of wooden crates and cardboard boxes. "Is this all you want moved out of here?" Paul asked and sneezed.

"Yeah, that's all there is. Let's leave the boxes piled here for now. You got time for a ride? There's some trackings I want to show you." Bert gestured outside. "I'll just shut the store down for a few hours. Here, have a beer."

"Sounds good," Paul said, and followed Bert outside toward the truck. Once settled in the seat, Paul drank the beer and watched as Bert drove north of the town. He continued to sneeze.

"You still sneezing?" Bert questioned.

"It comes and goes," Paul said. "It doesn't seem to be a cold though." He tried not to show his uncertainty about his new physical ailments. When he was younger his mother had feared he had a tendency to be a hypochondriac, what with the stomach ailments, headaches and skin rashes.

"Sarah can help you with that sneezing. Maybe it's just the new climate," Bert mused, popping open a new beer. He drove with one hand on the steering wheel and continued talking, "Anyway, can you imagine what the first white folks felt when they settled here in the mid-nineteen hundreds?" Bert asked and spit a chunk of tobacco out the window. "Yup, seems crazy that they would want to be out this way," he continued. "Didn't want to deal with the hustle of town twenty miles down. Just wanted their own experiences and the woods." Bert sighed and scratched at his forehead. "My family came then and my granddaddy set up a sawmill over that aways." Bert pointed toward a pile of wooden debris with tall birch trees that lined the road.

Paul looked out the truck window and saw the cement remains of a foundation. He had the feeling of looking into the remains of a ghost town and felt exhausted with thinking about where the people went.

Bert turned on a dirt road that ran along the lake edge. Paul was surprised by the water's closeness. He hoped Bert was steady enough to drive and not land the truck in the water.

Bert guzzled from his beer. "Yes sirree! Logging operations when they ran the logs during the spring river runs. I once hoped to be a river driver. Dreamed of having cleated shoes so I could walk onto the wet logs and break up jams. But my Daddy wouldn't hear of it. Old Dad said he needed me at the store and the farm."

"You were able to farm this land?" Paul questioned. He could understand the logging, but had a harder time thinking of farms in the dense forest.

"Enough for our family," Bert said. "Even with the short growing season there were gardens in the summer and canning in the fall. Mabel the cow kept our family of five supplied with milk. A gaggle of chickens gave us eggs." Bert gunned the accelerator as the truck climbed a steep, rocky section of the road.

Paul laughed, thinking about how his own family would starve if they had to grow their own food. He looked at the trees which pressed along the sides of the truck. What must it have been like to be the first white settlers in an area so dominated by winter that even the Indians stayed away except for summer? Paul wondered as Bert made a sharp right and headed in an easterly direction.

"This here is one of the old railroad beds. The tracks were torn up years ago," Bert said. "Lost our lifeline."

"What's that?" Paul questioned. He was beginning to feel the affect of the beer.

"Well, the rail line was the biggest connection. The train would shoot through every day. Massive black steel with a tower of coal smoke pushing out overhead; four freighters and two passenger cars. People would get off the train and head out in all directions. They disappeared, then later would re-appear and wait patiently for the train to blow into town again. You just ain't seen nothing like it. It made our town," Bert said. He pointed to a flat area where cement blocks lay in broken piles. "That used to be the station."

"The woods seem so still now," Paul said.

"You said that right," Bert replied. "Awfully quiet. With all our progress we lost a lot of what people did for work." Bert sighed and drummed his fingers on the steering wheel. "I'm getting on in years, so these things don't matter so much to me personally. I can stay in the store or leave or even get rid of the post office and survive, but it's the others I worry about: the young ones, you, Sarah, and my three kids who had to leave to get jobs. Seems like some of these changes take us over." Bert looked at Paul and steered around a sharp bend. He continued to talk, "Like some of the decisions are made by people outside of here. The railroad was one example—a link that is gone. Makes me sad." Bert burped. "Cause we love this land as much as our families."

"What about the post office, Bert?" Paul asked. "Do you think the transfer will be good?"

"Paul, we have to watch this one carefully," Bert said cautiously. "I'm an optimist by nature though, and I look forward to seeing the new postmaster cause that office is a link we can't lose." Bert swigged beer and threw the can behind the seat. He turned toward Paul and said, "Most people in town agree with me. There's something about a zip code that's important. It gives us an identity." Bert rolled the window down and spit a chunk of tobacco. "All's we got now are the weekend tourists and weeklong campers. I'll sell them a postcard and they want a place to mail it from." Bert peered at Paul, "You know something? People even tell me they mail to themselves just so they can get the postmark as a souvenir. I wouldn't want to take that away from them. Little things like that keep me going."

Bert grabbed a fresh chunk of chewing tobacco and suddenly brought the truck to a stop alongside the lake front. "This is what I wanted to show you," he said. "Come on, follow me."

Paul left the truck and walked beside Bert. The lake water bordered the edge of the sandy road.

"Look at this, this is one mighty big track." Bert's boot nudged at the dusty edge of a trail of large hoofed prints, formed together like half moons with a ridge in the middle. "I ain't seen nothing like this in decades. Bigger than a deer, horse or cow. I figure it must be moose."

"A moose?" Paul questioned. "When was the last time there were moose here?"

"Generations ago they roamed freely but gradually we lost 'em. The state is hot on reintroducing them, but lots of people complained about the potential for car crashes." Bert grinned. "A few years ago they found one and called it Roger. Roger fell in love with a cow a little south of here. Regardless of where they would move him, that moose would wind up back at the cow's field, hoofing around and in love."

"Well," Paul said and looked around. He sneezed and wiped his nose. "You'll have to keep me posted. Bears and moose in one summer? This is getting interesting."

"So much for our home," Bert said and walked back to the truck. He reached inside a cooler. "You want another beer?"

"Sure," Paul said and reached for the can.

As the truck winded through the backwoods, Paul told Bert about Francine. "Yeah," he said, "I'm not sure what's going to happen with us with me being up here." He shrugged and sipped his beer, happy to have someone like Bert in whom to confide. "The thing is, I really like it up here. I'm still hopeful that she will too."

"Well, if you're fixing to stay here, you'd be better off to have someone who loves this landscape, and wants it as home." Bert spoke cautiously. "If not—you're writing yourself a prescription to be nuts for a long time. Here have another beer."

Paul laughed. "Francine could go into any camping or mountaineering store and come out perfectly attired for a northern trip. She has an uncanny need to be fashionable."

"Lot's of places for that up here," Bert concluded and laughed.

Paul became increasingly happy and giddy as Bert drove through the woods. Paul knew he had a good friend in Bert. An hour later Bert dropped him off at the front of the cabin and Paul opened the truck door to get out.

"You realize," Bert said cautiously, "this area has a mighty strong pull. You came here to take some courses, but it sounds like in such a short time you're already thinking of staying. That's fine," he said. "You just don't underestimate that the bear encounter and your befriending that cub changes you. Breathing this air, day in and day out, only adds to it. You ready for that kind of change?" Bert asked, wiping at his mouth.

Paul smiled and swayed outside the truck. "I guess I'll have to see what this all means." He peered at Bert and wished that he had had a father like him. "It certainly forces something." Paul could feel his eyes shifting, trying to focus. "Thanks again for the ride and orientation. It means a lot to me." He hiccuped and waved goodbye.

Chapter 12

Wrapped in a wet sleeping bag, Charlie spent a restless night in a tent with the Platter family. The midnight storm continued relentlessly through the early morning hours. Between the sounds of Mike's mother-in-law's snores and the drip of rain, Charlie dozed intermittently. He reflected on earlier suspicions of Booker.

During their first meeting, years previous, Booker had droned on with questions of, "Do you know what I mean?"

"Yes, I know what you mean!" Charlie had exclaimed, exasperated and bored by having to spend hours in training with Booker. Booker had relentlessly jabbered on about the use of coded symbols for the bulk mailings, boxes and containers. So what if Booker had been at the office for fifteen years. Charlie knew immediately that the poor slob's inner batteries ran on low. He worked hard to not be easily distracted by Booker's shifting eyes and horsey smile.

Within two months, Booker had questioned Charlie. "You sure seem to be doing a lot of private shipping from this office. Can I help you with any of it?"

"What do you mean?" Charlie had asked distrustfully.

"Box, whatever."

"Okay. You can postmark those packages over there," Charlie grunted.

"What is this stuff anyway?"

"Postal work."

"I know that," Booker said.

"Well, this office is a lifeline with connections everywhere." Charlie remembered laughing loudly. "You know? Something for everyone: gifts, postcards, boxes, large and small."

Back then, it didn't take long for Charlie to realize Booker could be an asset, especially in establishing a local demand. With an easy-going manner, Booker was just the type of defenseless guy that Charlie had needed. Booker also had a unique ability to socialize with the congressional staff who were always pestering them.

Charlie thought about his past with Booker as he lay in the tent and listened to the unabated rain. He realized that without day-to-day contact, Booker single-handedly could jam the operation's networks. Charlie knew that Booker's self-absorption and tendency to forget details required constant management.

Thoughts churned through Charlie's mind in rapid disorder. Unable to sleep, he finally concluded it was necessary to deal with Booker's stupidity by providing just enough tidbits for Booker to operate. That's the solution! he realized. Confine Booker to a limited public relations role, Charlie thought. Charlie fell asleep with the conclusion he would find whatever horse was ready for battle.

Charlie woke at dawn and sat up quickly. The road had to be clear, he thought, looking at the sleeping lumps in the tent. Mike snored loudly under a Mickey Mouse sleeping bag. The two kids slept peacefully with their feet nestled under their father's face. The idea of hanging around another minute with the so-called vision seekers got him moving fast. He crawled toward the entrance and found his shoes. He quickly unzipped the tent's door and scrambled outside. Charlie bent and zipped the tent closed again. He whispered, "Good riddance," and stood upright.

Charlie was dismayed by the late-spring frost that had left a dew cover on the grass. Men and women nodded at him and drank coffee, but noone bothered to offer him any. So much for Christian charity, he thought, surprised to see people asleep in blankets on the ground. Charlie headed toward a port-o-john and passed a group of Harley Davidson motorcycles. How'd they get to park in here? he wondered, angry that he would have to walk a distance toward his car. Somehow he found the thought of bikers looking for Mary to be faintly amusing. He stood in line for the outdoor toilet behind a group of people who refused to talk with him. All these seekers are an uppity lot, he realized, concerned that they needed to call for a vision to really get down dirty and have a big party. Charlie wondered how many of the men and women he saw had hangovers.

Disgusted by the outdoor facilities, Charlie rushed toward his car, unlocked the door, sat down and swiftly maneuvered the vehicle away from the lot. The car edged on past two cops who stood in the early light. What an abyssmal mess, Charlie thought. He drove past a line of cars, trucks and mobile homes.

Exhilarated, he sighed. Ah, the ability to get away! He was particularly joyous about not having to spend the morning hearing about the significance of the rain and the feel of the Madonna's revelation. The night before, he had stayed solidly quiet when there were whisperings about how the rain washed away the people's sins.

"Escape, escape," Charlie chanted and drove onto the highway. Two hours went by before he decided to stop for breakfast at an exit. Charlie followed a food symbol which pointed to the left of the ramp. Annoyed when there was no restaurant directly off the highway, he finally found Betty's Diner after about five miles. He stopped the car, went in and ordered pigs in a blanket.

"Is there some way I can get back to the interstate if I continue to head north on this road?" Charlie shoved an empty plate away and questioned the waitress who refilled his coffee.

"Sure is," the waitress said and pushed a clump of grey, stringy hair behind her ear. "You're heading north?"

"Yeah, I want the thruway."

"Then just go left out of the parking lot and about six miles up you'll see the interstate sign. That way you won't have to travel south."

When Charlie left the diner, he saw the clouds had cleared. He was surprised at how green and lush the landscape was as he drove in the direction the waitress had suggested. The car moved along at a fair clip until Charlie spotted two state troopers at a road block. The flashing lights distracted him as he groaned, "Oh, now what? This can't be another spiritual convergence."

He pulled behind a small compact and saw a black hearse on the dirt shoulder. The window lowered easily as a cop peered intently into the car.

"Sorry for the slow down," the cop motioned toward the hearse. Charlie saw a middle aged woman crying hysterically beside a man in a grey trenchcoat. The cop's voice distracted Charlie.

"Did you see anybody walking down the road alone?"

"I saw some people, no one in particular though. Why?" Charlie asked, increasingly uncomfortable with the cop's intense gaze.

"Appears this hearse was abandoned," the cop said.

Charlie could hear the woman yell loudly.

"What do you mean you can't find the driver?" the woman wailed. "This here is my brother. Why is he left along the road?" The woman stamped her foot.

Charlie noticed the car had New York plates. That woman is probably a neighbor of mine, he thought. It made perfect sense that the hick town he was moving to was a place where people would lose their dead kin.

The cop appeared embarrassed, and motioned Charlie to move on.

What a weird trip, Charlie thought. He drove past the flailing woman and waved. Hell, he thought, she might be a patron of mine soon enough. The hood of the hearse was open. Charlie saw the man, who appeared uncomfortable and sweaty, as he reached into the mouth of the engine. Only in America, Charlie thought, and headed toward the northern interstate.

The exit off the thruway at Albany was easy to find. Within what seemed like less than one hundred miles, he saw a sign— *YOU ARE ENTERING THE ADIRONDACK PARK: A SIX MILLION ACRE FOREST PRESERVE*—and was surprised. A park where people live? A few miles later he passed another sign that said the road was a scenic highway. Too much scenery, Charlie thought and drove into country that became increasingly wooded and mountainous. Dismayed by the lack of commercial activity along the roadside, he began to miss the multitude of billboards and signs he'd seen earlier. This was no man's land. Overcome with nervousness, he reached into the glove compartment and found the pack of Camels he had hidden earlier in the week. Within seconds of lighting a match, Charlie inhaled. He quickly knew he didn't need to quit smoking.

Chapter 13

Deep in the woods, Sarah was finishing her work. Her Volkswagen passed slowly over a narrow road cloaked by a cathedral of pines. The car bounced through a rutted curve and entered an area where the trees shut out the sky. She was surprised to see a large forest-green building, surrounded by a stream, that blended into the landscape.

Sarah left the car and walked toward an open drawbridge. Men, women and children were visible in the windows. The deteriorating sign near the bridge said *FISH PRODUCTIONS.*

How could there be such a large building, smack in the middle of the woods, without even so much as a parking lot? In her confusion, Sarah tried to remain inconspicuous. Where did all those people live? she wondered. Her hope of finding additional buildings was abruptly stopped when a man in a lab coat appeared out of nowhere.

"What are you doing here?" he demanded. "This is private property. Didn't you see the sign?"

"No, I must've missed it," Sarah said cautiously, looking at the man. Small in height, he had blue-black hair that appeared flattened with hair gel against his head. "I'm working for the government and have been instructed to identify the number of dwellings in this area. I saw the dirt road and drove back," Sarah stammered. "Is this the only building here?"

"Yes, it is," he said. "The only building. Any more questions from you today?"

"Well, only one." Sarah stalled momentarily, unsettled by the man's black, piercing eyes. "Are there any homes for your workers nearby?"

"No, this is only dwelling. Now if no other questions, I must ask you to leave. You will list this as the only dwelling?" the man asked, glaring at Sarah. "Correct?"

"Okay," she said, shaking her head in agreement. "I'll only list the building by itself." She walked away.

Sarah felt the man watching her as she rushed back toward her car. "Let's hope he doesn't make a note of our license plate, Jupe," she whispered. Once on the main road she realized the job was continuing to be a real drag. "This work is getting stranger and stranger," she said, patting the dog's head. The dog hopped excitedly on the seat and muttered low growls. Sarah couldn't understand how the building could be in the middle of a dense forest.

Within minutes she parked in front of the *STORE GENERAL.* "Let's go say hello to Bert," she said. The doorknob to the store jiggled easily, but the door remained locked. Sarah noticed the small note—*AT WILSON'S PLACE,* and headed down the dirt road.

"Hey you found me," Bert yelled as both he and Paul waved.

"I saw the note."

"You've been a stranger," Bert said. "What's happening?"

"Nothing much," Sarah said, fidgeting with a braid. "I thought I'd stop by to say hi and see how you guys are doing."

"We're doing great. Paul agrees with me," Bert said.

"That's right," Paul said, flipping his welding helmet up to look at Sarah.

"I was here helping him with the final touches on a stove Paul's been working on." Bert motioned toward a homemade barrel stove sitting in the middle of the shed. "Besides being a newcomer who survived a bear attack, he's also a welder."

"Really?" Sarah questioned. She peered at Paul and was again aware of his blond good looks. Even though he was as tall as Bert, she found him to be more vulnerable in appearance. In his early twenties and hopefully single only added to her attraction. It was hard to look directly at him and not show her feelings of interest.

"Sure am," Paul said. "Thankfully, after the bear introduction, I do have a few other skills."

And I wonder what they are? Sarah thought, shamed by the images that danced across her mind. She sensed that he seemed more confident from having survived his move northward.

"You're still doing that census work?" Bert interrupted. "Any more excitement?"

"It's almost over. That is, if I survive," Sarah said, somewhat fearful that her lustful thoughts about Paul were maybe visible on her face.

"Survive?" Bert questioned. "You seen that Henry Ewing again?" he demanded.

"No, this one is even stranger," Sarah said, careful not to look closely at Paul. "I had to be, seven or ten miles away—I'm not sure—but anyway, deep into the woods. I went down this road, which was hardly visible from the main road, and bumped into a large building called Fish Productions."

"You're kidding! I never heard of that one," Bert said suspiciously. "You sure you ain't smoking any of that wacko weed that our friend Henry thrives on?" Bert laughed.

"Bert, believe me, this is real. Strangely enough, I swear I saw a lot of people inside the building with all this fancy equipment. Then a man in a white lab coat appeared out of nowhere. I didn't see him cross the drawbridge. He then told me that the building was the only structure on the property. He looked Korean."

"Whoo-eee!" Bert whistled. "Sarah this is a hot one. A place like that in the middle of the woods just makes no sense. You know how many reviews there are to get the proper permits?"

"Couldn't the building be visible from overhead?" Paul asked.

"I'm not sure," Sarah said, frowning. "There were plenty of trees which provided cover." Sarah shifted uncomfortably, unsettled with the directness of Paul's green eyes.

"I have an idea," Bert said, "we'll just have to arrange us a little plane ride over it. We'll see what we can find."

"That's a good idea," Sarah said. "Jupe, you be quiet." Sarah motioned to the barking dog. "Hey, remember the bear story you started to tell me?" Sarah asked and pointed toward the woods. "Is that the bear?"

"Sure is," Paul said proudly. "I've fed the cub for weeks now. She even lets me pet her and follows me around the property. Here take a look." Paul walked over to a dilapidated shed and pointed to a shelter he had set up for the bear.

"Looks like you have one unique pet," Sarah said.

"So, what do you think?" Bert called, fidgeting with a container of chewing tobacco. "You guys game for a plane ride?"

"Today?" Paul and Sarah asked in unison.

"No, not today," Bert sighed. "I have to make plans. How about in two days?"

"What about the post office guy who is due to arrive any day now?" Paul asked.

"Who cares! They never had the common decency to give me a direct date. If Mr. Dimwitt comes, he'll have to find me. I say we meet in two days on the porch of the STORE GENERAL at two in the afternoon. Is that okay with you guys? Will you be done with work, Sarah?"

"Sure. I have a bit more to do today, but I'll be able to be here for that."

"Good!" Bert said enthusiastically.

"Well, until then, goodbye," Sarah said. "Come on Jupe, stay away from that bear." Surprised at how thrilled she felt to be in Paul's presence, she looked forward to the plane ride. She drove away and hoped Bert didn't pick up on her interest in Paul. It would just be too embarrassing.

Chapter 14

►┼◄►─0─◄►┼◄

"I
t's God's carpet," Bert yelled over the din of the Cessna's engine, as the small plane coasted high above the treeline.

Seated in the back on vinyl cushions, Paul looked out the window at the green landscape. He had hidden his dismay during the several minutes it took for the rusty plane to start. Now his head hit the ceiling as the plane bounced on air currents. The plane's engine roared with an occasional sputter. Next to him, Sarah was pale. He nudged her. "You okay? There's a bag there if you need it."

"I hope I'll be okay," Sarah said, distressed. "Do you think the plane might settle down?"

"Hey, Peter, calm her down," Bert screamed to the pilot. "We don't need no one sick. Find us some calmer air." Bert sat expectantly in the front passenger seat and wore a large cowboy hat that smacked against the plane.

"We'll do our best for control," the pilot answered. "You got a special area you want to see?" He wore a Giants cap and a tee shirt that said *DON'T MESS WITH ME.*

"Just fly in a radius of twenty miles north of the store," Bert responded. "We're investigating a building. You any better back there?"

"Make chewing motions or if you got gum chew it," Paul suggested to Sarah, "it helps with the ears. Especially on the descent."

Sarah appeared grim and said, "I'll be okay. Remember, we're looking for a building that's surrounded by dense tree cover."

Bert pointed excitedly out the window. "You see that long open strip? That's where our railroad used to run. Ain't been one up here running for over fifteen years now. And there's the site of the old sawmill," he babbled. "Hey, Paul, they moved that mill at one point. Sarah, does any of this look familiar?"

"Like land upside down," Sarah said. "The only distinguishing thing was a sand pile. Let's look for that."

"You know, if you opened the window you could stick your head out for a better look," the pilot said. The plane sputtered as he played with the controls.

"Come on, Pete, who you kidding?" Bert demanded. "We gotta be serious in our search and you're giving us a death wish. Do you also propose to shut off the engine?"

Paul winced and thought about what it would be like with Bert's head out the window, the engine off and the plane floating through twisted clouds. He shuddered when he thought of how quickly the plane would plummet to the ground.

"Crash! That's what would happen." Pete snickered and twitched.

From the back seat, Paul saw the pilot's shoulders and biceps move continuously. He noticed the pilot's rhythm was only broken when he steered. The eery sensation of being trapped in a cartoon overcame him. Sarah seemed unusually quiet, and Paul felt shocks of electricity up his leg whenever their knees accidentally bounced together. He hoped they lived past the plane ride.

Paul thought about his family's reaction if he were to die in a plane crash. He imagined his father telling the mortician, "No flowers. If they want to do anything, let them contribute in Paul's name to the Animal Shelter." Fitting tribute, Paul mused, and knew his mother would go bonkers if anything happened to him.

His two younger brothers might even pause momentarily before they drew straws to get his room. Paul's passing on in a firey crash would give them the certainty that he really wouldn't be back home to claim that room. Otherwise Paul suspected they were taking bets on when he would leave school.

Sarah suddenly sat straight up. "There's the sand pile. I'm certain it is." She pointed to an area to the right of the plane.

"A pile of sand," Bert exclaimed, "but what else?"

"The building would have to be about two miles north through the woods." Sarah pointed.

"Hey, Pete, you game for getting in close up?" Bert asked.

"Why sure. Love to," Pete said. He lowered the plane and headed northward. The aircraft hovered close to the treeline, then dipped and rose in rolling motion.

"Lookee there! Is that what you're talking about?" Bert pointed excitedly to a building, covered with a green metal roof, and surrounded by large overhanging conifers. "That thing is sure hidden. I wonder why?"

The plane continued to dip down and climb back up in a circular pattern around the building. Paul saw a black haired man walk outside. "Look, there's a man," Paul said.

"Well, we seen what we came for," Bert yelled. "Pete, get us out of here now. We don't want to upset that guy below too much."

Pete's entire body spasmed in rhythmic twitches as he quickly directed the plane northward. Within minutes the plane coasted over the quiet landscape.

"Even from this distance that guy didn't seem too happy to see us. Lucky he didn't have a gun or we could've been history in the making. Like years ago when a helicopter was shot down and made national news. People like their privacy, I guess," Bert said.

"But what could that place be?" Sarah asked.

"Ah, people build all sorts of things in these backwoods. It's probably just something I never heard about. Don't mean there's a problem," Bert said. "Right, Paul?"

"Whatever you say, Bert."

"Anyway, since we don't know for sure, let's keep this one quiet," Bert cautioned. Paul and Sarah nodded in agreement.

As the plane coasted over the mountain edges, Paul tried to relax. He was surprised by the bright green of new leaves and the view of an old fire tower.

"Hey, look at that chair near that tower!" Bert exclaimed. "Can you imagine hiking through the woods with a metal office chair?" he asked. "It's strange what people will bring into these woods," he mused. Bert casually turned to Pete and, changing the subject, asked, "So is this all you do now—fly planes?"

Pete glared at Bert and said, "All I do? I'm making me a full-time living now flying all over the northeast. Sometimes even down to Florida."

"No need to be touchy. I was just wondering." Bert turned to Paul. "Pete here just finished flight school a couple of years ago. Everyone in his family was real proud to see him finish it."

Pete concentrated on flying, and within minutes Paul knew the plane was thousands of feet higher. Pete twisted his head back and forth and then yelped, "Here goes. Hang on to your shorts!" The plane dropped quickly in a spinning motion though the air.

Bert grabbed Pete's arm and yelled, "Cut it out! Just get us home. Now! There's no time for your funnies, Pete."

Paul's stomach moved up and down and Sarah clutched the vomit bag. Within minutes, the plane finally leveled out and Pete pointed it in the direction of the landing strip. The pilot radioed the tower, got the okay to land, and without any further incident landed the plane on the runway, where it finally coasted to a stop.

Pete angrily muttered, "There she is. You can all go now." He opened the door, walked away and left Paul alone with Sarah and Bert to scramble out of the plane.

"Mighty friendly," Paul said. He felt like his head was going to explode. What with clogged sinuses and plugged ears, he was unable to breath and felt unbalanced and in pain. He frantically swallowed and stuck his fingers in his ears. He hoped Sarah didn't think his behavior was too strange.

"Ah, don't worry about Pete," Bert cautioned. "I think he got mad when I said his family was proud. Must've brought back memories of it being the first thing he ever finished. I've heard he's medicated for what they call a bipolar situation. You know... if something triggers him up, he's up—down, he's down. We might've flipped him today."

Paul rolled his eyes and turned to Sarah. "Only Bert could find such an interesting pilot."

"Yeah," Sarah said, "I think our lives were at risk."

The group headed toward Bert's truck and slowly drove in silence back to the *STORE GENERAL.* The wind began to blow and afternoon clouds rolled into the sky. At the store, Bert invited everyone inside for a cold one.

Seated on an old stump inside the door's entrance, Paul sipped a beer and was relieved his life was no longer in danger. For the first time in hours, he felt his nasal passages clear, and his ears finally popped. Through a store window he watched as rain began to pelt down on the road and dust blew. "You know, Bert, people around here certainly have unique ways of doing things."

"Yeah. But don't go including Pete with the rest of us. He's one poor example."

Within minutes of getting settled, Paul saw a white car screech to a halt in front of the store. The rain shifted direction and beat down against the store's front windows. A large man, with an angry expression, climbed out of the vehicle. Paul saw him slam the car door and stomp through the rain. Paul immediately noticed the strained buttons of the man's shirt when he entered the store. Paul looked at Bert, but Bert stared at the stranger, expressionless.

The man walked toward the wall sign: *SOUNDLESS, USED ONLY TO CALL RABBITS AT A HIGH FREQUENCY,* and he picked the horn up and looked it over. Paul knew curiosity got the best of him when he blew into the horn. White flour flew out of the horn's core and covered the man's checkered shirt and patches of exposed stomach.

The guy stood angry and frustrated. "What the hell?" he screamed and turned and glared at Paul. "This some kind of practical joke or something? I was expecting a horn like General Washington used and what do I find but a joke!"

Paul worked real hard to keep a straight face. Bert let out a laugh and moved forward to introduce himself.

"You seemed real intent on that horn. I didn't have the heart to interrupt you," Bert said. He stepped forward with an outstretched hand. "Welcome to our homefront. I'm Bert Gendron, this here is Paul Wilson, and Sarah Moore. You up visiting?"

"I wish I was visiting now. This place is hell," he spat. "I'm Charles DeWitt. I've come here on reassignment to take over the post office."

"You! You're our new postmaster? Well, welcome, welcome!" Bert rushed toward Charlie, grabbed his hand and shook it. "Sorry about the horn introduction. You should've said your name first hand, Mr. Dimwitt."

"That's DeWitt."

"Anyway, as I was saying," Bert continued happily. "Paul's been helping me pack so we're all ready for the final transition. They never let me know when you would be here first hand. The whole town has been looking forward to your arrival. Yes siree! This is mighty exciting. Call you Charlie?"

"Yeah sure," Charlie said.

Charlie stood still in black wing-tipped shoes and wiped the flour off his face and chest. He looked stunned. Paul remembered his own fateful introduction to the town and wondered if the overweight postmaster had the stamina to survive in the new town.

"You know where your home and office is, don't you?" Bert asked. Before Charlie could respond, Bert said, "No better yet, we'll show you," and prepared to escort Charlie from the store. "Paul, Sarah, come on along for the tour." Outside, Paul watched Charlie sink back into his car.

"Isn't this fun?" Bert questioned. "We're watching the history of our little town being made. Come on. There's room in the truck for all of us. Folklore for the future, right Sarah?" They drove off the main road south of the store and up to a mobile home that had a wooden extension attached. "Yup, this is it. The new post office." Bert motioned proudly with his hand and climbed from the truck. "It's one mighty fine place. Yes sirree."

Paul watched as Charlie stumbled from his car and ran, fat and huffing, around the building. "You mean this is it?" he questioned as rain poured off his face. "This is not big enough to live in, let alone have a post office." The rain mixed with the flour on Charlie's face and shirt. Paul thought he looked pretty pasty to begin with.

"This is it for now," Bert said. "I sold this myself, so if you want more then you'll have to convince those Washington folks to give it to you." Paul could tell Bert was`disappointed about Charlie's lousy attitude, but Bert hid it pretty well. Bert asked, "You need any help unpacking?"

"No! Definitely not," Charlie said defensively. "I'll be fine. Let's schedule to meet tomorrow at nine for the final transfer of documents." He grumbled and quickly marched away before getting a response from Bert.

"Yeah, at the store," Bert called to Charlie's checkered back and slumped shoulders. "Is that doughboy a crank, or is it me?" Bert asked as they headed back. "Hope he gets more friendly. We don't need any black-listed employee of the government."

Chapter 15

›‹•‹‑·‑○‑·›‹•‹

T he yellow bulldozer perched near the side of Charlie's mobile home. He stood outside, picked lint off his khaki shorts and casually inspected the work. "Hey you! Stop! Stop!" he screamed, flailing his arms. The bulldozer operator ignored him. Charlie watched the machine's blade cut into the earth and was furious. He couldn't figure to get that fool driver's attention.

Days previous Charlie realized he hated the property and the small building. After contacting Booker from a payphone at the *STORE GENERAL*, he immediately pushed to get clearance to expand. "I'm going to change that damn rathole," Charlie said. Fortunately authorization had been miraculously cleared on short notice.

Hiring the bulldozer operator was the first step in a well-crafted building plan. But after careful instructions, Charlie couldn't understand why the driver, named Pigeon, still worked on the wrong side of the building. Pigeon was chosen because he didn't live too far away, owned equipment, was interested in any kind of work, and was cheap. Charlie felt increasingly angry that dirt was being moved that should've been left in place.

The bulldozer reminded Charlie of his fantasy of dominion over the earth. He knew the surrounding mountains and lakes were all useless. Ah— the joy of rearranging the dirt piles for his use. But did this driver do that? No! Pigeon had it all wrong!

"This is too much! Stop!" Charlie's love for the machine's power was now secondary to Pigeon's stark inabilities. He now feared that Pigeon's work would irrevocably alter building plans.

Pigeon let the engine idle, jumped down, lit a cigarette and walked toward Charlie. Dressed in a tie-dyed shirt, he inhaled on the cigarette and blew smoke circles. Poking a left finger at Charlie's chest, he demanded, "What are you jumping up and down for? You know you're disturbing my machine meditation. I need perfect concentration to do my best work."

"What do you mean? You're digging the wrong side of what I told you earlier," Charlie screamed above the engine's roar. "You made a big mess now!"

"Wrong side? The room will be the same on either side of the building. Just another square anyway. Turn it into a fish pond," Pigeon muttered.

Charlie watched as the unkept man walked away in untied, dirty hightops. He secretly hoped Pigeon would trip on his laces.

"I don't want no pond," Charlie called. "Now you move to the other side or we're done for good."

The driver climbed on the bulldozer, took a few haphazard swipes at the hole and slowly moved the machine backwards. Pigeon shifted gears and moved to the other side of the building. Large ruts pitted the open yard. Charlie stood silently, and thought Pigeon's name fit well—a flighty scavenger at heart, ready for any new scam. For all the morning troubles with him, Charlie still sort of liked the guy, but the damn hair had to go. That was for sure.

Finally comfortable with Pigeon's work, Charlie walked inside the small building and looked through the boxes he'd received from Bert three days ago. All the papers were complete and it was clear the transition could be made smoothly within the week. Both men had agreed the old office should stay open until the following Saturday when Charlie hoped the excavation work would be done.

The building shook on its foundation as the bulldozer scraped the dirt outside. Charlie turned on the radio, increased the volume, and was sickened by the sweet strains of classical music. He turned the dial quickly, found a country station and hummed along.

He sat down at the kitchen table in front of his preliminary construction plans, picked up the phone book, and flipped through the yellow pages, looking for a contractor. "Not too many businesses listed in this hick country," he mused.

He thought about the only business in town, the STORE GENERAL, and realized Bert was an old, transparent fool. He remembered the flour incident and felt himself heating up all over again. Even in his anger, Charlie knew he had to maintain a proper demeanor. He suspected everyone already talked about him as the 'Doughboy.'

"Doughboy! Can you imagine?" he exclaimed. Charlie wasn't so much concerned with Bert as he was with the young people. The Sarahs and Pauls were the bright, inquisitive types that Charlie hated. He didn't need their curious eyes.

Charlie finally found a company located nearby. "'Tree-Builders,' now there's a name," Charlie said. Grateful for having the phone turned on the day before, he picked up the receiver, untangled the cord, and dialed.

"Morning, I'm calling about your building company," Charlie said to the sleepy voice on the other end. "I'd like you to come see my plans and what I'm doing at the new post office." Charlie talked loudly and rapidly explained the preliminary building plans. "So can you stop by later?" he demanded. "You say your name is Waldo? Okay, we'll see you later then." Surprised about possibly waking somebody at close to ten-thirty in the morning, Charlie was still happy with Waldo's knowledge of the construction trades.

Charlie walked outside, stood with hands on hips, and surveyed the work. Pigeon now wore dark sunglasses and appeared to be lost in thought. The bulldozer roared as Pigeon forced the gears into forward position, dropped the shovel and pushed large mounds of dirt to the northern corner of the lot. A large area to the right of the building was hollowed and piles formed a boundary with the surrounding woods. It looked like Pigeon created a new vista as part of his handiwork. Stupid, Charlie thought—it was useless to leave any artistic signature on the mounds that would soon be covered with tall grasses.

"So much for beauty and symmetry," Charlie grumbled, waving for Pigeon to stop. Within minutes, Pigeon put the machine into neutral and jumped down.

Pigeon sauntered over and asked, "What's up now? You look like you're directing a speed race."

Charlie looked at Pigeon and feared Pigeon's body parts had the potential to disconnect and spin off. Pigeon walked as if his knee joints were loose. Just hope he doesn't unravel here, Charlie thought, and said, "Mighty nice job. I see you have a flair for the artistic, but you gotta recognize that with all the work planned there will still be changes when you're finished."

"I reckoned there would be," Pigeon commented. The young man took off his glasses and looked suspiciously at Charlie. "But my final mark is my signature for an eternity. It not only has to look good for you, but for all the birds, animals, and those from above who see down. Who knows? I could be making a small landing strip for some UFOs. One can't be too careful with the details. If you know what I mean?" Pigeon smiled and walked away mumbling.

"Well, I have a builder arriving soon. So, if you can finalize the finishing touches," Charlie called to Pigeon's receding back. How does that guy stay together? Charlie wondered and paced in front of the building. Lost in thought about the stupidity of a post office connected to a mobile home, it finally dawned on him that a change in plans was necessary: have Waldo move the wooden office forward, get rid of the existing mobile home, which was too small and useless, and purchase a large modular. The details of the new plan consumed Charlie and he rushed inside to call Booker to start the paperwork for the purchase of a modular. He was relieved that his rapidly constructed building plans could be thrown away.

The bulldozer's rumble had been long silenced when Charlie heard a truck pull into the driveway. Through the front window, he saw an overweight man in his mid-twenties jump out. The man waved to Pigeon, who stood with hands clasped in a silent prayer, and headed toward the front entrance. Charlie answered the knock.

"You made it over quickly. I'm Charles DeWitt," Charlie said, standing at attention.

"Morning Charlie," he said, extending a flabby hand. "I'm Waldo Umer."

"Great, come on in." Charlie ushered Waldo into the small living room. "Coffee?" Charlie asked. He motioned Waldo to sit down on the couch, hoping that Waldo's scruffy, dirty clothes wouldn't stain it.

"Sure, more caffeine to keep me going. Nice place," Waldo said and surveyed the room. He tugged at the wide elastic that held his hair in place, shook his hair free, and pulled it back into a new ponytail.

"You think so?" Charlie asked, disgusted with having seen Waldo's dark hair loose. "The place came furnished, but it's too small for my liking. I was planning an extension, but since I talked to you on the phone I changed my plans. I'm going to get a modular," Charlie said. He placed a mug of coffee in front of Waldo. "I'm primarily going to be needing mason work. Are you interested?"

"Sure, how fast do you want it?"

"As soon as possible."

"Then you'll probably need a crane to set the modular."

"Probably. Do you know where we can get one?"

"Pigeon can do that," Waldo said, sipping his coffee.

"You mean he also has a crane?" Charlie asked, suddenly envious of Pigeon's equipment.

"Pigeon's got it all. Inherited it from his daddy-o. He does good work. That is if you don't get in his way."

"I've noticed," Charlie said.

"Well, when do you want me to start? How big a foundation are you looking for?"

"I'm driving north today to the mobile home distributor I saw in the yellow pages. I want this done real fast and am willing to pay anything. I'm getting the post office in about a week, so hopefully it won't take too long. The wooden extension will stay, but I want it separated so the modular will stand alone. Follow me and I'll show you."

Charlie walked through the door which led to the post office structure. "This area needs some finishing touches: a counter, wooden slots in the back, and an area that could be used to divide mail."

"I see no problem with finishing this room up," Waldo said. "Maybe a day or two of work. The mason stuff will take longer though, depending on the size of the modular. What do you plan to do with the existing mobile home?"

"I haven't thought of that yet. You know anyone who might be interested?"

"Yeah, me. I'll even take twenty five percent off my charges. Probably can get Pigeon to move it too."

"This is getting to sound better and better." Charlie smiled and walked outside with Waldo. Pigeon was seated on top of the largest dirt mound in a lotus position.

Pigeon stood when he heard the men approach and said, "I feel something strange here in the land. A funny current that I tried to change with my sculpting."

"Well, that's nice," Charlie said abruptly. "But Waldo and me were talking and there's more work here. What with my plans for the foundation and all. Can you come back later?"

"You need more work done?" Pigeon asked, standing balanced on one foot as his fingers twirled dreadlocks. "I'll come back. Yeah, maybe I'll be able to finally correct these negative currents." He stared ahead with a peaceful expression.

"I'm going to purchase a modular. I'd like to have your crane and other equipment to pull this home out for Waldo," Charlie said.

"Yup, sounds good." Pigeon looked up and walked toward the bull-dozer. "Call me when you need me." Once seated Pigeon started the engine.

Charlie stood in awe of the machine's loud rumbling. He smiled at Waldo as the ground shook and the bulldozer moved off the property trailed by black smoke.

Chapter 16

"Plop, plop, plop," Bert said, pounding on the outside railing. "It rained all night. Continually beat on the metal roof of my house," Bert said, looking at Paul. Seated together on the *STORE GENERAL* porch, Bert guzzled a beer in the early evening. "Did you hear about the activity down the road?" Bert asked.

"No, what's up?" Paul asked. "I've been busy with classes. Even though it's summer they demand I take other courses: chemistry, calculus, dendrology; it's all too much," Paul sighed. "I'm learning how to identify every tree that grows around here including how to manage, grow and cut them." Paul peered at the Milwaukee can in his hand. "I think the registrar confused me with forest management, but that's life." He took the last sip of beer and threw the aluminum can in a pile to the right of the store's entrance. "This is my first Friday afternoon free in a couple of weeks."

Bert laughed. "My heart bleeds for you young careerists. To remind you, I've heard that story before. But now what I have to say is new to me too."

"About Charlie?"

"Yeah! He's gone ahead and employed Pigeon. You know who Pigeon is, don't you? The guy with all the equipment up the road."

"You mean the place that looks like a scrapyard surrounded by cranes, bulldozers, and dumptrucks? The guy that looks like a scarecrow?"

Bert laughed and handed Paul another beer. "You've pegged him. Do you know Waldo?"

Paul pulled the aluminum plug, took a sip and responded, "No, I don't. Does he live here in town?"

"Nah, on the outskirts. He still uses our post office, though. You must of seen him—short and fat, drives an old truck with a wooden bed. He's one of those reefer growing, reefer smoking characters who revolves each day around an eleven o'clock wakeup. Punctuality to him means arriving somewhere at around noon, working for a few hours if the mood strikes, and only if the weather ain't too good. If the weather is good, he's gone to who knows where."

"Now there's an exotic life," Paul said, laughing. "What's he doing for our friend Charlie?"

"Putting in a foundation to support the modular that Charlie found at a mobile home dealer." Bert laughed loudly. "If you stop by you'll see that the post office is now separated from the mobile home. Between you and me Waldo is working overtime. I even saw him drive by earlier today cause he's getting the mobile home as part of the arrangement."

Paul sipped the beer and wondered if Charlie had that much power in Washington to be able to get a new home so quickly. "Won't that cost a lot?" he asked.

A couple walked down the road. Bert waved hello before answering. "Cost? It's you and me paying for it. Don't forget the post office is the government and our friend Charlie seems to have his connections."

Paul followed Bert's gaze and saw the man from Los Angeles, known as Julio. Julio Somalez had long greasy hair, uncontrolled facial growth and a body covered with baggy, dirty clothes. His wife, Olive, towered above him by about twelve inches, with long stringy blond hair that hung to her waist.

"Where are those two always headed in the evening hours?" Paul asked.

"Don't know, but I'll wager along with getting their nightly aerobics they've already become friends with old Charlie," Bert said. "You know?" Bert continued. "We have a long tradition of fools venturing northward. Murray's fools the oldtimers called them."

Worried about being included in the group of newcomers, Paul asked, "Why do you lump them all together as fools?" Paul's tongue twitched against his bottom teeth. He secretly worried Bert might think him a fool. The constancy of his new allergic symptoms only added to his discomfort. He wiped at his nose with a handkerchief. After a night of sneezing, his nose was red and sensitive. He sneezed and worried about having the beginnings of asthma.

"Bless you once. And I don't lump nobody together," Bert said defensively, "history does. Now don't you go taking any of this personally, but the term Murray's fools links directly to old Pastor Murray who knew about the goodness of the wilderness. He promoted our land as a place where God lives. People, especially those with big money, came in droves in the past century. They were all looking."

"Aren't you being a little bit harsh about their experience?" Paul questioned. "Wasn't it Thoreau who said something about the preservation of the world being in the wilderness?"

"Whoa! Ain't you being a bit learned?" Bert peered at Paul. "I was just saying that you, Julio, Charlie, are all part of a long tradition." Bert opened another can of beer. "Trains and highways—that's what changed us. The wilderness shrunk with connectors. Roads made it possible for you to come in a couple of hours."

Paul sat in a drunken haze feeling guilty. He thought of how he came north to find a place with some peace and quiet and now maybe his own desires couldn't mesh with the surroundings. Maybe he was just an oddity to Bert. Coupled with the other eccentrics that seemed to surface again and again, Paul wondered about his own future.

Leaning forward Paul ventured, "Do you think me having the bear is a violation?"

"Nah, but Bear, that's what you named her right? That bear will just turn into another attraction if you're not careful. Keep a low profile." Bert stood up and burped loudly. "Enough drink for tonight. I'm headed home now for a nap."

Paul watched Bert walk down the road and wondered if he could really ever belong.

Chapter 17

Geneneral chaos ruled while Charlie established the dual fronts of home and office. For weeks he had operated postal services and was unsettled by the banging and shrill equipment noises that greeted customers. The renovation of the property was taking longer than he ever could imagine.

Aware of the town's curiosity, Charlie talked about the changes he planned: "We're going through some minor alterations, but everything will be for the best when it's all done," he often repeated to customers. Most people shook hands and cautiously said they had waited generations for the government to send a real postmaster. Charlie proudly responded—"Yup, I went through two months of official training for my post."

Tuesday, during the last week of June, wasn't any old day for Charlie. It was the Tuesday Charlie acknowledged he was fed up with everything. Plans, change—whatever—it all made him crazy. "What's going on here? What's going on here?" Charlie mumbled to himself. "Same questions over and over."

Charlie realized he could take or leave the townspeople and was bored by their politeness. The only accepted distractions were old Thelma from down the road, who brought sweet zucchini bread and cookies, and his new friends, Olive and Julio. Despite the overriding boredom, Charlie did his best to remain cheerful. He knew the future operation depended on his acceptance.

But what about Bert who still called him Dimwitt? And the people who hung out regularly at the store. What did they say about him when he drove by and saw them drinking beer and laughing?

Charlie stood and organized mail in the sorting booth Waldo had completed. One separate unit was for general delivery mail, an option that Charlie grew to hate within short time. He was angered at how the tourists, who camped at the nearby campground, came daily and looked for any mail sent their way. He was particularly disgusted with the folks who needed to send postcards off, happy with knowing that the town's official postmark and zipcode would be an authentic souvenir. Charlie believed that sending a postcard to one's home was a sign of stupidity.

A loud slam of the door broke Charlie's revery. Pigeon stood before him dressed in shorts with long, hairless legs.

"I'm getting fed up with all the moving of dirt and deconstruction out there. When am I going to get to build?"

There he goes again, being tempermental, Charlie thought. He spoke soothingly, "Pigeon, Waldo assures me that the mobile home will be moved momentarily. Why not help with the foundation? The new unit can only arrive when all this is done."

"I want the mobile home out of there." Pigeon stomped a skinny leg; his body shook in place. "That home's in the way. If I hit it now, I'll leave an open gash in the metal siding."

"Be more careful then," Charlie said and fidgeted with a first class stamp. "We have to synchronize everything so I'm able to have power and water."

"I told you before, there's a negative current here that I just can't right. You should wait till a planetary lineup if you want real synchronization," Pigeon said, and walked out.

What was it with Pigeon's flapping knees and ankles? Pigeon looked unhinged.

After the mail was sorted, Charlie called Booker. Unable to contact him for three consecutive days, he knew Booker had loafed off. He was pleased when the secretary, Cyrelle, finally found that good for nothing.

"Where the hell have you been?" Charlie screamed. "I've been trying to reach you for days." Charlie became increasingly frustrated with Booker's response that he'd been pretty busy of late, in and out of the office, and things just not being the same. Charlie finally snarled, "Look you better get used to being alone cause I don't care about what's happening there. You should see this place. Mud and strangers doing work everywhere. It's too much!"

"Yeah, but the investigation is heatin' up," Booker whined.

"What do you mean?" Charlie yelled. "Is it happening right now?"

"Not really," Booker yelped.

"Are congressional members still using our vouchers?" Charlie fidgeted with a button on his oxford as it broke in half. "Can't you slow down the personal services?"

"I guess it's possible."

"Good then. Can't the cash instead of stamps be stopped?" Charlie demanded, frustrated by Booker's denseness. "What's the weather like anyway?"

"Been real sunny three days straight. You should see how green the grass is."

"You dummy, I don't mean the outside weather. Don't you remember?" Charlie questioned, increasingly exasperated. "That's my code for asking if there's any suspicion or heat I should know about."

"Right on," Booker mumbled.

"So you mean all of our fronts are still carefully in place? And all you're doing is continuing to exchange money for vouchers plus a little shipping for favors right?" Charlie screamed, "And you're going to just keep the public relations front up then, right? Keep all the staff happy and minimize any direct action." Charlie was relentless in his pursuit of Booker.

"Hey, you know?" Booker interrupted. "The staff knows you are gone. Know what I mean?"

Charlie became increasingly agitated. "Quit repeating you know what I mean! I hear you Booker! Now listen here! You keep the favor mill going," Charlie said and wound the phone cord in his hand. "I'll keep you posted on any new directions. And stay near the office during the day if I need to reach you. This place up here is a hell hole and I've been subjected to a bunch of weirdos doing the work on the building. The townsfolk are all from another time period and the relentless visitors and campers get to me most," Charlie ranted breathlessly. "I think I might have a network of some friends. You stay clear."

Charlie hung up the phone and paced back and forth in the small living room. He realized for the umpteenth time that Booker was an idiot who was only valuable as a public relations front. A beep, beep distracted him and he realized the radio control signaled someone had entered the post office. What a brilliant system, Charlie thought. The radio enabled him to not have to spend all of the working hours in the post office. He left the residence and trudged back to the office.

An overweight man in a dirty tee-shirt stood inside the building and peered at the bulletin board. Charlie was immediately intrigued with the man's strong physique. Why he's a dirtier, meaner reflection of me, Charlie thought. It's like looking into a dirty mirror.

"Hi, I'm Charles DeWitt, your new postmaster."

The man looked up and said, "Issa tha so? How didja get ordered up here bein' a governmen' employee and all?"

"Well, I'm here on orders from Washington," Charlie said proudly. "For your service."

"Ha!" The man laughed coarsely and shook his head. The front door of the office opened again and Bert slid inside.

"Fine work that Pigeon is doing out there," Bert said, gesturing toward the back of the building. "I see him meditating now on top of the hill; he keeps telling me there's something mighty strong in a negative current in this building. You sure you're not near any wetlands or anything?"

"No way," Charlie said abruptly. "How are you doing today Bert?" he asked, happy to change the conversation.

"I'm just fine. And how about you Henry? Ain't seen you in ages."

The man jerked his head up, peered suspiciously at Bert and mumbled, "Fine, just fine with our governmen's investment in our town. Buildin' and everything."

"So I gather you've met Charlie Dimwitt then and heard about his plans to enlarge this office?" Bert asked.

"It's Dewitt," Charlie said.

"Right, well Charlie meet Henry Ewing. Henry's been with us for close to twenty years now. I see him only a few times a year though, so fix your eyes. And if you need anything from him, remember to ask."

Henry remained motionless and glared at Bert. Henry finally turned to Charlie and said, "Just gimme a book of stamps so I can get goin'."

Charlie handed over the stamps, collected the money and watched Henry angrily leave the building. The door slammed loudly. "He sure is a friendly type," Charlie said.

"Oh yeah, Henry is one of us." Bert grinned. "Especially when he takes to shooting at garden snakes. Mighty fine gun collection. He's a veteran too."

Charlie's ears perked up when Bert mentioned Henry's interest in guns. Anyone who's interested in firearms usually has an irrepressible notion for self-preservation. My kind of man, Charlie thought, and made a mental note to befriend Henry no matter what it took.

"So when is the modular due to arrive?" Bert asked.

"As soon as Pigeon finalizes the excavation and Waldo completes the foundation."

A loud rumble filtered through the office, followed by a crash. Charlie and Bert ran outside and saw Pigeon hopping up and down from one foot to another.

"I told you there was a problem here. Something mighty negative that resulted in me sidecutting that building. Lookey that hole!" Pigeon bounced in place and whistled excitedly.

Charlie rushed over to the trailer and saw pressed steel had caved into the living room forming a metal curled lip on the side of the building. "Look what you've done now," Charlie screamed. "Wrecked the building on me and Waldo. How's anybody going to live in it now?"

Waldo surfaced from the corner of the lot and slowly rambled over. "Charlie, there ain't no real problem here. We can fix this in no time and the trailer will be as good as new," Waldo said and glared menacingly at Pigeon. "Now you be more careful and don't wreck any more stuff."

Seemingly calmed by Waldo's comments, Charlie wandered back toward the post office and left Waldo in conversation with Bert. "These people piss me off," Charlie muttered.

The remainder of the afternoon passed quickly as Charlie made lists and drew elaborate schemes to reroute activity to the northern office. He crafted a strategic plan which included some local townspeople. He worked the phone to set up connections to the old base in Washington. Five minutes before shut down at five, Charlie's radio beeped. He went into the post office and saw a small man with a cardboard box.

The man approached the counter. "Can you please insure box and mail first class to New York City?"

Charlie noticed the return address said Oklahoma. "You visiting?" Charlie asked and passed seventy five cents in change back to the man.

"No, I work up way. Have lot of relatives; they like office here. They use zip code for the gifts: birthdays, showers, new year. You see me in future," the man said, and turned around and left.

How many relatives could there be in Oklahoma? Charlie wondered. He watched the man slide into a perfectly maintained black Cadillac with pointed fin tails. Charlie could see that the man's head was hardly visible over the steering wheel. He watched the car slowly drive out of the lot.

Chapter 18

▶━◀━◆━◆━◀━◀

Five hundred dwellings? Sarah realized the whole thing had just become too complicated! Hours had passed and she still was not able to connect the buildings into a quadrant; her limited cartographer skills left much to be desired. "Why do I always wait till the last minute?" she mused out loud, turned around and accidentally jarred a bowl of popcorn which crashed to the floor. Increasingly frustrated, Sarah threw the chair back, kicked at the popcorn, and ran outside into the dark night.

The moon hung creamy and full above the yard. She felt the caress of the clear sky, and wondered, like so many times before, about the strong feelings that kept her in the northeast mountains. After weeks of searching for dwellings, she was still only slightly ahead in having the money for wood and a new stove which would be so necessary for the winter.

She could still hear her father's reassurances—"Sarah, you know that the twenties will be a time of yearnings and testing of the waters. Call me any-time." But she couldn't call him. She couldn't tell him about the mountains. She couldn't tell him about her weird job. Her father drove a shiny Mercedes, ate steaks in fancy restaurants, played golf at a country club, and had a new, thirty-year old wife. Sarah just knew he couldn't relate to her life.

Her divorced mom's aggravation had been another thing. "So just what are your plans, Sarah?" Her mother had an incredible ability to probe and the phone calls increased if her mom had been drinking. Her mother never accepted being divorced and was rageful with being alone in her mid-fifties. Sarah had tried to get her to go on a diet, to give up drinking, but all without success. Instead her mother preferred to dig at Sarah, almost as if she were resentful of Sarah's youth. Even as a teenager, Sarah knew her mom wouldn't be much help. Decisions like going to college or heading out west were made independently and yet were still subjected to her mom's biting questions.

Sarah couldn't remember if the problem began with her mother when she was real little. There had been something too restrictive in her mom's admonitions to only use four pieces of toilet paper each and every time. Did the problem begin then? Sarah wondered.

Or did it start in the days before kindergarten, when her mom decided to treat Sarah like a grown-up, teaching Sarah to refer to her genitals as a "pippen." On days that Sarah was not scheduled for a bath her mom would ask, "Did you wash your pippen, Sarah?"

Sarah had been very disturbed on the first day of kindergarten when she was introduced to her teacher, an attractive woman named Miss Pippen. Even as an adult, Sarah still felt uncomfortable with her memory of that first school day, pleading with her mother to not be forced to go. Her mother had always said Sarah seemed afraid of her own shadow and couldn't understand Sarah's ability to live independently as an adult.

"Damn," Sarah muttered, and wished for the distraction of a boyfriend or family member to call. Ain't no one like that though, she thought.

She unhappily reviewed the two years of loneliness since her breakup with Michael in San Francisco. He had been a steady type; an investment banker who appreciated her seemingly calm and eccentric side. He ultimately refused to leave his refurbished brownstone and come with her to the mountains. After close to two years of dating, he and Sarah kissed goodbye and she took off in the Volkswagen. They never bothered to write or contact each other again.

That's just the way things went, Sarah thought, and trudged back into the house. Jupe greeted her with a wag of the tail. Sarah went into the kitchen and with a Herculian effort finalized the details of the drawings. At three in the morning, she finally fell exhausted into bed. The remainder of the night passed as images of shacks, garages and various sized homes filtered through dreams. She woke chilled with the image of a man who stood threateningly outside the door. Hours passed on and a phone rang, loud and insistent. Sarah stumbled past images of being lost in a rain storm at a fair.

"Hello!" she stuttered. "Uh, Joe? It's you!" She groaned.

"You missed an appointment," Joe yelled. "I've got a schedule to maintain!"

"I hear you Joe. The maps are finished. They just took longer than I expected. Sorry about this morning."

"Sorry?" Joe questioned. "You'll be in town shortly?"

"Is within the hour okay?"

"That's fine," Joe said. "I'll see you shortly."

Sarah hung up the phone. "Jupe, why didn't you wake me? Now on top of everything I feel horrible about oversleeping. Joe is such a nitpick." She washed, dressed quickly, and petted the dog. "Jupe, you're coming right? Joe's mad at us. But guess what? Today is the last day! And hopefully I'll never have a reason to talk to him again."

Sarah drove the fifteen miles to the village where Joe lived. She had prepared for the interminably boring questions he would ask about the details of the work. With all the maps and paperwork in hand, she knocked at the apartment door and was greeted by Joe holding his thirteen month old girl.

"Come in."

"Thanks."

"My wife, Emily, got called to work after I spoke with you. Things are a bit hectic here with Dylan being alone with me."

"Sorry I was off schedule."

"Whatever," he said disgustedly. "Have a seat at the table."

Sarah sat and noticed a framed listing of Joe's good and bad points that seemed to have been prepared by his wife. She handed over the maps and watched as Joe quickly inspected her work. She noticed a black underline under the work "impatient" on the framed list.

"This work looks good," he said and tugged at the baby's hand.

Sarah was pleasantly surprised with Joe's positive response. "You mean? Eh, you mean everything is okay?"

"That's right. If there are any follow-up questions I certainly know where to contact you." He reached for the baby as she tossed a pen on the floor.

By the time Sarah was ready to leave, Joe placed his daughter on the floor. The girl crawled over and began to pull on his pant leg. Joe distractedly said goodbye and lifted the baby. Why, even Joe experiences disorder, Sarah thought.

"Let's go Jupe! We're done! Want to go shopping?" The dog jumped excitedly and growled. Sarah drove down the steep hill, headed toward the center of town, and found a parking space in an unpaved lot. People on the street inquisitively looked her. She didn't think the Birkenstock sandals, long denim skirt and flowered tee shirt she wore appeared out of place. Maybe it was the tiny bandana wrapped around Jupe's neck, she thought. Sarah stopped in front of a thrift store and watched as Annabelle ran outside, dressed in a chef apron with a large painted lobster on the front. The apron covered polyester pants and a white frilly blouse.

"Look at that dog!" Annabelle yelled. "Here jump!" Jupe stood in the groundhog position and hopped. Passerbys stopped as Annabelle demanded, "Don't be sorry for that dog. No! That dog is happier—missing leg and eye and all. She ignores handicaps. We should learn something from that dog; she has a better life than us." She tossed a dogbone to the animal. "Remember I can't have her in the store, though."

"That's right," Sarah said. She was amazed by Annabelle's enthusiasm. "Jupe, you stay here and sit." Sarah motioned to the dog and walked into the crowded store. Inside the doorway, there was a counter covered with half-opened boxes, a variety of toddler pants and sweaters, and a pair of rain goulashes. Sarah immediately felt crowded in the rectangular space filled with long tables that stretched down both sides. The walls were covered with pictures of Jesus and school pictures. Pieces of clothing hung on display from hooks in the wall. Sarah looked through the display of dresses at the back of the room.

"You know I think I'm going to be able to find Mr. Axel's sister," Annabelle said excitedly.

"Really?" Sarah listened to the current version of Annabelle's endless missions to help others. Annabelle had helped the community for generations: ministering to the poor and lonely, sending hundreds of christmas packages to the senior citizen and nursing homes, and most recently acting as a conduit for the many people who had lost loved ones during their lives.

"Yup," Annabelle smiled and fidgeted with a long measuring tape wrapped perpetually around her neck. "We're getting very close. His sister might be in Ohio."

"That's wonderful, Annabelle." Sarah smiled and quickly inspected the clothing on the rack. She paused at a mini-dress made of silver lame with a two-inch bright fuschia tape that ran the length of the dress on both sides. Sarah was amazed at how both amazingly ugly and highly flammable the outfit appeared. This is it, she thought, and moved toward the register.

"Well, this is a very nice dress," Annabelle said. "I sold the exact same thing the other day. Three dollars."

Three dollars? The price seemed ridiculously high, especially in light of the customary quarters that Annabelle usually requested. Pay the money though; it's for a good cause, Sarah thought. She handed over a five dollar bill.

"Tax too. Twenty one cents. I have to pay the governor." Annabelle folded the dress into a paper bag and handed the change over. A new customer came through the door and Annabelle immediately began to repeat the success story of locating the sister in Ohio.

"Bye, Annabelle. Thank you." Sarah waved and walked outside.

"Hey Jupe! We have the outfit for the Tinker Bell costume for Halloween. And you can be the pirate! Still close to two months away, let's hope Bert still has his party." The dog wagged its tail and hopped after Sarah down the sidewalk.

Chapter 19

"I'm pissed and I'm out of here," Charlie yelled. Angry about Waldo's inability to complete the foundation work, Charlie decided to take the day off. Waldo had repeatedly proven that he was unable to follow the simplest instructions. What a farthead! Charlie thought.

"I'm washing my hands of this situation," Charlie huffed. He decided to take a Sunday drive. Happy to be away from the office, he headed for Ticonderoga.

The car sped along a road that bordered Lake Champlain. In early afternoon Charlie saw signs for Fort Ticonderoga. He tried to imagine what it had been like for revolutionary troops that had fought in the surrounding forest and on the lake. He knew the fort was strategic in its southern location on the lake. Ah, to have captured it from the British, Charlie thought. But what about the loss to General Burgoyne? Charlie questioned. And what progress had there been for Burgoyne's defeat at Saratoga? He traveled down the entrance road and past monuments that recognized the French and British. Charlie was in awe of the fortress. It reminded him of the strength he practiced daily in his work as postmaster.

He knew he kept a supply on the front lines of his postal buyers. With enough sense to know that a people divided were useless, Charlie was a warrior. He didn't even want to think about the secrets he knew about the congressional aids and other Washington staff.

Charlie followed the road to where it ended in a dirt parking lot. He left the car, looked over at a picnic area, and wondered, was that once a burial ground? A tractor moved over the lawn, and Charlie was uncertain if the driver was male or female. The lake wind rustled through Autumn leaves. Charlie passed through a wooden structure that housed the giftstore.

He looked through the window at the layout of the stone fortress and noticed the facility looked almost empty. "What's this?" he demanded of the woman who took his entrance fee. "I thought there'd be two brigades here today. That's what your advertisement said."

"I'm sorry, but that happened yesterday," the woman said. "If you'd like, you can tag along with a school tour that is scheduled to start."

Charlie reached out, took his change and walked away. "The ad said today," he muttered. He felt angry and tricked. For the rest of the afternoon, Charlie was never able to forget the feeling that he'd been taken for a ride. All the carved bull horns and various sized cannons were interesting, but a part of him remained distracted and angry. It wasn't until he heard the young tour leader, dressed in woolen outer garments and black boots with white tops, that Charlie became intrigued. When the man pointed to the stairs that Benedict Arnold ran up in the name of God and country, Charlie waved his fist and exclaimed, "Yes!"

The drive home in the shadows of the setting sun was pleasant for Charlie. He drove and thought about colonial soldiers marching in formation. Huh, huh, right, left, right; he drove inland away from the lake in an orderly fashion. Charlie landed on his small plot of land, owned previously by the British crown, and now used by him through the U.S. of A. government. As the car turned into the driveway, he was treated to the sight of Waldo, sprawled on top of the rectangular foundation. Charlie saw a Labatts bottle stuck in Waldo's hand.

Charlie's inland march from Lake Champlain ended in chaos. Filled with rage, Charlie yelled at Waldo.

"Why, you lazy, good-for-nothing," Charlie screamed. "When will you ever be finished?"

Waldo rolled off the row of bricks, as fat and spasmodic as a junebug. "Everythin' will be done in its own time!" He stood and his head bobbed. "In fact, the modular can now be scheduled."

Charlie stepped back, peered at Waldo, and laughed. "You drunk! Why I thought you were loafing off, and instead you're celebrating. Got another beer?"

"Sure," Waldo said, grinning happily. He swayed over to a rusty truck and handed Charlie a cold one from a cooler. "An' Pigeon says he'll be here first thing in November after Halloween to move this hummer out."

"Why do we have to wait so long?"

"Who knows? Pigeon claims he's busy and we had to schedule. Don't worry, this place will soon be spankin' ready for tha' new home," Waldo spoke drunkenly. "Everthin' set with that surveyor?"

"Ah, who cares about him?" Charlie huffed. "He claimed we were off the property boundary about a foot. I told him he was full of it and to scat home."

"Well, won't be the first time someone bumps a line," Waldo said, laughing.

"The property belongs to the government so they can sort it out in due time," Charlie said. "Now I'm looking forward to seeing Pigeon work that crane." Charlie sipped his beer. "Why does Pigeon have all that equipment anyway?" Yeah, why? he thought jealously. "It's the furthest thing from what he seems interested in—what with all that meditating and talk of bio-rhythm crap."

Waldo rolled in place. "It's all inherited from ol' granddaddy on his Mother's side; he was one of the finest excavators around. Pigeon is the only family member left and he controls everything."

"Why doesn't he sell it off?"

"Who knows? We think he likes the control. Maybe he's attracted to the machines' vibrations."

Charlie laughed hysterically when he thought of Pigeon's twitchy body getting a physical thrill from a machine. "I don't care how he gets off; I just want him to finish the work in quick fashion. Actually," Charlie continued, "I'm looking forward to saying good riddance to the lot of you. I've lived too long in that home with a gash in its side. This should've been finished months ago, and it's now fall."

"Come on, Charlie." Waldo finished the beer and threw the can on a pile of garbage. "Whatsa problem? You're gettin' a new house, my services have been reduced 'cause of the exchange of the trailer. Who's paying for everything, anyway?"

"Ah, what's it to you?" Charlie asked.

"Everything. Nothing," Waldo said drunkenly. "By the way, we move the trailer one week from this coming Wednesday."

"That's quicker than I thought."

"Didn't I say earlier right after Halloween?" Waldo questioned. "That's then, you know? We're fixin' to arrive at about nine next Wednesday, shut everything off, and move her out. You're goin' to need a place to stay for the night."

"I'll get a hotel room in town. In fact, I better finish everything now." Charlie walked toward the mobile home and called, "Thanks for the beer." He soon heard Waldo gun the truck out of the driveway.

Chapter 20

‹─•─◦─•─›

"Now, this is tradition! Come on let me finish you up," Sarah murmured. She placed a black eye-patch on Jupiter's head and positioned a yellow-felt coat on the dog's back. A small pirate's hat completed the outfit. "You look great, Jupe!" The dog happily wagged its tail and jumped. "Say cracker." Sarah shook a box of animal cookies. The three-legged dog stood in a groundhog position, growled and grabbed the cookie. "Good girl! Now, it's time for me to get ready."

Sarah reached into a bedroom closet and took out the silver dress she had bought two months earlier. The night before she had cut and sewn the bottom of the flammable material to form a short jumpsuit. She pulled on a pair of fuschia stockings, stepped into the sleeveless costume, and belted her waist with a bright red scarf patterned with green christmas trees. A pair of satin purple Chinese shoes, bought the year before at Martha's Vinyard, added the final complement to the costume.

"What do you think, Jupe?" Sarah asked, in a squeaky voice. "Do you think I'll pass for Tinker Bell with sex appeal?" She pirouetted in the room. The outfit revealed just the right amount of leg, she thought happily. But the rough material was a little scratchy against her nipples. Not enough to wear a bra, though, she figured. There was always the old bandaid option. She laughed remembering her half-year of wearing bandaids as a teenager to cover pubescent nipples. Her strategy had blown up when she was felt up for the first time. Billy had looked at her incredulously and questioned, "Are you wearing bandaids?"

In the bathroom, Sarah recalled the lines of a poem. Something about if here is all there once is; why does there seem so far away? Can't figure that one out, she thought, and smeared white clown makeup on her face. She streaked red and fuschia lipsticks over her cheekbones and lips. She used black mascara and a royal blue pencil to outline her eyes, then pulled her hair into a blond ponytail and sprayed it with gold glitter paint.

"We're looking pretty good, old pirate." Sarah examined her reflection in the mirror in the bedroom and thought the outfit was pretty revealing. She hoped for just the right amount of attention from Paul. But would he even be there? In what kind of costume? she wondered. Would it be possible to finally get him to notice? How many weeks had passed since she last saw him?

"We probably should get going." With the box of crackers in hand, along with a bowl of green-bean salad, Sarah left the house. Lured by the light of a third-quarter moon, Sarah drove down the road toward destination *STORE GENERAL*. Past a lineup of cars, she parked in front of the airport field. "Come on, Jupe," she said, positioning the hat on the dog's head, "let's go." She headed for the entrance, pulling at her jumper.

"Eeey, hee, heee!" The sounds of eery laughter and shattering glass escaped from the building.

The dog barked.

"It's okay, Jupe. Come on."

Sarah entered the darkened store followed by the dog. The room was lit by the ghoulish smiles of electric pumpkins and plastic skeletons that hung along the walls. Candles inside carved pumpkins flickered and threw shadows on the boxes of merchandise shoved into corners. A large metal table in the middle of the room was covered with a pumpkin table cloth. Sarah couldn't make out who the costumed people were.

For the third year in a row, Sarah was amazed at how Bert made room in the store for the party. She realized Bert and his wife, Carol, had the party to get everyone together with the benefit of a masked appearance. At the first party, Sarah had dressed as a clown with a colored wig. The following year she came with a monster face. This year, she wanted to be sexy instead of ghoulish, and recognized rather than all sweaty and hidden under a mask. Yet it was precisely the potential for recognition that unnerved her. Sarah headed toward what she knew was a heavily vodka-spiked brew.

"I have no heart, will you help me?"

Sarah looked at a tin man who accosted her. Was his costume put together with aluminum cans? she wondered.

"Help you? I would have to jump story lines. Do you have a yellow road to get me there?" Sarah asked in a squeaky, suspicious voice.

"Get you where?" the tin man asked. "I've been travelling for ages and I'm not sure. I lost my friends."

"Well, I'm busy with the rich; busy with the poor. Helping everybody to fly for magic. Can you fly?" Sarah realized she was talking to Paul. A momentary heart flutter combined with a feeling of heat. Could her reddened face be visible under all the face paint?

"Fly? I've been a stranger to all on land since I lost my friends. I'll keep the search going," Paul mumbled.

"Do you believe in fairies," Sarah asked suggestively.

"Fairies? You mean there are creatures who can help me?"

"Only if you have hope."

"Hope? Well, well! For now I'll keep the search going." Paul's voice cracked as he walked away.

She was disappointed. Sarah turned and saw an overweight revolutionary soldier dressed in tattered wool and carrying a musket.

"The fighting is something we still have a chance with," the man's voice boomed. "I saw the changes at Saratoga and played a role in the French's new interest." He leered at Sarah. "I'd hope to see you in my woods any day."

"Is that so?" Sarah said. She quickly turned away and pretended to look for the dog pirate. Whether government official or revolutionary soldier, Charlie's presence always made Sarah feel as if she were dropped into a vat of oil. He was creepy. Sarah peered at the floor and saw the various clown, fur covered, ballerina, and booted feet that populated the room. Jupe stood on hind legs in the middle of a group of monsters and clowns.

"How mean are you Captain Hook?" a monster's voice called as the dog hopped in place.

"Pretty bad," Sarah said and approached the crowd. "And in desperate need of a reward." She handed the dog a cracker.

"Well, ooeey!" the monster yelled. "Lookee ol' Tinker Bell. Can I fly with you? You must help me not have any troubles," the low voice demanded. "Are you a fairy?"

"Well, if you didn't ask, I wouldn't tell," Sarah said. Bert held an Old Milwaukee can in his furry claws. Reassured that she was near somewhat friendly ground, Sarah stood and jabbered in a squeaky voice about life in the forest. It was only when the monster left and Sarah looked at the other costumed people in the crowd that she realized everyone else was indistinguishable.

Orange and black balloons popped intermittently as Sarah participated in a volley. The night wore on. She noticed that the clowns, Batman and monsters became increasingly more disoriented. A wild man with orange teased hair and a painted chest ran through the crowd. A tongue from a freshly killed pig hung from his mouth. Somewhat sickened by the sight, Sarah headed toward the store's entrance.

Close to the front door, she was startled when Paul stumbled in front of her and fell to the floor with a loud clang. "Oh no!" Sarah squeaked. She bent to help him. "Are you okay?"

"It's just my pride," Paul mumbled thickly. "Take me to the forest for care! It's my ankle too," he said, and pointed to his right foot.

Sarah helped Paul toward a corner where he leaned against a pile of boxes. He swayed toward Sarah and whispered.

"I really love it up here." Paul spoke in a revelatory tone. "Classes, the town, the people, but my family has abandoned me and my girlfriend thinks I went to Mars."

Sarah bristled, protective and territorial, when she heard Paul mention a girlfriend. A girlfriend? Where? she thought anxiously. She concentrated on looking confident and interested in whatever he had to say. She desperately hoped that her attraction to him was not visible.

"Francine would live out her life in a catalogue," Paul said. "It's only because I'm up here that she's been looking at Bean and Eddie Bauer. The model of outdoor gear! Yup that's her." He hiccuped.

"Has she been up here yet?" Sarah asked suspiciously, somewhat surprised that Paul was willing to talk about his girlfriend.

"Up here? She can't even find her way to the highway." He laughed loudly. His masked head shook. "She'd like to visit but I don't want to go down and drive her up, then go back making two round trips. Enough about me though," Paul said. "It's just another adjustment to being in the north; an adolescence of sorts. What about you?"

Sarah guardedly said, "Oh? I've lived here for a couple of years. I really love this place and found I can't live anywhere else. Do you want another beer? Or brew?"

"Sure. Beer would be fine."

"Okay." Sarah walked toward the keg in the middle of the room and returned with two large cups of beer. The candlelight threw shadows on Paul's stiff metal form, and Sarah felt an inward tingling of excitement.

"Thanks." He extended a metal hand. "You know I sometimes feel its not just that others find this place strange. It's also that there's a certain amount of difference in everyone who's here."

"Yeah, I often think of it as a jump to the side into a different time and space dimension. Maybe it's only beyond space and time that people like Charlie are permitted anyway." Sarah shuddered as Charlie marched by, pitched forward and unbalanced by his large stomach. "Man, I don't know about that guy." She watched Charlie thump a grey mouse on the back. The mouse's legs and arms flew in all directions with the impact.

"Hey man! Quit being so forceful and negative!" the mouse yelled as Charlie pumped the mouse's hand.

"Look at him! He's mighty strange," Paul said. "I heard he recently checked the property boundary line, found the line extends onto a neighbor's land and told the surveyor to scat. Yup, that modular is going in no matter what!" Paul talked drunkenly. "Bert claims this will be a landmark day in the town. You know? A shift into the future."

"You're right. And an expensive shift at that," Sarah said. "Years back my friend dragged me around all those mobile home sale parks. We'd walk through the units and I'd fantasize about the orderliness of doing the wash off the kitchen and lighting a fire in the fireplace." Sarah talked dreamily, "Sort of a plasticized, mass-produced version of the white fence." She sighed. "Then I checked the price tags; forty thousand and up."

"That much for framed plastic and veneer?" Paul asked. "How could Charlie get that when there already were useable living quarters in place?"

"Who knows? But we're being billed for it. And if he's getting the modular it costs a lot more." Sarah smiled and could feel the white paint crack on her increasingly dry and itchy face. "And why is it taking so long anyway? Hasn't he been here over four or five months now?"

"What are you two whispering about for so long?" Bert loudly demanded. "This is a party and you're supposed to socialize!"

"Bert! We were talking about the post office. What else?" Sarah exclaimed. "Paul was just telling me about why it has taken so long for Charlie to complete everything."

"Been working since early summer. Can you imagine?" Bert questioned. "With Waldo's slowness, it's been way too long to get a foundation in. Charlie stayed in the old trailer even though the gash Pigeon made had to be fixed with slats and plastic."

"And we know he'd like a new one," Carol said, and joined the group. "What else is new?" She was dressed as a tall, Raggedy Ann doll. "To briefly change the subject," Carol said, "did you know that Emma is over there?"

"Where?" Bert asked.

"There." Carol pointed to the corner. "The squat woman dressed as a prison guard." Carol continued, "Well, she snootingly told her husband that she is not going to take his fancy, pancy ways anymore."

"You're kidding!" Bert said. "Did you know this, Sarah?"

"Uh, I don't know them at all," Sarah said.

"I certainly am not kidding." Carol motioned. "Heard her myself. Seems she finally woke up to the reality that he has been having an affair with that drunk who lives twenty miles south of here."

"No!" Bert exclaimed. "Two years to find that one out?"

"That's right," Carol said smugly. "We're lucky a cat fight didn't break out here tonight between those two. Many times we heard their yells in the night air, and we just don't need it here tonight." Carol glanced in the direction of Emma who danced slowly in place. The rhythms of country music echoed through the room.

Sarah saw that Emma's husband, Louie, stood sullenly in the corner dressed in a Tiny Tim outfit. He picked at the long hair of a black wig that hung over a shoulder. He drank a large cup of beer in two swigs and stared at Emma as she swayed toward the stereo and flicked the volume switch. Within seconds Sarah was surprised at how the music switched to the eery sounds of screeches and breaking glass.

"Come on Bert," Carol motioned. "Let's go get that stereo under control."

"You need me for that?"

"Yes. You leave these young ones alone now to talk."

"All right." Bert sipped from the beer can, winked at Paul and Sarah, and trailed after Carol. "You be good now," he spoke huskily through the heavy plastic and fur mask. "Gotta listen to the wife for now."

"Interesting stories." Sarah peered at Paul. "By the way, how's your ankle?"

"My ankle? Oh yeah—much better. In fact, do you want to come over for a coffee? Unless Emma and Louie get into it again, things seem to be dying out here. You could lend me a hand walking."

Sarah could see a smile through the cut corners of the metal mouth. "Yeah, that would be fun. Let me go see where that pirate dog is though."

"Okay, I'll wait here."

"Come here, Jupe," Sarah called softly and walked around the room. "Oh there you are," she said and picked up the dog who had been asleep behind shelves filled with cereal boxes. "Paul invited us to his house," she whispered. "You can stay in the car and sleep."

"I found the pirate who wants to go shipside for the rest of the night." Sarah held the dog and followed Paul to the front door. The trio walked outside as the door slammed. The night sky was cast with stars and a quarter moon. As they began to walk down the road, Bert ran up—half monster and half human.

"Fire! There's a fire down the road," he yelled. "Must've started when some of the guys went home and continued partying." Without the mask, Bert appeared sweaty and out of breath. "We need you two to help!"

"Well, rather than rust up with getting wet, let me change." Paul looked at Sarah questioningly. "Sarah will you help me out of this thing?"

"Sure, no problem," she said, thinking anytime.

"Okay you two. No hanky panky with that costume you hear? We need you at the fire."

Sarah stood fixed beside Paul and felt a tingling embarrassment. Undress Paul? Even if it was only out of a costume it would be closer than she'd ever been to date. "Wait just a minute," she said, "while I put Jupe in the car." The moon cast strips of light on Paul's metal costume as Sarah moved away, disappointed that the option of a quiet cup of coffee had been lost.

She returned quickly. Cast in the smell of smoke they headed toward the cabin. Sarah heard a scurrying noise in the brush and jumped back.

"It's okay; don't worry, it's only Bear. She's stayed around. You met her before, didn't you?"

"Yeah, the cub I saw during the summer."

"Well, she always checks on my whereabouts. Can you give me a hand up these stairs?"

"How did you ever get this costume on? Let alone walk and stay in it all evening?"

Paul stumbled into the kitchen, reached above his shoulders and pulled the mask off with a loud snap. "All the parts are connected. So if you detach each arm from the shoulder, and do the hands first, I'll be free." Paul placed the head on the table and grinned. "Bert helped me with it. It's been pretty hot."

Sarah tugged each hand off and then reached up and pulled the left arm. She fell backwards with a metal sleeve in her hand.

"You okay?" Paul asked and stuck out his other arm.

"Sure. But you have to be careful now to not go around telling people that I undressed you." Sarah laughed, pulled on the right arm and saw that Paul wore longjohns under the metal. She fantasized about what could happen if they didn't have a commitment to Bert to help stop the fire. Her hands felt scorched after trailing across his body.

"The front and back panels also have to be pulled off from the upper shoulder."

Sarah yanked the two metal pieces apart as Paul stood motionless. "Now about your bottom," Sarah said suggestively.

"What about it?" Paul's voice floated flirtatiously as he caught Sarah's eye. "Same thing except everything joins at the side hips and below my waist."

Could he read her mind? she wondered and blushed. Sarah felt a spark when her hand brushed against Paul's abdomen. After observing him on previous occasions, she was still surprised by the flatness of his stomach and the tightness of his hips. Sarah reached down, yanked at the bottom of Paul's left leg as the metal clattered to the floor. She repeated the movement on the other leg and Paul stepped out quickly.

"Free at last! Free at last! Thank you Sarah," he said. He reached over quickly and grabbed her in a big hug. "Thank you!"

Shaken by the feel of his arms around her, Sarah watched as Paul moved quickly toward the back of the cabin to dress. Taut hamstring muscles were visible under the thin longjohn material. Within minutes he came out in the usual flannel shirt and jeans and bent over to tie his hightops.

"Now, let's go see that fire," he said, standing upright.

Sarah swallowed hard and followed Paul out of the cabin. Close to the center of town the bonfire sparked against the moonlit night. A crowd of monsters and clowns formed a chain of connecting arms and passed water buckets filled from the nearby lake. They were trying hard to control it, but the Autumn wind fueled the fire. Charlie, now drunk and disheveled, stood at the head of the line and barked out orders.

"Everyone, keep it going faster," he screamed. "Where the hell is the fire department?"

It was very clear to Sarah that the wood pile was threateningly close to the small house that belonged to Bert's cousin, Marylou, and her husband, Walter. She heard Bert's voice in the darkness. "The fire folks will be here shortly. It's late and everyone is probably out and about."

Sarah quickly took a place in line in front of Paul. "How did this happen?" Sarah asked the wild man on her right.

"Walter was in there partying with some friends. Got a knock on his door to find out there was a fire outside. Somebody must've flicked a cigarette butt in the pile or something." The man, streaked with orange paint and dirt, handed Sarah an aluminum can filled with water.

One of the nearby town's vintage firetrucks screeched into town with flashing lights. Five men clung to the side of the truck, talking loudly as they jumped off. The driver got out and hurried toward the front of the line.

"What's this?" he demanded.

"What's it look like?" Charlie yelled. "Or does fire look different at two in the morning?"

Sarah thought Charlie was a jerk as usual, especially when he tried to say he was the one in charge. She was relieved when the driver stumbled toward the fire engine and pulled at a hose as vehicles with flashing blue lights drove into the town.

"Come on, let's pump this lake," the chief yelled.

Sarah was surprised at how smoothly the process went, considering the men all appeared slightly giddy. Within minutes water flowed in powerful streams that squelched the fire. A heavy smoke fanned over the crowd and streaked faces with a combination of soot and dirt.

The sudden darkness of the halloween night permeated Sarah. She suddenly believed the night spirits had descended on the town, wrenched free from the cribs of October grass. An understanding of loss and lack of connections overwhelmed her as she walked away from the water line.

As the flames died, she felt tired and cold. The long night of drinking in a skimpy costume, the contact with Paul, and the culmination in a night fire had taken its toll. She felt a little disoriented as the Halloween creatures blended with moon shades.

"Heading out?" A voice sounded from the darkness and Sarah found herself being crunched by an arm around her waist. She stopped, as Paul looked down, and she felt a flutter inside and the tug of Paul's presence.

"Yeah, I have to go now."

"After all this, that's probably understandable," Paul said.

Sarah couldn't figure if he was disappointed that she was leaving. She felt saddened by the fact that the spontaneity and closeness they experienced earlier had been lost. Sarah felt increasingly nervous with him.

"Hopefully I'll see you around town soon. Tonight was sure fun. Bye, Sarah." Paul reached out and touched her arm, waved goodbye and walked in the direction of his cabin.

See me around town? Sarah questioned. What does that mean? Does that mean he wants to see me around town or that he will see me around town? Is there any wanting here? She watched Paul's form recede into the darkness. Frustrated that she never got to have the coffee with him, Sarah slammed the car door and started home.

But out on the dark road she drove slowly. She felt overwhelmed by emptiness. The moonlight only made her feel worse, as if she couldn't escape from her isolation and uncertainty. The car picked up speed as she passed through a curve. Sarah braked and swerved to avoid the three sets of raccoon eyes that peered at her. Upset and shaken, she wondered if anyone would have found her if she had crashed off the road.

Chapter 21

In the days immediately following Bert's Halloween party, Charlie packed stuff into cardboard boxes during a move he labeled Operation Countdown. He had quickly made a reservation at a local hotel and tried to think of what furniture could be passed onto Waldo or sold. Careful to have picked a unit with home furnishings, Charlie knew it was best to get rid of as much stuff as possible.

On his last night in the mobile home, Charlie was surprised when the phone rang, loud and insistent. "Hello," he yelled. "Who's this? Booker? Is that you? Why are you calling me so late?"

"I have some problems down here," Booker exclaimed. "Thought you'd want to know. The heat's really on. There's problems," Booker ruminated.

Charlie paused for a minute and then screamed, "You got problems?" Charlie paused for a minute. "I've got problems— the modular is coming tomorrow. It took not one week but more than four months to get ready!" Charlie shrieked.

"But, some congressional aid keeps snooping around," Booker whispered. "Asking lots of questions."

"Ah, just give him the money for the stupid mailing," Charlie raged. "You know?" He paused thoughtfully and then continued, "Money in exchange for the stamp vouchers."

"But, that's just it," Booker whimpered. "This guy asks about the vouchers. He seems all suspicious and all."

"They're nothing!" Charlie yelled.

"But, but he's questioning if our procedure is right," Booker stammered.

"Who cares?" Charlie said. "You and me have bigger things to worry about." Charlie paced. "Look! Now you listen and listen good! I'm switching everything up here. I think I've finally seen one of our biggest suppliers."

"Does he know you?" Booker asked.

"No, stupid! He doesn't know me! We were just paper to those in the network. Just paper names." Charlie's free hand gestured wildly. "You think I'm going to come out of the blue in some fucking hick town?" Charlie slammed his fist on the counter. "Sure!" He winced with the sudden smarting of his hand. "He'd fall right over if I reveal that I'm code name Jefferson in the mail network. That ain't the way it happens," Charlie sneered. "Booker, you better sit tight till I give you further notice," he cautioned. "Just give those aides what they want. They're only fronts anyway for the big leagues."

"But they're fronts who can result in me gettin' arrested," Booker whined.

"Shut up, Booker! You're rattling scared!" Charlie shook his head. How'd he ever let Booker in on things? "Now listen to everything I just said and get it together! You're really getting on my nerves."

Charlie slammed the phone down and paced in the small living room. "He's such an idiot," he yelled.

After his belongings were packed, Charlie relaxed with a vodka tonic and a whirlpool footbath. Waves of water surged over his feet. He contemplated a plan to move operations to the north. But how could he keep aides from becoming suspicious? He thought about using stamp vouchers for money and soon realized he had a solution to his problem. Money for drugs; money for drugs... he thought sleepily.

Soporific from the vigorous foot massage, he fell asleep and woke hours later chilled by the cold water. He stumbled into bed and fell asleep for what seemed like seconds before he was awakened by a loud banging noise. Dressed in a Christmas nightshirt covered with a grinning Santa, he stumbled toward the door, opened it, and saw Pigeon and Waldo smiling up at him

"You ready to move, Santa?" Waldo asked.

Charlie stood and wiped his eyes. "Yeah, sure. Just need some coffee and to get dressed. You guys eat yet?"

"Of course we ate," Waldo said. "You never offered us anything in the past, so what's different today?" The men followed Charlie into the building.

"Today is different," Charlie said, and headed into the bedroom. "We're moving." He reemerged dressed in slacks and a white oxford shirt covered with stains. He walked over to a sink and poured water to make coffee.

"You still going to a hotel tonight?" Waldo asked.

"Yup, as soon as I can shut the office down for the day."

After the coffee was ready, Charlie sat with Pigeon and Waldo and went over the plans for the day. Pigeon seemed like a wild, caged bird from the effects of the caffeine.

"You training for a marathon or something?" Charlie demanded. "You haven't been still for a second."

"Nah, I'm just revvin' up for the work ahead," Pigeon said. "It's all part of how I psyche myself."

"Well do whatever you need to do, but just remember to get that trailer out of here in one piece," Charlie said.

Charlie finished his coffee. "We ready?"

"As good as ever," Waldo said. "Right, Pigeon?"

"That's right," Pigeon said. He stood and stretched from side to side.

Outside strong winds flaunted the end of Indian summer. Charlie realized Pigeon had already parked his various toys in the yard: crane, dumptruck, bulldozer, and front section of a semi-hauler.

"Yup! We're ready for anything," Pigeon said and flapped his arms in place as his legs spun out. He regained balance and yelled, "Is everything disconnected?"

"No, that's what I need to do first," Waldo said fatly. "Power, water; all of it has to be off before we move on."

"Well, get it right," Charlie muttered, and walked inside the post office and opened for the day. Throughout the morning postal customers were treated to the sounds of the bulldozer as it pulled at the trailer and Waldo screamed at Pigeon. Because of the equipment, parking space was limited. Charlie waited for the day's incoming mail which he knew would arrive at 10:30. The driver, Steve, arrived on time with the delivery.

"Sure looks busy here," Steve said, and handed over the incoming bag. Charlie exchanged a large white bag of outgoing mail. He thought of the packages, coded with first class destinations of Oklahoma, Washington D.C., New York, that he was placing in transit.

"You finally getting that new place?" Steve questioned.

"She's arriving tomorrow," Charlie said gleefully. "Just a little behind schedule, but we'll soon be set for years."

"Well, good luck with it. I'll see it first hand tomorrow."

The rest of the morning progressed without incident. Charlie sorted the mail, placed it in the various boxes and chatted with customers who came to buy stamps. He again recognized that stamp usage at the office appeared quite low. What could he do about the decrease? he wondered, short of selling stamps at his social club. Located an hour away in a nearby city, he could request that the club purchase stamps from the office. He was pleased with such a logical solution. Smart of him to hint repeatedly that use at the office had been skyrocketing, he thought.

Charlie looked up as the silver home passed before the window. He ran outside and rushed toward the road. "I'll direct from here," he said.

'Whoa!" Waldo shrieked. "Why don't you stand down that away to stop any traffic?" He pointed to the right of the driveway.

"No! I'm the director," Charlie shouted. "Now you head down there." Charlie gestured forcefully.

"You're acting like we get a lot of traffic or something."

"Yeah, yeah," Charlie muttered. "We can never be too ready," he cautioned. "You give me clearance and I'll check the other direction and motion Pigeon to drag the home on to the road."

The conclusion of Operation Countdown began smoothly as Charlie flagged Pigeon to move out. The silver mobile home lumbered past. Charlie could see Pigeon's head spin from side to side.

"Keep your eyes ahead!" Charlie yelled. He ran beside the hauler.

"Get your disorder out of my way," Pigeon screamed and gunned the engine. The machine gyrated to the side of the road as the home spun in the opposite direction. The hitch appeared ready to snap.

Pigeon could easily drive him nuts. "Keep her straight," he bellowed, running beside Pigeon. One more minute with Waldo's fat laziness and Pigeon's flapping complaints would lead to total distraction. What with the entire town thinking it was a field day, and Bert probably on the store's porch surveying the action, it all was too much! The machine finally straightened and tugged the mobile unit down the road. Charlie bid good riddance to the mobile home as it moved into a curve and was soon out of his line of sight.

Chapter 22

Paul heard a thunderous noise as the *STORE GENERAL* rattled. Cans, posters and lighting fixtures shook. Outside the window, he saw a semi-hauler drag a mobile home and maneuver through the turn at the center of town.

"Hey, Bert! There it goes!" Paul pointed outside.

Bert looked up from where he carved a duck and hurried toward the door. "Let's take a look!" On the porch, Bert whistled loudly and thumped Paul on the back. "Yes! This is one mighty day! You thought it was thunder? But no! It's old Dimwitt's trailer making way for the new."

"Sarah told me on Halloween night that Charlie possibly could be paying over forty grand for his new home," Paul said. "Where do you think he's getting the money?" Paul sneezed and peered at Bert.

"Don't know." Bert shrugged. "Something about old Charlie makes me suspicious. New home?" Bert's eyebrows arched questioningly. "Let's hope the cost is coming out of his pocket," Bert said, walking back into the building. "You seen Sarah since the party?"

Paul followed inside. "No. Have you?" He wondered if Bert had given any thought to the possibility of him and Sarah being an item.

"Nah, Sarah's like that. Sometimes you'll see her frequently and then she disappears. Never know." Bert shrugged and looked at Paul.

Bert was watching him intently. Careful to disguise any interest, Paul said, "Sarah seems real nice, but I have to figure out this Francine thing before I make any new friends."

"You've seen Francine lately?" Bert asked nosily.

"Nope. I've talked to her now and then though. She keeps sending me these letters, cards too. Now there's a life spent in the Hallmark aisles," Paul said, laughing. "And she's real good at it."

"Sounds interesting." Bert's lip twitched.

"Yeah. She's coming up in a week. I'm excited about it."

"You're kidding! You're fetching her?" Bert demanded and sat down.

"We're still negotiating the terms." Paul laughed, embarrassed by Bert's interest.

Paul thought about whether he and Francine had a future together. He hoped that the recent silences on the phone and increasing discomfort were only because they hadn't been together in so long.

"What do you think it is? What makes someone want to be up here?" Paul looked questioningly to Bert.

"I don't know! Reckon there must be a level of attraction to place. Either you got it, or you don't. For me it's been different. I've always been here." Bert jabbed at the wooden duck. "The biggest thing for me was hoping that my kids would stay. You know? That they'd find jobs and not feel they needed to be exported somewhere else. Transplants up here are another matter, though. You still wondering about Francine?"

"Yeah, what with her coming."

"You'll know immediately. Some folks like the outward appearance," Bert mused. "The trees are pretty kind've thing. But it's the cold and winter that sticks, when everything is white and you're dealing with snow and ice for months on end. Then stuck with a cabin fever. Let's see," Bert continued, "she'll be here mid-November. Might be certain to have snow."

Paul smiled and thought of Francine. "I better emphasize to her that she wear hiking boots and that this place is not a fashion show." He hoped he and Francine were not looking at ending their relationship. For the life of him he wouldn't know how. Over the phone? In the northern town? he questioned. The distance can't be that much of a problem, he reassured himself, still hopeful that the relationship had a future and that maybe they could see themselves together in the north.

"Hey, you been watching all the activity at the post office?" Bert interjected. "Olive and Julio seem to be walking there nightly. Fast friends, real quick with old Charlie. Why, I've even seen Henry out and about more than usual. Old Charlie seems to be a magnetic attraction. Has he mentioned the increase in sales?"

"No. I haven't heard anything. I try to stay away."

"Yeah." Bert smiled. "But you still need stamps."

"There's always the post office at school."

"Well, sure, but then you miss all the action." Bert grinned. "And you still can't answer how he got the stamp usage to go up in the fall when the tourists are mostly gone."

"How'd he do that?"

"Told you you wouldn't know!" Bert clapped his hands. "And I don't know either. Must be through Henry and Olive and Julio. Maybe ol' Mr. Hoofer, too. They're buying stamps to cement the friendship." Bert laughed loudly. "Remember that you and me are witnesses to a new office being formed. And these are all just random occurrences for Charlie's profit, huh?"

"I don't know," Paul said. "But enough watching for one day. I have work to do."

"Catch you later," Bert said.

Paul headed down the dirt road and wondered if Bert implied that Charlie was somehow scamming the postal operation. If anybody should know about the use in that office, it was Bert. Bert ran the place forever, before Charlie.

Chapter 23

The tall stalks of corn and rows of blackened leaves of beets, beans and zucchini had beckoned for attention for weeks. Determined to avoid Paul, and yet confused by the strong attraction, Sarah worked in the garden. She bent over and felt the dried broccoli pull up easily in her gloved hands. Increasingly angry, she ripped plants from the ground. In addition to being confused about Paul, she was disturbed by the fall temperatures, below freezing mornings, and early dustings of snow. After two years in the north, she still believed the descent into cold happened too quickly.

"We can't sidestep this one any more." She stood, pulled the gloves off and threw them on a stump. "Jupe, we gotta find a stove. And Paul is the only one I can think of who makes one we might be able to afford. How did you let me wait this long anyway? We're into November now!" The dog followed Sarah toward the car and waited to jump inside. Sarah remembered how her friend, Janet, really wanted the cabin's stove back. Sarah knew she could no longer beg for time.

An imaginary conversation with Paul spun through her thoughts while the car moved along the tree-lined road. Just looking for a stove. Oh yes! We've been very busy since Halloween. What with the vet's office and the few people we see in private practice! There's been no time! So we let this one slip! That stove—what do you call it? The prototype—would be perfect. How have you been able to do all this and go to school? You're a welder? How interesting!

Within minutes the town came into view and Sarah almost crashed into a traffic jam in the middle of the road. Surprised by the line-up of cars, she braked quickly, screeched to the right, and came to a stop in the sandy shoulder. It's Charlie again, she thought; he finally did get that modular. Sarah sat and watched as the wooden structure was backed into the postal lot while Waldo ran haphazardly around, pointing in all directions.

"Back up! Back up!" Waldo yelled.

From the distance, Sarah saw Pigeon seated inside a crane in what appeared to be a contemplative position. The crane's claw hung high above the foundation and swung in the early morning air. Charlie strutted back and forth and screamed directions to the driver of the truck who pulled the modular's back section. The back doors and windows were visible while the open middle was covered with plywood.

That guy is a nutcase, Sarah thought. And fat too! Jams up the entire town. Stops all activity so nothing can get done so he can get a new home. "Let's go Jupe. We can walk from here."

The dog jumped out of the parked car and followed Sarah past the confusion toward the town's center. Charlie yelled at everyone and everything that moved. Sarah realized he was one of those types who acted big until someone said shut up. She passed the truck as the driver jumped out, ran up to Charlie and did just that.

"Would you shut up? I can't concentrate!" The heavyset driver stuck his face two inches from Charlie's head.

Charlie grimaced and sputtered, "Ah, I'm just trying to help."

"You'll help by shutting that mouth," the driver said.

Sarah watched Charlie walk away, looking deflated. She was surprised by Charlie's meekness next to someone who was stronger, and probably even angrier and crazier. Was insanity needed to combat Charlie? she questioned.

Bert waved from the store's porch. "Where've you been? Come out to see all the action?"

"I had no idea." Sarah approached quickly. "You've got quite the jam here."

"Ah, Charlie's been jabbering about this since the first hour he set foot in this town. This is the new home he's been yelping about. Pretty slick, huh?" Bert tapped his foot on the porch and motioned toward the modular.

"Why did it take so long to get?" Sarah asked.

"Who knows. Probably had to finagle money from somebody in Washington. He also used Pigeon and Waldo to do the prepatory work and we both know what that means." Bert laughed loudly and pointed. "Hey look, there's Paul. He was here yesterday when the old home left."

She felt her breath catch. She watched Paul walk down the dirt road. Yeah gods, she thought. He's one of the nicest looking guys in a pair of jeans.

"Sarah. How are you? It's been ages since you rescued me from my costume." He smiled broadly. "How have you been?"

Similar to a replay on a tape cassette, Sarah continued the conversation she had earlier in her mind with Paul. "I'm doing fine. You seem much better than when you're trapped in that metal costume." She hesitated momentarily, uncertain with how to order a stove. "I, uh, I really need a new stove and thought I'd stop to see if you have any."

"Well good! I'm glad you came by." Paul spoke enthusiastically. "I've got a couple I can show you. Do you mind missing all this action?"

"Yeah, you'll miss a lot," Bert said. "Charlie has put himself into a screaming fit. Surprising huh? That man is going to have a heart attack one day when he's running around like a pit-bull." Bert motioned. Charlie was scampering in front of the hauler with a bloated and reddened face. He reminded Sarah of the jellyfish that slid across the sand on the Jersey shore.

"He's one sorry sight on this day in history." Bert took a sip of beer. "A man's here for a few months, and jams the whole town up."

"Sounds like a disgrace to me," Paul ventured.

"A disgrace? It's just a way some outsiders maneuver when they know how they can use us. That's the main question to you both—how is Charlie using us?" Bert brushed grey hair away from his eyes. "We've survived lots of abuses, and his self-interest ain't new, but he sure is one hell of a maniac. How did we go from me running a little post office to that whale building himself an empire?"

"Bert, do you know more than you're telling us?" Sarah questioned.

"Nah, I'm just an observer."

"Well, I just know that Charlie makes me squeamish enough to stay away from this post office. He smacks his lips when any young women go in the building!"

"You've given up your box?" Bert questioned.

"For now," she said. Sarah shivered, disgusted with the memory of Charlie's vacuous eyes. "He is harassment."

"Well that sure isn't a problem I have," Bert laughed. "Horny old Charlie. What about you Paul?"

"Nope I think it's all women with Charlie. Maybe we can get him a number in Montreal or something," Paul suggested.

The thought of Charlie in a French brothel made Sarah laugh. "Yeah, could you imagine him all dressed in that revolutionary costume living out some fantasy of who knows what?"

"Now there's a thought! Colonial power! Anyway," Bert ventured, "Pigeon stopped by the other day and told me all about his work on Charlie's building. Even though we know Pigeon's thinking is a little shifted, he made it real clear he ain't too happy." Bert suddenly stopped talking and watched the crane's metal move above the treeline in the distance. "Geez!" he exclaimed, shaking his head. "Would you let Pigeon operate a crane near you? He even said Waldo is a lazy, good-for-nothing that doesn't follow through on his promises, and is in need of rehab."

"Pigeon is the guy who lives up the road with all the equipment?" Sarah asked. "I've never talked with him much." She did remember stopping at his place during her census work. Even though noone answered her knock on the door, she had been surprised to hear loud thunderstorm music from inside the house.

"You probably haven't missed too much," Bert said and shrugged. "He either appears totally unhinged or deeply calm when he goes into a trance state. The trances are new the last couple of years; that along with his claims his dead folks live in the spheres of Saturn."

"Another interesting neighbor?" Sarah questioned.

"Sarah! You be nice now," Bert stressed. "All the neighbors don't have the bear attack story or schooling like our friend Paul, but they're our family nonetheless."

"Even if I live up the road?" Sarah asked, hoping to change the subject. She stood awkwardly and tried to wrestle with the notion of having Paul as a member of her family. Brotherly love would be a little hard to come by she realized.

An engine roared as the hauler slowly pulled away from the town's center minus the modular. "Wonder if the other half arrives today?" Sarah mused.

"Whenever it arrives probably only makes a difference to Charlie," Paul said. "Did you hear he is renting a room in town?"

"At whose expense?" Bert questioned. "You two go ahead and be nosy for me cause I've got to get inside now," Bert said, shooing the two young people away. "Paul you be sure to fix her up with a good stove. It's your responsibility to make sure Sarah is warm for the winter." Bert's laughter resonated. He wiped his hands on his apron and headed back inside.

Sarah hurried to catch up with Paul. "That Bert is a character," she said.

"Sure is! I obviously wouldn't have survived without him. That's a fact. How long have you known him?"

"I first met him years ago when I was doing a month long research project for the college in town and worked on a French-Canadian lumberjack festival. Bert lent me a number of the old saws he had in the barn for my display. He also drove me around to see some private landholdings that had been logged. When I came back two years ago, I stopped by and with some promptings he remembered me. He's always been real helpful." Sarah saw Paul's cabin in the clearing.

"Hey, don't be startled when you see Bear. You remember her from Halloween? She stuck around. I think her winter schedule is off a bit," he said and laughed. "But she's otherwise harmless." Paul bent down at the edge of the clearing and called for the animal.

"You said you have some stoves finished?" Sarah asked. She was unwilling to acknowledge her fear of the bear.

"I sure do, but the one is covered with a tarp. Without a garage I've been working outside or in the shed. This is it." Paul lifted the blue plastic and proudly displayed the rectangular stove. "I call it the Mardi Gras."

"Why's that?"

"I've been to New Orleans and liked the town; it needed a name."

"It's beautiful. Airtight?"

"Guaranteed."

"How much are you selling it for?" Sarah asked cautiously, fearful that she could never afford to purchase such a quality stove.

"Two hundred and fifty."

"Wow," she said. She couldn't possibly find that much money. She looked at him, trying to conceal her desperation. "Uh, I don't have the money."

"Well, we can work a deal." Paul hesitated for a brief moment. "You obviously need a stove and I have a stove. So, I'll rent it to you for a dollar a day, and when you pay it off, the stove will be yours."

"Rent?" Sarah looked questioningly at Paul.

"Yeah, rent." Paul smiled. "No interest either. You'll just need to pay me monthly."

"Well, that's awfully ge-generous of you," Sarah stuttered. How could someone so attractive, be so nice? Sarah couldn't believe her luck. Finally appreciative of his openness, she awkwardly accepted his deal. "Let's shake," she said and grinned. "This one is too good to pass up."

"Sounds good. I can even deliver it to your house."

"You can? This is like a dream."

"Well, I have to finish this one up. Paint it and all. But that should be done within the week. How about next Saturday?" Before Sarah could respond Paul ran toward the cabin. "Hang on a minute, I think that's the phone. Come on inside." He leaped up the stairs and Sarah followed him into the building. Paul picked up the receivor and Sarah discreetly watched him.

"Hello. Yeah, hi Francine. I was outside." Paul paused and listened. "Yeah, but this is a bad time to talk. You going to be in later? I'll give you a call then." Paul hung up the phone with an audible sigh. He looked at Sarah who sat at the kitchen table seemingly absorbed in reading Newsweek. "Okay, so what were we talking about?"

"The delivery of the stove."

"Right!" Paul flashed a smile. "Do you need any stove pipe?"

"No, I'm okay, but you might think otherwise when you come to my house."

"Where is your house anyway?"

"Oh, about three miles down the road on the left. The cabin is set back a bit from the road. It's vinyl covered, with a long driveway, surrounded by trees."

"Can you leave your phone number in case anything comes up?"

"Sure," Sarah said, reaching for the pen and paper.

"Would you like a cup of tea or coffee?"

"I really should get going," Sarah said, stalling with the desire to stay. There was something, too, that made her want to run far away and seek cover. Afterall, there was Francine.

"Well, I'm glad I ran into you again," Paul smiled. "If I don't see you within the week, I'll stop by next Friday."

On the drive home Sarah became obsessed with Francine. She tried to imagine the extent of Paul's relationship with the woman and was surprised at how quickly he got off the phone with her. She hoped that her feeling about their relationship being in bad shape was true and still hoped that Paul was really single.

Chapter 24

➤➤➤ ❖ ◄◄◄

What a rathole, Charlie thought. Fifteen degrees in mid-November for two week previous? Settled in his new home, Charlie was quickly chilled by the reality of the impending winter. And that nosy Bert had predicted it would get even colder. Charlie hoped he was wrong, especially since the night now was a balmy Indian summer.

The spaciousness of the modular pleased him and helped barricade him from the cold outdoors. "This is really it," he sighed, pleased with his choice of living room carpet. He entered the kitchen and fondly touched the oak veneer cabinets. The newest appliances: microwave, dishwasher, garbage disposal, were all neatly positioned in the cabinets. The sink was situated under a window that looked out into the woods. "This is perfect," he sighed, eyeing a picture of his wife who died six years previous. The comfort of the new home gave him a feeling of invincibility.

Charlie looked up from dusting the living room and saw two shadows in the outside light. He opened the door and stood on the unfinished wooden steps. "Post office closed at five," he barked into the night.

"We know that Charlie!" A voice boomed from the darkness.

"Well, well! If it isn't Bert coming to visit me after all," Charlie said. "Who do you have with you?"

"Paul Wilson."

"Yeah, Box 369," Charlie said.

"That's right," Paul ventured.

"So what's up?"

"Well, we figured 'cause you're settled you might be interested in some hunting with us," Bert said. "It's big game season, but I thought you might want to start out small. Sort of introduce you to our region and all." Bert grinned and his teeth shone in the darkness.

"Hunt?" Charlie asked. "Come on in. You haven't seen the inside yet?"

"Nope. Come on, Paul," Bert said.

Charlie led the way into the living room. Bert whistled loudly,"This place is mighty fine. Don't you think, Paul?"

"Sure is," Paul said, wiping his nose. "Everything fits together like a magazine picture."

"Yes sir! A picture of perfection! Charlie you've done good," Bert spoke happily and clapped his hands. "Now what do you say about snipe hunting with us tonight? It's real warm for November and we have a sprinkle of rain that has just started. Perfect conditions and Paul needs an introduction to our hunting patterns too. Three of us are needed to do the job right."

Charlie stalled for a minute. He questioned, hunt with Bert and Paul? His thoughts raced around a mental picture of being a big game hunter in pre-revolutionary days. He thought of bringing home the various pheasants and deer that his wife would cook on slow burning kettles. Warmed by a fantasy, Charlie smiled and thought of himself as a hearty provider. So what if he never hunted a day in his life. There was always time to start, he thought. And so what if Bert rambled too much. Maybe this was the time to prove he wasn't a 'Doughboy.'

"Well? What do you say?" Bert asked and pulled a toothpick from a vest pocket.

"Sounds great!" Charlie said enthusiastically. "What do I need to wear? Can I take my musket?"

"A light raincoat would help. Take the musket if you want, but you might not need it. Like I already told Paul, there's two parts to this." Bert chewed thoughtfully on the toothpick and looked at Paul.

"Two parts? Like what?" Charlie asked. He suddenly felt suspicious of the two men who loomed inside the immaculate room.

"Well, one person stands in the swamp with a burlap bag and a flash-light. The other two of us will flush the birds out from the surrounding woods. The light attracts them, so when they scoot out they'll head to the bag. Which part do you want catcher or flusher?" Bert smiled and continued to pick at his gums.

Catcher or flusher—who does this guy think he is? Charlie stuttered, "Do, eh, I have to stand in the swamp?"

"I have an aluminum chair in my truck that we can put down for you. You saying you want to try catching then?" Bert asked.

"Yeah," Charlie smiled. "Let me get my coat."

"You okay with being a flusher with me, Paul? We have to walk through the tag alders. It'll be rough, but the reward is worth it."

"Sure, Bert, anything sounds good to me," Paul volunteered.

Charlie followed Bert and Paul outside and walked toward the center of town. A fine mist of rain and fog permeated the darkness. The only visible light was the twinkling of a neon Labatt sign in the store's window.

"Paul, you take the middle seat beside Charlie." Bert gestured toward the truck.

Charlie lumbered in beside Paul out of breath. He felt squished when Bert sat in the driver's seat. Charlie began to drum his fingers on the dash-board.

"I forgot the musket," he yelled as the truck began to back up.

"You sure you still want it? What with holding the flashlight and bag, what are you going to use the gun for?" Bert asked.

"Yeah, I guess you're right. I'll forget it for now." Charlie's body mushroomed into the seat and he felt Paul pinned against him.

Bert grabbed the gearshift and put the truck into reverse. "You know what these snipes look like? Don't you?" Bert questioned. "Small birds with tiny legs and feet. They move pretty fast so hunting them's a job. Paul did you try the stew I had going a few weeks back, when there was that cold spell?"

"I don't think I tried it. You mean that brew you keep going on the stove is to eat?" Paul asked incredulously.

"Sure! I do my best cooking there in the store during the colder months. Venison stew: rabbit, muskrat, deer, bear, partridge, snipe—all these things are free fixin's that you'll have to try sometimes. North country food I call it. Good stuff." Bert winked.

Charlie sat and thought about the strange smells he had encountered in the store. He realized the smell was not just wood burning but a combination of the stews Bert prepared. Poison! Images of the colonial cookbook he bought at the Yorktown battle field assured him proper recipes were available. He sat back happy with the memory of having read a snipe recipe.

The drive into the woods brought back Charlie's feelings about the uncertainty of troops bunked at a battle site. How long would the hunt take? Were his fellow men enough for the job? Was there trust for his compatriots? Questions rattled through Charlie's head.

"Snipe's a mighty tasty bird too," Bert continued. "They're fast, though. So, you have to be awfully quick on your feet." The truck eased into a parking space in the dirt pull-off above the swamp. "We're here. Now remember to be quiet." Bert jumped out of the truck followed by Paul.

Charlie opened the passenger door, stood and attempted to catch his breath. Oh the excitement! The dark muskiness of the swamp mixed with the vision of himself as a warrior on the track of blood. The sounds of nightlife filtered through the rainy mist. He heard an owl hoot eeerily in the distance.

"Here you go: flashlight and burlap bag," Bert said. "I'll carry the chair."

Charlie and Paul followed Bert down the steep pass toward the swampy low ground. Balsam ground cover soon gave way to swampland that pulled at Charlie's rubber booted feet.

"This is it," Bert whispered to Charlie. "You sit right here." Bert placed the chair down in the muddy water. "Now you remember to stay here with the bag and the light shining into it. Paul and me, we'll go and flush them birds out. You'll hear us in the woods, but we'll be heading all around. Remember don't leave—even if you don't hear us. Any questions?"

"So, I just sit here and wait?" Charlie asked excitedly.

"That's right. Unless you want to flush them out with me," Bert offered.

"No. I want to be the catcher," Charlie said emphatically.

"Sounds good to us," Bert said. "Right, Paul?"

"I guess so, Bert." Paul shrugged. "I'll go with you."

Charlie sat down heavily in the aluminum chair. Threads of nylon webbing strained under his weight as he rocked back and forth. He carefully planted his boots ten inches apart in the black slime. Water swirled and a malodorousness made him nauseous.

"You've got to stay quiet," Bert cautioned.

Charlie watched as Bert and Paul escaped into darkness. The fetid night sounds filtered in slowly. The distant owl and the tree noises, coupled with Bert and Paul's hoots and cries in the surrounding woods, filled the vacuous blackness. Charlie sat in the chair, held the flashlight and bag, and waited for the hunt to be completed. Within minutes, he no longer could hear voices. He was extremely pleased the two men traveled the distance for the hunt.

Except for the light from the flashlight, all was dark. Each sound took on monstrous proportions as the woods became alive with threatening shapes. Charlie tried to contain his nervousness. Is that a bear? A moose? A panther? Charlie's imagination made him both afraid and nauseous. Unable to reconcile himself to being a warrior who could be sick or afraid, he forced himself to sit quietly. A scream echoed in the distance. Was it a loon or a wildcat? Charlie wondered. He became convinced that a mink lurked in the shadows. Minutes passed by as days. Where are those men? Where are those stupid birds? Charlie realized he hadn't heard any voices for quite some time. He looked down and was shocked to see the flashlight flicker out.

Charlie spent his first hour ever alone in the night woods and the final fifteen minutes in complete darkness. No birds? Charlie couldn't figure what happened to Bert's plans.

Charlie shuddered at the noise of feet high above. "Hey, is that you guys? I'm over here," he called He stood up and was sucked into the swamp's undercurrent. He attempted to regain his footing in the murky water and felt a slithering movement. He jumped back, fearful of a snake.

"Charlie! Any luck? We heard a lot of movement all around the swamp. How many birds do you have?" Bert called hopeful.

"None," Charlie grunted.

"None?" Bert questioned. "What happened? Where's the light?"

"The flashlight burned out about fifteen minutes ago. I didn't see any birds prior to that."

"But Paul and me heard lots of them. Lots of them running toward the bag. Right, Paul?"

"Sure did. They are a little bird; shifty and real quick on their feet." Paul laughed softly.

"Well," Charlie huffed. "We will have to come back again sometime with a stronger flashlight."

"That's right. You know hunting is what they talk about in the Bible. It's like faith—the thing hoped for but not seen." Bert paused reflectively. "Paul and me saw those birds so now we just have to get you to see."

"I can see fine," Charlie said angrily. He shifted in the swamp. "But I want results."

"But we might have to wait for spring for that," Bert cautioned. "I heard the weather is again going to change cold tomorrow and we need warm rain for this." Bert chuckled and shook his head. "Next spring might do us better."

"I see," Charlie said gruffly. He heard strange, night sounds but was fearless in Bert and Paul's presence. "And there's no other options?"

"That's a case," Bert said. "Case closed."

Chapter 25

Did time move too quickly? Sarah wondered. Or too slowly? Did time move at all? One week had passed since she spoke with Paul, and still no sign of the stove. Friday came and went, and rather than call on Saturday, she decided to stop by instead.

It had gotten cold. She zipped her coat up higher. "This is the start of winter, Jupe," she announced ominously. She was pleased when the car engine fired and warmed.

She coasted out of the driveway with one arm out the window, scraping at the windshield. As the windshield warmed, frost slipped toward the hood in runny patches. The view finally cleared completely when she stopped in front of the *STORE GENERAL.*

"You wait here." She ran up the stairs, entered and was surprised to see Bert's wife, Carol, seated near the stove. Steam misted above the wood stove from an iron pot with boiling water. "Carol! It's been ages," Sarah exclaimed excitedly. "Other than seeing you on Halloween, I have not seen you since last summer."

"I've been busy, but today Bert got me to watch the store so he could go hunting." The older woman smiled softly. "Usually he just shuts it down. Today he felt differently. And I said to myself," she shrugged, "why not? I can just as easy do my embroidery here." Carol motioned to a landscape of trees and a farmhouse on a linen cloth in her outstretched hand.

"Oh, that's beautiful!" Sarah exclaimed. "Is it a Christmas gift?" Sarah looked at the tall woman who appeared to be in her sixties. "It sure would be nice as a gift." Sarah was still amazed at Carol's clear, unblemished skin, and blue eyes.

"I'm not sure yet, but a gift sounds like a good possibility. I've been doing a lot of this lately." Carol's hand weaved a needle through the cloth. "You're right, maybe I should start giving everything away. But enough about me. How about you? I haven't seen you since the Halloween party."

"Summer ended about the same time my government job did. Fall came too fast, and now it seems winter is here. I hate it!" Sarah exclaimed. "I'm in need of a new stove; in fact I'm desperate! Makes me want to gorge on all the red licorice you can sell me," she said, heading toward the candy container. "So I'm stopping to see if Paul is finished with the stove he promised me." Sarah walked toward the cooler and returned with a six-pack. "This is my offering to him," she smiled anxiously, placed the Molson beer on the counter, and handed her money to Carol.

"Why, Bert never told me Paul makes stoves. But then again I probably don't know much about Paul. Other than that he and Charlie went snipe hunting with Bert, and that maybe Paul is single."

"Snipe hunting?" Sarah questioned. Wasn't that a scam? she thought. Did Carol wink at her when she mentioned that Paul is single? she wondered.

"Yeah, you know those little birds that you see near the ocean? Or so Bert says." Carol paused. "Anyways, Bert convinced them the birds are choice game and I guess he got Charlie to sit in a swamp with a burlap bag and flashlight. Nothing ever happened of course. Do you think Paul knows what Bert is up to?"

"You mean the tricks, Carol?" Sarah asked, chewing thoughtfully on the licorice.

"Yeah, you know how he can be," Carol said and smiled.

"Sure do. I'm certain Paul will figure it out."

"Let's hope so!" Carol said, and Sarah laughed with her.

"Who is Bert hunting with today?" Sarah asked. She was suddenly alarmed that maybe Paul was gone for the day.

"I think he headed out by himself."

"Carol, thanks for the update," Sarah said. "Hopefully it won't be ages before I see you again."

"If I don't see you before then, have a nice Thanksgiving." Carol spoke softly and immediately returned to the embroidery.

"You too," Sarah called. The door slammed behind her.

"Well, Jupe, I think we're ready. Let's walk. If you see a large bear don't go on the attack! Just stay outside."

The dog hopped toward the corner of the house and sniffed at a bush. Sarah walked on the porch, knocked, and after a few minutes heard voices and rumblings from within the cabin. The sound of a woman's voice made Sarah realize he had somebody with him. Escape was impossible, so she stood uncomfortably still when Paul threw the door open.

"Hi, Sarah! What are you doing over this way?" His tone was friendly, and he ran a hand through uncombed hair.

"Well, uh, I thought I'd check on the stove. But it sounds like you're busy. I can call or stop by some other time." Sarah could feel the beginning of a blush.

"The stove?" Paul asked. Sarah saw that confusion clouded his eyes. "Today is Saturday?" he questioned. "Oh, Sarah, I'm sorry! I was supposed to deliver it yesterday! And to think I didn't call! Here, come on in. It's cold with the door open."

"I can come back," Sarah offered reluctantly.

"Nah, come in."

"Well here's some beer." Sarah shyly presented the six-pack.

"A present? That's great!"

She followed Paul and observed how lean he looked in black sweat pants.

"Francine came to visit, so I'm a bit off schedule. Come on in." He motioned to a dark-haired woman. "Francine, I'd like you to meet a neighbor, Sarah Moore. Sarah, Francine Puzzi, a friend from my hometown."

"Oh, hi," Francine said. The woman sat sprawled on the couch and picked at her hair with a comb. She glanced at Sarah and appeared bored with the introduction.

"Nice to meet you," Sarah said. She was gripped with a sudden uncertainty. Francine's red fingernails and competitive, coal-grey eyes made Sarah feel edgy. How much aggression could there be in a look? she wondered.

"Oh, it's so interesting to meet you," Francine said.

The woman appeared distracted. Sarah knew her own rubber boots, baggy pants and heavy Woolrich coat contrasted with Francine's black lycra pants and white shirt emblazoned with a gold-sequined lion. And the choice of shoes! A pair of laced white boots with two inch heels; wasn't Paul concerned about Francine tipping over? In comparison to Francine's tight trimness, Sarah felt large and awkward. Did Francine expect her to slowly turn into an abominable fur creature and leave a pool of water? Anything to get rid of her?

"Do you live near Paul's family downstate?" Sarah questioned.

"Yes. This is my first time up here." Francine laughed confidently.

"Yeah," Paul interjected. "I picked her up at the train station on Friday. Sarah, I've been rude. Do you want coffee or one of those beers you brought?"

"If the coffee is made, I'll take a cup; hold the beer for another time." Sarah smiled and sat on the chair opposite the couch. She had quickly decided to try to get a better feel for Paul's girlfriend. "So this is your first visit?"

"Yes, and unfortunately it might be my last. Paul doesn't have much longer in school, you know? And I've been very busy with work."

"What do you do?"

"I've just been promoted to manager of a boutique where I've worked for the past two years." Francine examined a cuticle on her thumb and impatiently pulled at a small piece of skin. She flinched momentarily.

"A clothing boutique?" Sarah asked.

"Yes, with real trendy clothes. You know the type," Francine squealed, "colored leather skirts, sequined tops; real hot stuff."

"What's hot?" Paul asked and entered the room with a mug of coffee. "Here you go, Sarah. Do you need sugar or milk?"

"No, this will be fine, thanks."

"Oh, Paul," Francine giggled, "hot! The kinds of clothes we carry at the boutique. I was telling Sarah about my job, and that I might not be able to visit you before the semester ends and you leave here."

"Leave here?"

Sarah watched Paul carefully.

"Yeah, when your classes are finished. You weren't planning on stay-ing?"

Sarah envisioned buckets of cement pouring into the channels of Francine's mind. A heaviness permeated the room.

"Well," Paul said, hesitating. "I, uh, I have time to make that deci-sion." Paul's mouth twitched.

Sarah sensed she and Francine positioned themselves on opposite ends of the playing field. What to do? What to do? Suddenly at ease with the ad-vantage of living near Paul, Sarah relaxed into the conversation. "So," she looked directly at Francine, "do you like it up here?"

"Like it up here?" Francine whined. "Well the A-ron-diacks are cer-tainly beautiful. But I told Paul I get a little scared with all the quiet. It's cold too. Don't you think?"

"We do get a lot of winter, but you learn to dress for it." Sarah looked down at her feet.

"I see," Francine said disappointedly.

"Well?" Paul said questioningly.

Sarah imagined him as a conductor who tried unsuccessfully to control the uncertainties in the room. Francine seemed like a nice enough woman, but Sarah was somewhat disappointed that Paul was with someone who ap-peared to be stuck on herself. Maybe he doesn't realize it, Sarah thought.

"Sarah, I'm almost finished with your stove," Paul said "I, uh, I should bring it over within a few days."

"Sarah is getting a stove from you?" Francine asked with a look of as-tonishment. "When did you start making stoves?"

Sarah was interested in how Francine's mouth appeared opened and amazed in a wide "O," circled with red lipstick.

"You look surprised, but you've always known I have an interest in welding. I started making some stoves over the summer. The results were better than I imagined, and now Sarah is buying one."

"Buying one?" Francine's voice was rich with amazement.

"That's right! I'm dabbling in the stove business."

"Isn't that interesting and nice," Francine cooed.

"Have you seen the bear yet?" Sarah asked, changing the conversation. Let's see how this topic floats, she thought.

"What bear?" Francine questioned.

"Remember, I was attacked when I first arrived here?" Paul said ques-tioningly. He sneezed and appeared trapped. "Uh, well the cub stayed around and now lives on this property. She's harmless, but her winter schedule seems off, and she is still up and about."

"That's it!" Francine exclaimed. "I definitely am staying in for the rest of the day. I have no desire to see a bear in the woods. And after your experience how can you be friendly to one?" Francine waved her hands indignantly.

"This is totally different Francine. The cub won't attack—she thinks I'm like a mother. The bear has strangely enough bonded with me."

"Bonded with you? Oh Paul! You sound like a new father; this is too much!"

"Guess she doesn't like bears, eh Sarah?" Paul asked.

Sarah looked from Paul to Francine and sensed the tension in the room. "Well, I probably should be going now," she gulped the coffee, stood and handed the mug to Paul. "Nice meeting you, Francine. I hope you enjoy the rest of your stay."

"I'm leaving tomorrow," Francine said icily.

"Well, hopefully the weather will hold. Paul, thanks for the coffee. I'll talk to you later. Bye Francine."

"So nice to have met you," Francine said and tossed black curls .

"Sure has been. Bye you guys." Sarah, followed by Paul, walked toward the cabin door. The door opened easily and she stepped onto the porch.

"See you soon," Paul smiled broadly as the door stayed open a crack.

"Bye, Paul." The door closed quickly. "Jupe! Come on it's time to go." The dog hopped over. "No bear? That's one lucky bear, Jupe! She couldn't ever stand a chance against your fierceness."

Chapter 26

▶━▸━०━◂━◀

Charlie knew the snipe hunting was a turn around. For days afterwards, he was excited by the memory: pitch darkness, mud, water, and trees combined with a readiness for the hunt. Conflict and victory had been his challenge. Cast as a main character, he replayed the hunt as he hummed and sorted the mail.

After months of planning, he finally executed deliveries through the office: the goal of Operation Transit had been achieved. Large boxes now arrived daily on the small United States postal truck. Charlie was certain that in time he would even find a local supplier. Charlie saw an empire ultimately disconnected from Booker and knew it didn't matter to anyone in Washington.

"You got a new one here Charlie," Bert called. "Another white collar trafficker of stolen funds."

"Yeah, he came yesterday," Charlie said, startled and somewhat annoyed he didn't hear Bert enter the office.

"Well, you know more and more of this seems to be happening. Criminals—all of them—in suits no less. You know that savings and loan bailout was shoved down our throats and for what?" Bert angrily pushed white hair away from his face and continued, "To fix the largest bank robbery in the history of this country! Just for a day I'd like to go back to criminals you could see. The ones on horseback with scarves covering their mouths."

Here he goes again, Charlie thought and recognized Bert had a fascination with the criminal mind. Yea gods! He always picked out who was new on the FBI most wanted list and had something to say about it. And today it's banking! Charlie yawned and continued to listen to Bert's outline of the problem.

"You know what it is don't you?" Bert questioned. "Banks going out of business—people lining up in hopes of retrieving their life savings. Thousands in line for a few jobs."

"Yeah, yeah," Charlie said disgustedly and continued to sort mail.

"Ain't just on the news," Bert continued, "it's everywhere. Put that with these suited folks doing drugs and we're breaking apart at the seams. Remember the old 'just say no' pitch. What did we say no to: poverty, no jobs nowhere? No sirree," Bert talked rapidly, "we're in denial about our problems."

Charlie yawned again and hoped Bert would leave. He feared Bert's increasingly suspicious talk and hated Bert's nosiness.

"So, it really does seem that postal use is up here then, huh?" Bert inquired.

"That's right. Both in stamp usage and parcel post." Charlie spoke with pride.

"Funny. I had the office for years and never saw an increase. There would be a little change during the summer, what with the tourists and all, but there was never any big change. What's different?"

"Nothing special," Charlie shrugged. "It's just that having a real office with an American flag on display makes a difference." And that's the truth, Charlie thought defensively. "I don't mean to say anything was wrong with your operation, but it didn't really give the impression of a real life post office."

"And now we have that?" Bert drummed his fingers on the counter and looked around. "Complete with the modular in the back?"

"That's right. Washington knew I needed a nice place to live in to draw business and make this place prosperous."

"With a blacktopped driveway too?" Bert pointed outside to the recently paved driveway.

"Yup, blacktop. People are attracted to a certain way of doing things. My customers don't want to get stuck in mud or snow. I'm even going to be doing the plowing when all the snow comes." Charlie didn't understand why he needed to defend the changes. Wasn't it apparent to Bert that he had lacked the ability to run a professional office.

"Plowing?" Bert questioned.

"Yeah, I'm getting a plow to do the job." Charlie knew he couldn't hide his enthusiasm. This guy is a pain and a wimp too, he thought.

"Amazing!" Bert exclaimed.

Charlie was relieved when Bert finally bought a book of stamps and left the office. Geez, he certainly is a pest, Charlie thought; comes in here almost daily and sniffs around and pokes at all the good things that have been done. Maybe Bert was used to not getting anything from the government office, but Charlie knew his way was different.

The morning passed quickly as Charlie hummed and carefully packaged small boxes. He closed the office between twelve and one o'clock, and used the time to eat and kick back on a sofa to watch the early afternoon soap operas. The television blared as Charlie dozed. Within what seemed like minutes, a loud noise woke him.

He heard yelling. "Ain't the government here to serve me now?"

Charlie stumbled toward the window and saw Henry Ewing pace back and forth. This guy looks plenty mad, he thought, and decided to walk outside before Henry broke the window.

"Hey, Henry it's been some time. The office is shut for the lunch hour." Charlie spoke soothingly.

"Shut? What for? I have need to get some stamps now and I was never shut off when I worked for the government. Nope! Day in an' day out in hot swamp country waiting for instructions to go attack some village. You're here to wait on me."

"You're so right! And what can I do for you?" Charlie asked.

"I said I need stamps!"

"I'll make a special case for you then. Here follow me inside." The back door opened easily and Henry stumbled inside and walked directly to the counter. He threw his money down.

"Here you go. You been hunting much?"

"Nah. I don't like going into the woods to sit around. I like to shoot what's on my property. How about you?"

"Been out snipe hunting recently with Bert."

"Snipe hunting?" Henry looked up as his jowls shook.

"Yeah," Charlie spoke proudly.

"Come on!" Henry exclaimed. "You mean those little birds?"

"That's right," Charlie continued, "with the stringy legs that you see at the ocean. They make an excellent stew. We have to go out again when it warms up. My flashlight died and we didn't catch any, even though Bert was able to flush quite a number out of the swamp." Charlie paused, breathless with the exhilaration of the memory of the hunt.

He looked at Henry and suddenly felt uncomfortable. Why did Henry appear angry?

"I thought you were a fool before, but now I know it for certain," Henry snarled. He quickly spun around and left the office. The door slammed.

He's mighty touchy, Charlie thought. And in need of a good dentist too! Charlie continued to hum and pack the small boxes.

Chapter 27

The distracting, whiny, self-centered chatter reduced Paul to a fraction of his former self. It did not take him long to realize Francine had the unchallenged, uncanny ability to create insanity! How could she complain for three consecutive days? he wondered.

"Paul, don't you realize the cold and snow are a burden?" she questioned repeatedly. "How can you be here?"

Paul felt trapped on the last morning when she said, "There's nothing to do outside. Come on, let's go back to bed."

"There isn't time. Besides, you'll miss your train." Paul awkwardly watched as Francine spread body oil across her legs. "You put much more of that stuff on and you'll feel like a seal. Or worse yet, you might slip away."

"From you? Slip away—never!" Francine shrieked. "Even if the cold gets to me and your water pressure stinks, I'm still with you," she said jokingly.

That's the point, Paul thought and reflected on their conflicting attempts at intimacy. And why did she oil herself before a shower? For two days he had felt trapped by Francine's dissatisfaction. He found it easy to retreat into silence, surprised that Francine seemed so different in his new home. He longed for their earlier closeness that possibly seemed lost forever.

"Whatsa matter?" Francine questioned for the umpteenth time. "Did I say something wrong?"

"Nah," Paul said, and looked up as she squirted a thin stream of oil along the length of her leg. "Uh, I just wish you'd stop referring to the people here as woodchucks."

"Woodchucks." Francine giggled. "But don't you think these people look like they climbed out of a hole somewhere?"

"You can think whatever you want, but some of them are my friends."

"Sorreee! I didn't mean to offend!" Francine yelled and headed toward the bathroom.

After Francine was dressed, they drove to the train station in silence. Francine clung tightly and kissed him at the station. Uncomfortable with her intense public display of affection, Paul pulled away, held her shoulders and said, "We'll keep in touch. Okay?"

"Okay." She walked backwards, blew kisses, turned and sashayed toward the conductor. Paul felt relieved when her smug wave was visible in the window. He chewed on his bottom lip and happily waved goodbye.

On the drive home he felt confused about the relationship. The attachment he had once experienced with Francine seemed gone. He questioned if time could possibly provide any answers.

As he drove into the mountains, snow began to fall steadily. The sky turned dark grey with clustered storm clouds. The road became increasingly white and visibility was poor. This would've been it, Paul thought, and imagined Francine's alarmed reaction to the storm. Can't say she has a survivor's instinct for life up here.

Over his short stay in the north, it became increasingly obvious that he was not really interested in going back home. Francine's reaction confirmed the reason he moved north—to be independent from family and to carve out a comfortable life. He didn't see how Francine could possibly fit in this picture.

Paul arrived home and was greeted by the bear which lumbered out from behind the shed. "Why aren't you in a cave or something?" Paul asked. He bent down, snuggled against the matted fur, and immediately began to sneeze. "You hid most of the time Francine was here," Paul said, in awe of the animal's presence. "Can't blame you much. She wasn't too friendly, huh?" he asked, amazed by how huge Bear had become. Snow swirled as the animal moved into the woods. Paul wiped his nose and was fascinated by the connection he felt to the animal. He walked into the shed to complete Sarah's stove.

"Hey Paul, you here?" The sound of Bert's voice distracted him.

"In here," Paul called.

Bert came into the shed, shaking a snow-covered wool cap. "Quite a day isn't it? Where's Francine?"

"On the train headed home," Paul said, looking up at Bert. He felt a strange sense of relief. "And not sure to be seen again."

"She seemed like a nice girl when I met her briefly."

"She's a great girl, but I never heard one woman complain as much as she did in three days. Everything was wrong!" Paul sighed, "It really bothered me, as if I was with a different person. Whatever it is, I hope it passes soon. I miss the old relationship."

"You sound frustrated," Bert said, "how about a beer?" Bert reached into his pocket.

"Frustrated isn't the word. And yes, I'll have a beer." Paul sneezed and wiped at his nose with a handkerchief.

"How much more do you have left on the stove?"

"I'm done finally. Just need to load it. Want to help?"

"Sure."

"It's getting late so I plan to deliver it tomorrow."

The two men lifted the stove and carried it on to the truck.

"There. That's one nice stove." Bert grinned. "You learn quick."

"Thanks Bert. Would you like to come inside? I'm sure there's another beer for when these are finished."

"Can't pass that one up."

They headed toward the cabin and entered the warm kitchen. Paul thought again about the cabin's coziness and still was amazed at Francine's reaction when she called it a shack.

"It's looking good in here. A little different than when you first arrived," Bert said, laughing.

"Yeah, that certainly was one introduction."

"You know? I always feared you wouldn't be fixing to stay and that you'd want to leave. Forget the studies and all."

"Couldn't happen. It just made me think about why I'm here and then I actually came to appreciate it. Seeing Francine made me even more certain about where I want to be." Paul looked at Bert and wondered if he sounded convincing to his neighbor.

"So you gave her the boot then?" Bert questioned.

"Not yet. I'm still hopeful she'll like it here."

"Then it's just a matter of time?" Bert probed.

"I'm not sure," Paul said. His tongue picked at his bottom lip as he shifted uncomfortably on the metal chair.

"Hey, not to change the subject, but did you hear that Charlie claims his postal use has gone up?" Bert asked.

"You've mentioned that before."

"Yeah, well the news is that now that the driveway is paved he's getting a new truck for plowing." Bert laughed heartily.

"How'd use go up in November?" Paul just knew that Bert was itching to have him ask.

"Beats me," Bert said, shaking his head. "Maybe folks are sending Christmas cards early." Bert pushed hair away from his eyes and looked questioningly at Paul. "Charlie claims 'cause people now know it's a real government office because of the way the building looks. I had that office for years and use never once went up."

"Sounds fishy. Where did he get the money to do all the work anyway? And now a new truck."

"It's like the thing with Francine," Bert grinned widely and tapped a large cowboy boot on the floor. "Only time will tell."

Geez, Paul thought, Bert is starting to sound like a cliche.

"Anyway," Bert hiccuped, "no more beer. I have to get going. Promised Carol I'd take her shopping. You sure you won't need help with that stove tomorrow?"

"I'll be fine." Paul followed Bert to the door. "See you later."

"Catch you then." Cold air blasted into the room when the door opened and Bert waved goodbye.

The following morning came quickly. Unwilling to get up, he relaxed in the warmth of flannel sheets, happy to be alone in his bed. When he finally left the bed, he was surprised to see three inches of snow and a brilliant white landscape outside the window. He shuffled around the cabin and dressed slowly. Paul breathed easily and wondered if his allergies were worse in Francine's presence. She had been annoyed with his constant sneezing.

He ventured outside the cabin and was surprised by the intensity of sunlight that sparkled against frozen limbs. He hoped for a day where anything could happen. The truck backed easily out of the snow covered driveway and he headed south past the store in the direction of Sarah's house. Three miles down the road, he found a driveway situated between large spruce trees and backed up close to the house. In the nearby garden, he saw the remains of deadened vegetable leaves covered with snow. He left the truck and walked toward the front door.

He called, "Hello. Anyone home?" and realized the house was vacant. A note taped to the door said: *PAUL— IF YOU HAPPEN TO COME BY FEEL FREE TO INSTALL THE STOVE. OLD STOVE CAN BE LEFT IN THE OUTSIDE SHED.* The brass knob turned easily as Paul opened the door, walked in and was immediately impressed by the room's neatness. He saw a couch, two end tables and a wooden-burl coffee table in the living room. A wall shelf held neat stacks of books. In the corner a stove was connected to piping that went through the ceiling.

He quickly disconnected the metal pipe, saw it was visibly corroded and pulled the stove away. Creosote and pieces of rust fell on the floor. What a mess! He walked outside for a hand cart and once back inside positioned the stove on the cart, maneuvered it out of the building, and deposited it near the shed.

He heard a noise, looked and saw Sarah pulling into the yard.

She scrambled out of the car. "I see my note helped." The dog followed and barked repeatedly.

"Sure was. I already have the old stove by the shed."

"If you give me a minute to get some work gloves, I can help you move the new one."

"That's great." Paul watched Sarah walk toward the house. Dressed in a plaid coat with hiking boots, she had a clean but relaxed look. She was more solid than Francine. Strong. And there was a warmth to her personality that he was drawn to. Take note, he thought. Sarah has adjusted to life in the woods. Could Francine ever make the transition? Paul compared the two women and felt traitorous because of his attraction to Sarah. His heart fluttered and he remembered it hadn't been twenty four hours since he last saw Francine.

"Well, I'm ready now," she said, smiling. "Where do you want me?"

Paul stalled for a minute on the word want. He had the crazy feeling his heart had been seered by the bright intensity of her smile. "Uh, how about we both get up on the truck?" he suggested.

"Okay." Sarah easily climbed on to the platform.

"Here," Paul said, "let's both just pull it toward the edge. This blanket will help if we lower it."

Sarah scrambled to the ground, positioned the blanket and jumped back on the truck.

"Okay, let's bend and get this moved." Paul could feel Sarah's blond hair brush against him. Standing inches from her, her strength combined with his. "Okay, let it go." They simultaneously released and the stove fell with a loud thud. "Only a few more feet to go. The hand cart will help with that." Paul smiled reassuringly.

Within minutes the new stove was inside the building. "Hey, I also brought some new piping and you really need it. How do you get upstairs to disconnect this stuff?"

"Well, that's a challenge," Sarah said, seemingly embarrassed. "Not having a ladder, I use the chair and door knob to lift myself up so I can pull into the attic."

"The door knob?"

"Yeah." Sarah smiled. "Probably not a good idea especially since it can't hold you. I'll go." Sarah clambered into the attic space. "I'm going to pull the piping down."

"I've got it." Paul caught the length of pipe as creosote fell. "Here, let me pass the new stuff up. Will it go straight out of the building?"

"Yeah. Stovepipe used to travel through the attic; everything hung on metal coat hangers. The new chimney was put in a year ago."

"A year and this much corrosion?" Paul asked. "Anyway, I hope this pipe is the right fit. Here it comes."

Minutes passed as Paul listened to Sarah fit the pipes together.

"All together; I'm going to come down now," Sarah said. She jumped through the hole in the ceiling. "Time to move the stove?"

"Sounds good." Together they moved the stove toward the wall and placed the draft hole under the piping. "This is the finale," Paul said, "getting everything to come together just right at the end." He positioned the two pieces of metal together. "There! It's all done!"

"Wow! Can we get it going?"

"Let me put the fire brick in and then we can start it up," he said, somewhat startled with how happy Sarah was with the stove. "I'll just be a few more minutes." *It seems so easy to make her happy*, he thought, as another disturbing image of Francine flashed before him.

"Do you need help with anything else?" Sarah questioned. "If not I was just about to make a lunch. You interested?"

"Well... what are you having?" Paul asked.

Sarah stammered, "Uh.... some casserole, salad. I can even make a quick dessert."

"I'm definitely convinced. I'll finish up the stove."

Paul noticed that while she was busy and absorbed with peeling and cutting apples, Sarah didn't pay any real attention to him. He was amazed at her interest in preparing lunch. Days with Francine had forced him to assume daily cooking responsibilities. The usual campaign—too busy, not interested—kept Francine on a soapbox of being able to always talk about not cooking.

A slow fire burned in the stove when Sarah said lunch was ready.

"That smell is from the paint I used. It will go away in a few hours."

"Here, have a seat. I'm thrilled about this stove."

"I'm glad, but what's this—a full course meal?" The table was filled with a variety of foods: salad, lasagne, parmesan cheese and a bowl of meatballs covered in red sauce. "This is amazing!"

"It's nothing—actually it's leftovers, except for the salad."

"Leftovers?" Paul noticed her face had turned red again. "This is the best I've eaten since being up here."

"You probably should hold your praise until you've had a bite. It might just look nice."

"I doubt it." Paul dished food on a plate.

"Go ahead and start to eat. Would you like a glass of wine?"

"Sure," Paul said.

"Here, let's toast." Sarah lifted a glass.

"Good idea!"

"To warmth in the winter and my success in finally finding a stove. Thank you!" The glasses clanked together.

"Well, this whole thing has been neat. Meeting you, fixing you up a stove, and then having a real meal. Too much! What do you do when you're not visiting with Bert or now that the government work is finished?"

"I still have my part-time massage and acupuncture business. Part-time is probably a simplification—I only have a couple of customers I see on a regular basis. I also work at the vet's place down the road. Combined I guess it keeps me fairly busy."

The differences between Sarah and Francine were striking to Paul. With long blond, free flowing hair, Sarah appeared to be both solid and relaxed in her corduroy pants and turtle neck sweater. For months now Paul had imagined what her body would look like without all the clothes. He ate a forkful of salad and was distracted by his fantasy of her long legs.

"What was that?" He shifted uncomfortably, suddenly conscious of both his absorption and Sarah's suspicious look. "I'm sorry I missed what you said."

"I asked if you are enjoying school?"

"School? Oh yeah. It's been great. I'm really happy that I came up here," he responded quickly. "I've always hoped for a connection like I've

found here, but I'm also fearful of it. The fact that you're known by everyone is a bit scary."

"Yeah, I know what you mean, but I think I'm more settled with it
now." Sarah took a sip of wine. Paul noticed she casually flicked her tongue
along the glass rim. "Did Francine enjoy her visit?"

"Francine? Oh yeah." Paul smirked. "She left yesterday on the train.
I'm not sure if she found the cold to be appealing."

"It certainly is a shock the first time. I'll always remember when I came
up here with a friend one April, years ago, after first visiting in the fall. We
brought tents and were ready to camp, but wound up sleeping in the front
seats of our car. There was close to two feet of snow still on the ground!
And we were not ready for winter camping!"

"You survived it though?"

"Well, sure, but my expectations changed a bit. I've accepted the fact
that it gets quite cold here and dress accordingly."

Paul started to laugh. "I'm sorry," he said, wiping at his eye, "but
Francine was so unstable in those boots she insisted on wearing."

"Boots?"

"Yeah, those leather, high-heel boots. She believed they're a necessity.
The two times we stepped outside—when she arrived and left—she clung
to me to keep from falling," Paul said, somewhat uncomfortable with talking about Francine. "Anyway," he continued, "I guess it's a matter of pref-
erence and adjustment."

"Yeah," Sarah smiled, "those kind of things are sort of forced on you
up here."

"Hey, changing the subject," Paul said, "did you know that Bert and
me went snipe hunting with Charlie?"

"Yeah. Carol told me."

Paul laughed. "It took me a while, but snipe hunting is another of
Bert's challenges. You had to see Charlie! All excited—standing in the
middle of a swamp with a flashlight and burlap bag. We left him there and
went back to the store and had a beer. Later we went back and Charlie's
flashlight had died out, but he kept asking—'when are we going to do this
again?' As you can see, we're trying to bring him into the fold."

"So," Sarah ventured clumsily.

Paul simultaneously said, "snipe hunting..."

They stumbled over each other's words and collapsed in laughter.

Paul liked the way she laughed... when she looked at him his face felt
warm and he had to look away.

"More wine?"

"Sure. Why not? Getting back to Charlie though." Paul looked at Sarah. "You think he's creepy?"

"Creepy! That guy is a sleaze. He undresses women with his fat eyes and just always seems so slippery."

Undresses women? Paul wondered if his distraction about Sarah's body was visible. Nah, he reassured himself. Smile now, brightly, he thought, and do not shift eyes up and down.

"You think he's that bad huh? He's got one operation going there with his new home and paved driveway."

"I've probably overreacted to Charlie," Sarah said, passing the salad to Paul. "He's probably a nice guy and being new and all in town with no wife doesn't make it any easier."

"Yeah, it's important we give him a chance," Paul said. "We need that post office." He was not sure if it was the wine, the good food or the fire in the stove, but he suddenly sensed a longing for a feeling of peace and warmth. He looked at Sarah and realized it was so easy to be with her, but something made him afraid. He relaxed cautiously in the magic that weaved between them. He didn't want to leave. He wanted to stay with Sarah and have her, at least for a moment, blend into him.

"This meal is wonderful," Paul spoke softly.

"A small thanks for the stove," Sarah said, looking at him. "I can't tell you how much I appreciate you bringing it over and renting it to me. Being cold up here in the winter is no fun."

"Well, I'm happy to play a role in keeping you warm. Let's toast again."

"I think we need some more wine," Sarah said. She poured the liquid into the two glasses."

"Here's to Sarah being warm for the winter!" The two glasses clanked together. Outside the window it was becoming increasingly dark. "The change of clocks makes everything so dark early," Paul sighed. "It's like an onslaught of darkness."

Sarah shrugged, "That's for sure. Would you like some apple crumb?"

"Sounds great. You know, with the loss of light and all, I've always found this time of year to be a real challenge."

Sarah dished up two bowls of dessert. "That's why being warm is important." She handed the dessert to Paul.

"This looks great! Do you like to cook?" Paul questioned.

"Yeah," Sarah said, smiling openly. "I guess I do like it."

"You're pretty good at it," Paul said. This woman is too much, he thought.

"Cooking helps me to relax."

"Do you get bored cooking for yourself?" Paul asked. He didn't know how to probe if Sarah had a boyfriend.

"Not really," Sarah mumbled, "but it's sure nice to have someone to cook for."

Paul sensed Sarah was hesitant to talk about being alone, but hoped for a small space in her life. Did he really know with any certainty if he wanted Sarah? Or if she wanted him? He glanced at her and suddenly became overcome with uneasiness.

"Would you like to sit in the living room and listen to some music?" Sarah asked.

"Can't touch another bite. The meal was great," Paul said. "I'll take more wine, though." He reached for the bottle. Paul stood. "The stove seems to be burning real nice." Together they walked out of the kitchen into the living room.

Sarah turned the radio on to a jazz station. Slumped in the chair next to Paul, Sarah sipped at the wine. Music filled the quiet spaces.

"This is really too peaceful," Paul said. He knew his voice sounded dreamy and far away.

"What's that?" Sarah questioned.

"Being here in the north woods with the challenge of the long winter. Getting to know everybody." Paul peered at Sarah and felt that he babbled. "Being a visitor at your house."

"A visitor?" Sarah questioned. "As the stove man you're now in a special category." Sarah reassuringly touched Paul's hand.

"I don't know," he continued, "there seems to be something up here that I want. Something that I'm headed ever closer to finding." His hand felt on fire with her touch.

"So do think you might stay after school is finished?" Sarah asked.

"It's becoming more and more a possibility," Paul responded easily. Did her voice sound hopeful? he wondered. "I'm even looking into some work. Who knows? Livelihood can probably even come together."

"That's how I felt when I first came here. It was like a voice inside made it real clear that I needed to live here. I tried to deny that urge and live in other places, but it never seemed quite real. So when I left California two years ago I knew it was for good."

"Did you find there was a different acceptance?" Paul asked, wondering if Sarah had the same feelings of unease he experienced.

"Yeah." Sarah laughed. "Like I said to you on Halloween. It's a jump to the left—another dimension. I don't know why I've always felt that way, but there is something about the land, the culture, and the humor of people like Bert. Maybe it's that there are so few of us. So we come together to make an extended family," Sarah said, twirling her blond hair around a finger. "With the long winter, we learn to rely on each other in unique ways. I've never been sure why, but I know it's very real."

"That's quite a mouthful," Paul said and smiled. "What did your folks think when you decided to stay here?"

"My folks are divorced, and my Dad has a new life with a young wife.

He's pretty materialistic and would never understand this simplicity. My Mother is another story," Sarah said sipping the wine. "In our home you weren't supposed to go very far away and northern New York is quite a distance from my hometown of Greenwich, Connecticut. She's been real disappointed about my moving, but I've had her up a couple of times to visit. Mom thinks it's pretty—you know, 'the mountains are really blue, Sarah,' line, but she will never understand it, and unfortunately takes it as a personal rejection." Sarah suddenly stopped talking and looked at Paul. "I have two younger sisters and a brother," Sarah continued. "They think I'm nuts."

"Hey, you're the oldest too!" Paul said, looking closely at Sarah. He wondered if she felt comfortable talking about her background with him. "Your experience is similar to mine. I know my folks want what's best for me, but it will be interesting to see their reaction when I finally settle down. My two younger brothers and sister probably have bets I won't make it up here."

A feeling of tenderness overcame Paul as he looked at Sarah and he felt confused. Overwhelmed by the warmth in the room and the tingling in his body, he had a sudden urge to lean over and kiss her. Is she waiting? What are the rules here? Not naturally aggressive, and in a totally different element than when he was with the brassy Francine, he sat in confused thought. Jazz rifts filtered through the silence.

"Are you going to be here for Thanksgiving?" Sarah broke the quiet.

"I'm not sure yet," Paul said, sitting upright as he remembered his homework. "I, uh, unfortunately I have to get going. I still have a ton of school stuff to do before Monday." He placed the glass down on the burl table.

"Okay," Sarah jumped up. "Again, I can't thank you enough for the stove. Come by soon and check on it."

"I sure will and thanks again for the meal." Paul hoped the quickness of his leave was not too visible or disturbing. He leaned over and gave Sarah a quick hug. "You keep good and warm now," he said.

Sarah followed Paul outside. "Boy, it has gotten cold. Take care now."

Paul walked toward the truck. He drove away and wondered if Sarah knew that it was her closeness that upset him; that he needed to be distanced from the softness of her voice; that he needed to understand a projection of her; that he needed to understand himself before he could really connect to a person like her. He easily maneuvered the truck through the dark road, lured by the brightness of a full moon on the horizon. He feared that Francine now lived in the periphery of his life and sensed that Sarah had the ability to come close—too close.

Clouds spun over the moon and cast shadows over the road. Enveloped in the cold of the early winter, he ignored the sudden aloneness and emptiness. The coldness of the truck's cab stayed with him during the drive home.

Chapter 28

"What do you mean you lost the file? The only thing I left with you and it's gone." Charlie screamed into the phone receiver. "Booker you stuffed yourself with too much turkey and now you're sounding like one. What happened to your mind over the holiday?" Charlie paced back and forth.

"But there could have been a break-in at the office by enforcement," Booker said.

Charlie suddenly stopped dead in his tracks. "You mean drug enforcement? Uh, oh," he stammered. "Do you know what this means?" Charlie questioned.

"Not sure," Booker said.

"Any other evidence? Come on, Booker, answer these questions." Charlie quieted down momentarily, picked at his belly button and examined a lint ball. "That's all you've got to say? That's nothing! I'm hanging up now. You call me back when you have more information."

There's no sense in anything Booker said, Charlie thought. And to think of how he whines! What could have been simpler? A box of index cards of buyers and a smaller box of suppliers were the core of the network. Charlie had made certain there was nothing left in Washington, but that obviously didn't decrease drug enforcement's interest in the capitol office. Nah, Charlie thought, they could never pull the final thread to unravel the workings of the North Country office. Charlie paced, deep in thought. It was a perfect puzzle as long as Booker didn't slip and mention Charlie's name to enforcement. But what if he described the quick transition? What if someone put two and two together and realized the shift north happened during the first leaks of drug trafficking to the media?

That had been the beauty of the move. His solution came on a winter day as he had visited with the assistant postmaster general, Gorgo Rushton, and had heard complaints about the need for rural post offices and staff unwillingness to relocate.

"Can you imagine? Some nitpick in northern New York wants out cause there's too much paperwork? Some Gendron guy says his little town is in need of a postmaster." Gorgo had waved a letter and picked furiously at his eyebrows. "This here is paperwork," Gorgo had said and brushed a hand over mountains of paper.

"Well, if you have to respond to that request I'm your man." Charlie had spoken quickly, thrilled with the opportunity to move forward. "I'd love to get back to rural America."

"For what?" Gorgo had demanded. "Nothing up there but bugs, trees and folks complaining about their postal service."

"I want to pursue a quieter life. Hunt, have nights around a campfire." Charlie's hope for adventure had motivated him to fantasize.

Charlie now thought about how that first conversation with Gorgo Rushton was the beginning of the transition. It had not taken Rushton long to realize that Charlie would be an asset in the north. When Charlie had received the transfer order he had already carefully laid the groundwork to move his entire operation to the small rural office. Throughout the move Charlie had thought happily of being in control, free of Booker.

The only real surprise had been the twenty-below zero temperature outside in December. Trembling with the cold, Charlie repeatedly mouthed Booker's words until he wanted to bite somebody. Stupid, stupid man, he thought. Continually suspicious about Booker's trustworthiness, Charlie feared the reason for the northern move would surface. Inside his living room, a silver artificial tree shimmered with blue satin balls and white lights. Booker's conversation pranced through his head. "Gorgo can't find out anything," Charlie muttered and walked toward the iced over window. He looked through the frost and saw a plastic snowman aglow on the front stairs.

Charlie's face twitched as he paced in the living room. All the suppliers adjusted to the move. In fact, did any of the buyers have a problem? No one cared if the stuff came from Washington or some outside town as long as the boxes came on a continual basis.

Charlie carefully justified why the northern connection had made sense. He knew that when you were the government you were treated differently. No sniffing dogs or anything. Confident the investigation could not possibly extend to him, Charlie dismissed Booker's fears and charges. But just how many people feared the investigation? Charlie wondered. He thought about how nice it would look to have people throughout America know that stamp vouchers were being exchanged for cash. And for them to know that the cash was used for drugs! And all in a day's work, Charlie thought happily.

Chapter 29

Nothing made sense, Sarah thought. Weeks had gone by since Paul had brought the stove. Thanksgiving and Christmas had come and gone, and still no news from him. Sarah had hoped the stove would be the beginning of something bigger between the two of them. She was frustrated by how unrealistic her expectations had been.

The end of a visit with her family in Connecticut over Christmas did nothing to help her depressed mood. Although she was accustomed to the usual questions about her northern home, Sarah had still found it hard to justify her patchwork of employment. Her success at finding a new woodburner was a minor footnote to a family used to centralized heat and the best of America's products.

Her sister, Martha, happy with a new Mazda sports car parked in the driveway, was positively scornful of Sarah's beat-up Volkswagen. "Aren't you afraid to drive that car on the highway?" Martha had questioned, carefully inhaling on a cigarette. Two years younger, Martha lived near their mother in Connecticut, worked in New York City, and was inured to a daily ride on the tube into work as an investment banker.

When all the gifts were unwrapped at her mother's house, she and her two sisters and brother stared at each other while their Mom drank vodka tonics and smoked. Time had stood still and empty for Sarah, filled with a permeable sadness.

As Sarah had prepared to leave, her Mom had whispered, "You know if you want to move back here you're welcome anytime. There are nice schools nearby," her mother said, slurring her words. "I'm sure your sister, Janet, wouldn't mind sharing a room with you again. Think about it," she suggested and hiccuped.

Sarah thought about her mother's proposal and almost wretched with the idea of moving home to share a room with her sister. She didn't even try to imagine what her younger brother, Mike, would think of having two sisters at home, and couldn't entertain how Martha would gloat. The notion of sharing a home with them again, all of them smokers at that, made her feel ill.

A visit at her Dad's home, with his new thirtyish wife, Patsy, only added to her disorientation. Sarah had reluctantly watched as his wife tore at the gift wrapping.

"What is this?" Pasty asked, suspiciously holding up twined threads, beads and feathers.

"It's a dream catcher," Sarah said.

"Oh, how interesting!" Patsy squealed.

"You can catch good and bad spirits with it," Sarah mumbled, "or so Indian lore says."

"What's that Sarah—voodoo?" Her Dad's voice boomed across the room.

"Come on, Dad." Sarah sighed.

"Oh, look dear," Patsy exclaimed, "little itsy, bitsy tiger eyes. How thoughtful of you, Sarah. We'll put it in the hallway near the bathroom."

Leaving Dad and Patsy was a relief. The separateness of her Father's life only added to Sarah's loss. Sarah had never wanted two separate families and she feared that Patsy hinted once too often about having a baby.

During the drive back home, Sarah wondered about all the things she wanted and did not have. She couldn't understand why spending time with her family made her feel so empty and so uncertain about the choices she had made for herself. Tears came to her eyes and she had the overwhelming sense of being completely alone.

It began to snow north of Albany, and the car moved slowly over increasingly icy roads. The roads were congested and visibility was poor. She squeezed the wheel tightly. Within an hour the snow began to let up and the traffic decreased. When Sarah passed the entrance sign for the Adirondack Park, she breathed more easily. Two hours later, the clouds lifted and sunlight filtered onto snow covered mountain peaks. Away from the highway, the trip through a mountain pass was dark and icy. On the final lag of the journey, the car moved past the collossal ski jumps which thrust up abstract and prominent to the left of the road. Within minutes, Sarah entered the flatland which led toward home.

After parking the car in the yard, she trudged through a foot of fresh snow toward the cabin. A white envelope stuck to the door and fluttered in the wind. Sarah tore it free, and entered the cabin. A Charlie Brown christmas tree, fashioned with colored ribbons, popcorn strings and pinecones, stood in the corner. The inside of the building seemed even colder than outside and Sarah was disappointed the electric back-up heat had not worked properly. So much for frozen water pipes, she thought, and was downright giddy to see the water still worked in the bathroom.

Sarah quickly built a fire, and went outside to carry the pile of gifts and backpacks inside. She called her friend, Susan, who had been dogwatching for her, and left a message on Susan's answering machine that she would stop by to pick up Jupe in the morning.

As the fire began to burn steadily in the stove, Sarah added larger pieces of wood. She sat down on the couch and opened the white envelope. Colored balloons beckoned: *JOIN US FOR A NIGHT OF CHEER! GET RID OF THE OLD WITH THE NEW.* Sarah opened the card and saw it was an invitation for a New Year's Eve party at Bert's house.

Sarah went to bed knowing she would wear the red sequined dress her mother had given her. Short and stylish, the dress had hung in her closet for years. She fell asleep certain she would make an all out attempt to get Paul's attention.

Chapter 30

Paul sat in his cabin and drank a cup of coffee. He thought about how a journey to hell had colored his holiday season. Distracted by Thanksgiving, the relationship with Francine had become even more twisted and uncertain. It wasn't enough that he went home for a long Thanksgiving weekend at the end of November, but landing at Francine's parents for a meal had been too much. And her teenage brother had the nerve to video everything! Francine's squeals of 'Paul give me a kiss on camera' had had the feel of nails scratching on a blackboard. He cringed with the memory.

And then for Christmas he went back home and fell into the trap of having Francine to his parents' house for the holiday meal. Stupidity! he thought. What kind of message did he send anyway? he questioned, sipping the coffee. He had been thinking about breaking up with Francine and ultimately spent not one but two holidays with her. He shuddered thinking about Francine's relentless expectations about a gift.

"Paul, what's in this package?" she had asked, shaking a large box. She had torn the paper off, and pulled a blender from the carton.

"Oh, I love it," she said sarcastically.

"Yeah, I figure you like those low-cal drinks and can now make them," he had responded smoothly.

He remembered how later, during a dinner after Christmas, his mother had asked about his plans. "What are you going to do after the semester is completed?" she questioned, passing a bowl of mashed potatoes to his younger brother.

"I've decided to stay up north." Paul had reached for the bowl as silence descended on the table. He felt minutes tick with the precision of a baker's timer. "I think I have some real opportunities to make a fair living and I love it there."

"What about Francine?" his mother asked nosily.

"Well," Paul stalled, "we've not really talked about it."

"Did she enjoy the visit up there?" His Dad's voice boomed.

"Enjoy?" Paul questioned. "It was hard to tell. It was pretty cold and with the snow and all she refused to go outside. She whined quite a bit."

"Why is that?" his father asked.

"She might just be an urban girl, Dad." Paul shrugged.

"What are you saying, Paul, 'an urban girl'?" his father demanded. "Just what do you want for yourself up there?"

"Uh," Paul spoke uncomfortably, "uh, some quiet, work, a woman who fits."

"Fits?" the older man questioned.

"Yeah," the twins chattered, "like a glove."

"Be quiet you two," Paul said, glaring at the two teenagers, Jimmy and Timmy.

"Well," his mother interrupted quickly. "Well." She smiled brightly, happy to have shifted the conversation. "We'll stand by you son. Right dear?" Paul watched as she turned expectantly to his father. "We'll hope to visit you. Soon."

His dad shook his head, back and forth. Did his father agree or was the head shaking a signal of Paul's stupidity, recklessness and indecisiveness? Man to man, what did his father really think of a son who was confused by one woman? Did Dad really think the school courses would be of any use? Paul just knew the twins and his sister were calculating their returns on the bets they probably made about his ability to stay up north. He felt like kicking them.

Once back in the northern cabin, Paul felt relieved with the distance from his family. He finished his coffee and thought about how Bert's invitation to a New Year's Eve party gave him hope. The inability to confront Francine over the holidays had made him desperate for change and he wondered whether Sarah would be there.

On the night of the party, a foot of fresh snow lay on the ground as Paul walked toward the center of town. Lured by the white christmas lights that bordered Bert's house and sparkled invitingly in the frigid air, he realized it was mighty cold.

Dogs barked as Paul rang the bell. Within seconds Bert opened the door. "Paul, how you doing? Survive the holiday?" Bert asked

"Yeah, it was a pretty good Christmas. I went home." Paul shrugged out of his coat, and hoped his despair about the family visit wasn't too apparent. "It's nice to be back. How about you?"

"Can't complain. Got some fly tieing equipment, so I was happy. But I'll be even happier when I can give you some of my dandelion wine," Bert said, heading toward the corner of the room. "Got this from my old friend Walter years ago." Bert held an opaque glass bottle and poured wine into a glass. "It's homemade. Here you go," Bert said and handed the glass to Paul.

"Homemade?" Paul questioned. He hoped the wine wasn't anything like Bert's venison stews.

"Yeah, Walter was a neighbor. A good friend who passed away. A great winemaker," Bert said enthusiastically.

"Pretty strong stuff." Paul's face grimaced after the first sip.

"Yeah, and not just in taste. Here, come say hello to Carol."

"Paul," Carol looked up and hugged him, "you look great. Happy holidays."

"Happy holidays to you," Paul said. He bent down and kissed Carol on the cheek. "Nice party here." Paul looked around and saw about ten people in the room.

"We're still expecting some more folks. It's early yet. Sarah's here," Carol said and grinned. "Have you seen her lately?"

Paul choked on the wine. "Sarah? No, I haven't seen her in weeks. I was away for the two holidays. With the break in classes, I was able to visit my folks."

"Well, it's good to have you back. We had a quiet Christmas with lots of snow. How about downstate?"

"Hardly any except for an inch on Christmas Eve that was gone by morning." Paul looked up, surprised to see Sarah in the doorway. Yea gods, he thought, and watched her walk into the room dressed in a short red dress. The sequined material sparkled and molded her hips and waist. High heels made her legs appear endless. The blond hair that was usually in a braid or ponytail was blown dry and tousled. Paul looked longingly at her and felt confused as she approached.

"Hello, and Happy New Year," she said. She leaned toward him with a quick hug and smack of lips on his cheekbone.

"Sarah, it's been too long." Paul smiled, somewhat dazed by his attraction to her. "Happy New Year too—you look great!" Paul quickly noticed the details of how Sarah's dress formed a rounded neckyolk and exposed her shoulder, upper chest and back muscles. Definitely strong, he thought and watched as her biceps rippled just ever so slightly when she lifted the wineglass. "I've been real busy with school and the holidays so I'm sorry I never made it back to check on the stove. Everything okay with it so far?"

"It's been great. Best stove I've ever seen."

"That certainly is good news!" Paul fidgeted with his wineglass.

"Paul, Sarah, nice to see the two of you together talking," Bert said. "You need a refill Paul. What about you Sarah? What are you drinking?"

"Uh, regular wine. You better be careful with the dandelion wine, Paul. It's potent."

Paul smiled broadly. "That's okay. It's New Year's Eve. Anything can happen."

The house filled with people from the surrounding community. Bert dragged Paul around for introductions to the various cousins and neighbors who were still strangers. Paul quickly lost track of names as music filtered through the room and people danced in slow motion to the country tunes.

Paul experienced a sense of vertigo as time first stood still, spun and then erupted in the hour before midnight. With perspective and identity gone, Paul was exhilarated with a forced senselessness. Hope for the coming year was both distorted and framed by the wine's intoxicating influence. He felt surprisingly loose when Sarah surfaced in front of him.

"You're back. Oh no! You're not a fairy godmother who's going to make me go home at the strike of twelve?"

"Paul?" Sarah asked questioningly. "Are you feeling the influence of that wine?"

"Wine? Oh, yeah, this stuff is great!" Paul swayed in place. "It will soon be the new year. Do you have all sorts of resolutions?"

"Well, I always try a sort of mental house cleaning that energizes me through January and February. Beyond that I am not very consistent with promises of things to do or not do. What about you?"

"Me? I'm still caught in where to live; the what to do scenario. The old girlfriend scene. Maybe it will be resolved by the new year?" He laughed and felt the heat of Sarah's presence. "Maybe there's a resolution to solve all of this?" he questioned.

"You certainly seem to enjoy a sustained confusion. Has this been for some time now?" Sarah asked.

"Ah, it's all about changes and what I want out of them." Paul laughed. "I think I'm probably a real danger and risk to anyone until I know. Anyone who would get too close would see it all quite starkly."

"What do you mean?"

"I can't reveal that now," Paul said. "Want to dance?" He grabbed Sarah by the waist and began to pull her around the room. "So you think I'm drunk and need an excuse to dance with you? What about me just wanting to dance with you?" Paul murmured into Sarah's hair.

Paul felt Sarah blend into his movements as he thought about the new year on the horizon. The wine liberated a core of fear. He mellowed in the safe feeling of Sarah's arms. He and Sarah swayed quietly to the music. This is a place of dreams, he thought, when Carol suddenly interrupted.

"It's almost midnight. Everybody get your party stuff so we can watch the ball descend on t.v." She gestured. "Come on Paul, Sarah—the time is now."

Paul grabbed the blowers and hats that Carol passed out. "Here you go, Sarah," Paul said, handing Sarah a pointed green hat. He saw people standing with the goofy expressions that come from wearing paper hats covered with tinsel and sparkles. He and Sarah crowded around the television with people who chattered loudly.

"Ten, nine, eight, seven," Paul shouted, ticking the seconds off as the old year passed away.

"Midnight! Happy New Year!" The crowd chanted. People grabbed each other and hugged and kissed.

Sarah wrapped her arms around his neck, said, "Happy New Year, Paul," and kissed him long and hard. Paul knew with a intense clarity that he wanted her. He wanted her long, blond and naked but only on terms of his own freedom from Francine. The wine suddenly vacated his brain cells.

He cringed with the shocking realization that any new relationship had to start only after the old was dissolved. He pulled away and looked at her closely.

"That was nice," he exclaimed. "Can I have time?" He mouthed the words, slowly and fearfully.

"However much." Sarah smiled brightly. "I live here."

Chapter 31

February arrived too soon for Paul. Depressed by the grey stillness of the sky and the relentless snow, he scraped the windshield of his truck and prepared to drive to town. He hoped the winter parade would help to break his winter blues. He figured if the parade helped people overcome winter doldrums during the past ninety-five years, it could be quite a good tonic. There was nothing left to lose, he thought gloomily, maneuvering down the icy road. Once in town he parked and was slightly cheered to see Sarah visible in the crowd.

Any thoughts of walking over and casually striking up a conversation with her were shadowed by his feelings of uncertainty. He was pleased when she headed in his direction. "Do you really think this will work?" he asked, reaching out stiffly to shake her hand.

"Work?" She smiled questioningly. "This will be the best one here," she said, pointing to the sauna float. "We'll win a prize."

"How have you been?" he inquired. Did he catch a hint of distance in her eyes? "You haven't been around since New Year's Eve."

"Okay, I guess. Yeah, that night. One point I remembered being at a party and then a week of the flu followed by a relapse."

"You're feeling better?" Paul asked, wishing he had known she was sick.

"I think so."

Paul looked at Sarah and wondered if he really wanted a place in her life. He remembered their kiss.

"How have you been?" Sarah asked.

"Okay," he said, somewhat gloomy. "I've decided to look for work up here."

"You decided to stay?"

"Wouldn't leave if I was dragged by wild horses." Paul grinned and watched the crowd: clowns and costumed children packed the street. Did Sarah seem interested in his decision to be a full-time resident? he wondered, peering guardedly at her. "Have you ever been in the parade before?"

"No, but I've attended a few."

"Can you believe all the people?" Paul mused.

"Pretty amazing," Sarah said. "How did you hear about the float?"

"Bert advertised it like it was the second coming and then pulled out from actually participating. He said he'll video us. Did you hear from him too?"

"Of course." Sarah smiled.

"Did you see Charlie?" Paul questioned.

"Not recently," Sarah said. "Why?"

"Rumor has it he's going to join the parade today on horseback dressed as a colonial soldier."

"I guess that's what's good about the parade—it lets anyone come out and present their obsessions," Sarah said. "What about you?"

"I have a bathing suit, so I'm joining the sauna," Paul said. "And you?"

"I'm walking. Do you know where we are in the lineup?"

"In the middle, I think." He glanced over at the hot tub and sauna situated on a trailer hooked to a truck. Evergreen boughs and colored balloons decorated the float.

Relieved that Sarah walked into the crowd, Paul stripped down to his bathing suit and t-shirt . For some reason, when he looked the most ridiculous, he felt the most comfortable, particularly when he covered his forehead, eyes and nose with a half-mask. He climbed into the hot tub. In zero weather, the heat of the water was refreshing, and he was quickly unaffected by the cold. Other people scrambled into the tub wearing large cardboard cones atop their heads.

The float was motioned to move into the lineup behind a group of World War II veterans. It snowed heavily as the parade wound up the main street, past people who stood, hung from bar porches, and looked out windows that lined the route. Costumed bears scrambled down the street and threw candy at the crowd. Children screamed, "Miss Piggy, over here, this way." Miss Piggy sashayed and blew kisses at the men who whistled at her. Hot from the sauna, Paul stepped onto the road and walked alongside.

Dressed in woolen leggings and a grey coat adorned with gold buttons and metals, Charlie rode by and blew a bull horn. "Hey, Paul," he called, "you warm?" Charlie's horse threw its head up and down and pranced uncontrollably. At one point, the horse turned around and walked against the parade.

"Damn it, horse, turn around," Charlie swore and attempted to rein the horse to a stop. "Mind of his own," Charlie muttered.

"Yeah, mind of his own," Paul said. "Come on, Charlie, act militarily."

"This horse blows my cover," Charlie said angrily.

"How'd you cut in the parade if you can't control the horse?" Paul asked.

"What do you mean?" Charlie huffed. "Besides noone ever said anything about riding skills."

"My point exactly!" Barefoot in shorts and a sleeveless football jersey, Paul stood astride the float. He, the horse, and Charlie were captured on film by many of the people who lined the street.

The horse turned in circles as Charlie yelled for the animal to move ahead. He jabbed the animal's side with his boots and the horse reared. Paul motioned people back as the horse reared again. Within seconds Charlie was dumped on the ground and the horse ran down a side street, away from the crowd.

"Are you okay?" Paul asked, helping Charlie off the ground. "Whose horse was that anyway?"

"Ah, what's it to you," Charlie said, repositioning the musket on his shoulder. "Belongs to Hoofer," he fumed.

"Aren't you going to do anything to catch it?" Paul questioned.

"What for?" Charlie snarled. "That's a smart animal. He'll find his way." He stomped away, brushing snow and ice from his knickers.

Paul watched Charlie and felt a painful, sickening sensation radiate in his stomach. He knew with certainty that Charlie was dishonest. If Charlie didn't care about his friend's horse, how could the townspeople's future matter to him? Paul wondered.

During the final minutes of the parade, Paul felt distracted. He believed Charlie was a parasite but was uncertain of the details. Soon the loudspeaker introduced the float, "Number 29 passing through, titled "Imagination of the Carnival."

The coneheads splashed water and chanted, "It's over." Paul felt relieved when the float stopped and everyone disbanded.

He walked toward his truck and sensed he knew the direction in which Sarah headed. When fully dressed, he looked through the crowd and realized he had, once again, completely lost track of her whereabouts.

Chapter 32

Charlie sorted the mail and discovered a package with his name scrawled in Booker's childish print. What's this? Charlie wondered and opened the package. Inside a video tape was wrapped in plastic packing material. "This is the update. You need to know. Booker," was scrawled on the back of a Washington Memorial postcard.

Charlie stood in a numbed state of disbelief. "I can't believe it," he muttered. "That stupid old Booker lacks any collection of brain cells." And to think he had the nerve to send a video!

Charlie walked into the living room and placed the tape in the video machine. Within seconds Booker's face loomed toothy and pockmarked on the screen.

"Hey, Charlie, old boy! How are you doing?" Booker questioned, flicking his tongue outside his lip. "I got myself this camcorder and thought I'd set it on automatic to talk with you myself. This is important trade information so it's best it's not over the wire. You know what I mean?" Booker grinned, big and horsey.

What is he talking about? Charlie thought impatiently. Not over the wire, but in a video that can last forever?

"They seem to be investigating everything. By they, I mean the research people. You know what I mean?" Booker questioned. "The suits who seem bent on unraveling the threads of a coverup. They're everywhere—been sneaking around here like you don't know. I sometimes hear them whispering amongst themselves about the highest levels of office being suspicious. So, Charlie." Booker paced, pulling at his pants. "I don't know what to do, but thought you should know. I just keep repeating that I don't know nothing." Booker winked suggestively. "You and me both know I don't know nothing."

Charlie watched the camera zoom on Booker's face. He was tempted to punch the television screen out— anything to get at Booker!

"Well, I just thought you should know. So, I'm going to go now. I'll continue to do my best." Charlie watched as within seconds the screen went white, and then lit again with Booker at the Washington zoo, standing near a cage where monkeys screamed and jumped.

"What a jerk!" Charlie yelled and slammed the video button off. Charlie picked at his face. Of course Booker can't account for anything. There's nothing to account for, Charlie thought. There's nothing happening at that Washington office now! Vouchers exchanged for money rather than stamps didn't mean anything.

Charlie's thoughts rambled as he pondered his situation. He knew the majority of connections in the north had already been covered with his maintenance of a new, coded filing unit. The real advantage had been in the transfer of suppliers. When he was in Washington, he had to rely on shipments from New York City. Now, with a local supplier and all, things were clean. A network of travels into Canada made cross border trade possible. Charlie grinned happily and realized he never could've imagined that trade could be so easy.

From the beginning, Charlie insinuated he had government backing to move packages, and he was continually amazed at his new level of support. He mentally ticked off the local people with whom he already worked: Henry Ewing, ol' Hoofer, and the doctor from the facility nearby. The occasional plane shipments, with the help of the pilot, Peter, had expanded work horizons beyond Charlie's wildest imaginings.

Charlie doubted that such orderliness could be in jeapardy. Yet at the same time, if Booker were correct about the potential heat, Charlie wondered if he would be forced to quickly shut the northern office down and be gone? Charlie speculated about how Gorgo Rushton would respond if postal use in the north went down and the office lost money.

To start, Charlie decided he should stop selling stamps in other districts. If his office looked too good and the heat turned up, he ran the risk of being without a job. He shoved junk mail in the various boxes, suddenly alarmed he could lose everything. He speculated it could be time to unravel the connections he had made in the northern community.

He finished sorting the mail and left the office for an early afternoon nap. Once inside his kitchen, he reached into the refrigerator and took out a plastic eye mask that he routinely used to help with fatigued eyes. He sat down, positioned the mask on his face, and moved the recliner back. After all his rambling concerns, he decided to not be too bothered by Booker's admonition, and soon fell asleep.

Chapter 33

Charlie was angry the first day of spring arrived with a snowstorm that dumped six inches of fresh powder over a two-foot base. Disgusted by the gloomy weather, he had been increasingly worried by the extent of the investigation in Washington. Within the weeks following the receipt of Booker's video, it had become clear to him the office closure needed to take place. Busy with sorting mail, he hummed and looked forward to a life in a warmer climate.

Charlie gleefully remembered calling Gorgo Rushton and explaining postal use had slowed and the office was losing money. Rushton had actually commended Charlie, instructed him to submit past financials, and shut the office down effective April 30. With Rushton's quick support, Charlie easily dismissed concerns about an investigation that could potentially involve the northern office. He knew for a fact he would be long gone.

Charlie looked up as Paul walked into the post office. Uh, oh, the first person to read the closure notice, Charlie thought. He furtively watched as Paul approached the bulletin board and read the sign Charlie had carefully crafted. Charlie reread the sign: *NOTICE: RESIDENTS OF THE HAMLET WILL NO LONGER RECEIVE POSTAL SERVICES AS OF APRIL 30. IT WILL BE THE RESPONSIBILITY OF EACH RESIDENCE TO ESTABLISH THE APPROPRIATE BOX FOR RURAL SERVICE DELIVERY.*"

"Hey, they're closing this place?" Paul asked. "And we only have a little over three weeks to get another mail box?"

"That's right." Charlie shrugged. "We've been losing money and they're shutting her down."

"What do you mean? Why couldn't they notify us earlier and get our response?" Paul demanded. "What are the specs for setting up our mailboxes?"

"Come on," Charlie said, "you seem to think they owe you something. They were losing money, so they decided to shut the office." What a pain this kid is, Charlie thought.

"Owe me something? I'm a citizen; don't people in this hamlet pay taxes too?"

"So? They weren't enough to count. These decisions are made in higher places." Charlie spoke defensively. He was angry that Paul was wasting his time.

"But didn't you say use was up?"

"I was wrong." Charlie shrugged. "It dropped again. At the start of May, they'll send someone around to check on the mailboxes to see if they meet regulations."

"What do you mean?" Paul asked. "What regulations?"

"Oh you know: road set back, height, size," Charlie said emphatically.

"Do you have any written guidelines?"

"Nope. And let up with your busy questions. I told you I'm out of here in less than three weeks." Charlie's cheeks puffed as he quickly exhaled short breaths.

"You don't have anything other than this written notice?"

"Yeah, that's the way it is," Charlie huffed. "It's too bad, but I don't have much control over it."

"Why, Charlie, you never struck me as somebody to be out of control." Paul snickered, picked up his mail and exited.

Charlie couldn't believe Paul had the audacity to talk mockingly to him. Such nerve, he thought, and continued to hum happily and sort mail.

Chapter 34

Within days, Paul's news about the post office's closure rippled through town. He joined Bert at the store and talked while Bert whittled a wooden loon.

"Can you believe that guy?" Bert asked.

"Don't know," Paul responded. He looked up as a gray haired woman entered the store.

"Bertha Myers. It's you." Bert stood and kissed her on the cheek. "I haven't seen you since that fall day with Sarah and the rainstorm. How have you been?"

"Very good. I was away over the holidays visiting with my daughters in Massachusetts. I stayed right through the middle of March."

"We missed you at our New Year's party."

"I'm sorry I wasn't here to respond to your invitation. That's why I thought I'd stop by today." She stood still and motioned toward Bert. "Can I have a seat?"

"I've been thoughtless," Bert said, smacking his hand on his forehead. "Here, let me clear off this chair." Bert moved a pile of newspapers off a rusted lawn chair. "Here you go. You remember Paul, don't you?"

"Nice to see you again, Bertha." Paul smiled warmly and reached to shake Bertha's hand. "Did you hear about our post office?" Paul asked.

"Just that it opened. Why?"

"That's old news," Bert said interrupting. "The new stuff is there's a closure notice on the bulletin board. You tell her, Paul."

Paul hesitated momentarily, happy that Bert had given him a chance to tell the story. "Okay," he said, "Charlie had a written closure notice posted. After questioning him, he still refused to mail notice to everyone in the zip code."

"But why?" Bertha exclaimed. "What do you have to do?" She shifted uncomfortably on the metal chair.

"We've been instructed to set up boxes for rural delivery," Paul said. "None of us know what that means." He sneezed, increasingly frustrated by how his allergic symptoms had worsened in the spring.

"Bless you," Bertha said. "Does this postal situation affect me? I already have a rural box."

"Your mail doesn't come from here does it?" Paul inquired. He felt uncomfortable with having to tell the older woman about the town's problems.

"No, my mail comes from the office close to my house."

"You'll be fine," Paul said. "I don't know about the rest of us though." Bert continued to carve, flicking slivers of curled wood on the floor.

"So how's Carol?" Bertha asked, changing the subject.

"She's been fine," Bert responded. "Sort of at that point where any type of change gets to her." Bert sighed, jabbing at the wooden loon. "She's been doing nothing but complain about this postal situation," he said. "She keeps saying things like 'I don't know—there's something fishy here.' Keeps pointing out that things went on fine for the years that I ran the office and then smat!" Bert exclaimed, smacking his carving tool against his leg, "they close the new one in less than a year."

"That certainly is interesting," Bertha commented. "Is there any local involvement in what is going on?"

"What do you mean?" Paul asked.

"Well, there might be something underhanded here. I've seen lots of times when your postmaster visited my neighbor, Mr. Hoofer. That in itself is suspicious. Of course I missed a lot when I was away, but since being back there seems to be a considerable amount of activity. I've never seen anybody visit Mr. Hoofer in the time he's been my neighbor," the woman said, fidgeting with her purse strap. "Seems Hoofer is even letting Charlie ride his horse. I've never seen anyone on that animal."

"Hmmm." Paul reflectively stroked his mouth. "That's the horse Charlie had at the parade. The one that ran away; did it ever get home?"

"I wasn't aware of that incident," Bertha said, "but the horse is in the pasture. Seems Hoofer has even been feeding it."

"I got an idea," Paul said, "Maybe we should call a town meeting. Get everybody out to talk about things."

"Now that's an idea out of the blue," Bert said. "Where'd you think that one up?"

"Well," Paul said, ruminating on his hope to somehow alter events. "Maybe we can get people together to figure out why the office is being shut down. Maybe there's something we can do."

In the background the bird, Otto, squawked, "Customer is pretty; customer is pretty."

"Ignore that bird," Bert said. "That's a fine idea, Paul. We can meet Thursday night at my house. You lead, Paul, and we'll follow."

"Are you inviting the postmaster?" Bertha asked.

"Now there's another thought," Bert said approvingly. He winked at Bertha.

"Bert, can you leave for a few minutes?" Paul asked.

"Of course," Bert said. "I'll put my little clock up and point the fingers—back in twenty minutes. You joining us Bertha?"

"No. I have to go home now." Bertha followed the men out of the store. "You guys let me know about Thursday night."

"We will," Paul said. "Let us know if you see anything with Hoofer."

Bert peered down at his right boot, walked toward the stair and scraped his heel. "Something here on my foot," he exclaimed. "I knew something stinks here." He looked up and grinned. "Yeah, Bertha, we'll see you soon. And remember, Paul, you're the one to do the asking. You take the lead."

Paul joined Bert along the short walk to the post office. Charlie looked up from where he sorted mail.

"Hey, Charlie, we thought we'd stop by to ask you to a community meeting on Thursday night to discuss the office closure. You game?" Paul smiled.

"I certainly am not," Charlie huffed, standing up straight. "I am not even aware of all of the facts of the closure and you expect me to go before the community. No way!"

Paul towered over Charlie in height. "But postal code requires that you provide a community hearing when any closure is anticipated." He looked the postmaster in the eye and saw Charlie was unable to make eye contact with him. "Right?" Paul was thrilled he had researched the ins and outs of the postal code.

"What do you mean, require? I don't know anything about requirements," Charlie said, exhaling. "Like I said I am not willing to go until I receive a command from my higher ups about the need to address the community." Charlie shifted back and forth as he placed mail in its proper slot. "Here you go, you guys—your mail for the day."

"But doesn't this concern you?" Bert asked.

"Concern me? I just do what I'm told to do."

"That's it?" Bert challenged.

"That right. I was told to uproot myself and head up here to open this office and now I'm being told to uproot again and head out." Charlie spoke quickly.

"Where are you going now?" Bert asked.

"Don't know."

"You mean?" Paul exclaimed, "You've built a new home, you're leaving by the end of the month, and you now don't know where you are headed?" He was astonished by Charlie's lack of interest in the situation.

"Right again!" Charlie said. "You guys are getting close to winning a prize for accuracy."

"Come on, Paul. Let's get out of here. It doesn't seem we're going to get anywhere," Bert said. He threw his junk mail in the garbage.

"We don't seem to have many alternatives," Paul said, following Bert. "He is certainly set on leaving," Paul mused. "And out of breath at that."

"Yeah. I don't get it," Bert said and walked slowly toward the store. "He's here for not even a year, runs an office that I kept for over a decade, and now it's closing."

"We have to go ahead with that town gathering," Paul said. He was surprised by how certain he felt and anticipated meeting with his neighbors.

"Good luck with the organizing then," Bert said.

"I'll round everyone up," Paul said. He walked in the direction of his cabin and for the first time in days felt his sinuses clear. The sweet smell of spring balsam permeated the air. Paul felt delighted with the trust that Bert placed in him.

Chapter 35

How many trips were needed down dirt roads to speak with everyone in town? Paul wondered, as he bicycled, drove and walked through the hamlet. How could so few people know? Paul shook his head in disbelief, and headed toward his neighbors, Ethel and Mario.

"Closed?" Ethel and Mario exclaimed. Paul sipped lemonade on their screened front porch and watched their surprise.

"Why?" Ethel's perfectly groomed eyebrow raised questioningly. "Did you hear anything about this Mario?"

"Why no!" Mario emphatically waved his stocky arms. "Where did you hear about this?"

Paul knew the couple had lived in town for decades. He also knew their keen interest in events was an important barometer. "You mean you didn't know?" Paul asked. "Why, you guys know everything. If you didn't know, that means we have a real problem on our hands."

"In what way?" Ethel asked.

Mario, seated on a white wicker rocker, shifted back and forth, and laughed softly. "What problem?" he questioned.

"Well, you guys usually know everything, so I suspect it means there was a plan to close the office without involving or informing any of us." Paul concluded.

"How did you find out?" Mario asked. He rocked in repetitive motion.

"It was a small notice on the corner of the bulletin board. I mean, if you were rushing through, you never would've seen it."

"We never received anything in our box," Ethel said. "No postcard or anything."

"That's right." Paul sipped the remainder of his lemonade. "But did you know that you will be responsible for setting up a rural delivery box? And that you are required to have the box set off the road in a specific manner?"

"No." Mario laughed. "Why couldn't they send us something?"

"Bert and me, we're not sure what's being covered up." He knew his face expressed his uncertainty. "Thus the meeting," he concluded. "Can you come?"

"We'll be there." The couple agreed in unison.

Paul thanked them for the lemonade, said goodbye, and was followed off the porch by their black dog, Jennie. The dog stood in the middle of the road and barked as Paul walked toward old Hawk's house.

Old Hawk had been most convincing as he shuffled a worn boot in the dirt and spoke. "Somebody needs to be young enough and with enough energy to speak for us. Don't you hesitate to take on these forces."

"Thanks. Your words help," Paul said, somewhat uncomfortable with everyone's support.

"You'll be our voice," Hawk mumbled. "Just be sure you're ready for the task."

Conversations with other neighbors went pretty much the same way. After being in town for more than a year, Paul was surprised by everyone's friendliness. Did they really accept his leadership in addressing the office's closure?

The meeting night arrived quickly. Paul felt the town was electrified with activity. Cars were parked across the front of the INTERNATIONAL AIRPORT, parallel to the STORE GENERAL. He approached a crowd of people who stood outside the white ranch house. It didn't take long for him to catch up on local news.

"Hey, Paul, I heard you went snipe hunting with Charlie."

Paul turned his head and saw that a local, named Alan, had called him. "Come on Al! That happened months ago! End of last year in fact. Everyone needs one experience with snipe hunting in their life!" he exclaimed.

"That's right!" Alan laughed. "A good character builder! And it was important Charlie had that introduction, especially since he's reckoning to leave us."

"Is that certain?" Sarah asked and approached.

"Sarah?" Paul questioned. He was surprised by her refreshing, clean appearance. She was dressed in a denim skirt, t-shirt and vest. "You look great! I'm glad you decided to come, especially knowing your feelings about Charlie."

"My feelings about him have nothing to do with this community's need to have a post office. Do you know what we're going to do?" she whispered.

"Bert is going to open the meeting in a few minutes," Paul said excitedly. "He's going to hand it over to me." Paul peered closely at Sarah. "Hey, I'm thrilled you came. It's been ages."

"Yes," Sarah said, "winter passed way too quickly."

"That's a fact!" Paul exclaimed. He felt embarrassed by the electricity and desire he felt around Sarah. What a history of noncontact, he thought.

"Well," Sarah said and smiled, "we never did get together for any cross-country skiing."

"Swimming! Let's try swimming," Paul offered. Did he appear too interested? he wondered.

"You let me know, now." Sarah's hand ruffled through her bangs.

Sure, Paul thought, intrigued by how her fingers looked in her hair. But how did he appear to her? he wondered. Did he look relaxed dressed in a chamois shirt and corduroy pants? Or was his combined confusion and attraction evident? He questioned if Sarah found him attractive. "Okay," he said softly, still fascinated by Sarah's hair that seemed inches longer and even more blond than he remembered. "Swimming or even canoeing, I won't forget." He spoke cautiously and wondered if Sarah could ever be interested in him. He felt unsettled and alarmed, with a feeling of drowning in Sarah's presence.

"Paul," Bert rushed outside. "It's six-thirty now. Quit lounging about. You want to get started." He turned toward Sarah and uncharacteristically hugged her. "Hey, Sarah! How are you doing?" Paul was immediately alarmed by Bert's physical contact with Sarah.

"Bert? I'm, uh, fine. Nice to see you." Sarah stepped back from Bert's arms. "You okay?"

"Oh, we're fine. Lot's of changes here. Got to get the people inside." Bert moved around excitedly. "Give me a hand."

"Okay," Sarah said. She laughed and followed Paul. "I guess I'm here as an assistant. Jupe's here as a guard dog. She'll stay outside."

"Well, with that kind of protection, this shouldn't be too hard," Paul said, relieved to refocus on the meeting. "We're going to get going now," he said, gesturing for people to move into the house.

Once inside, more than fifty people sat on chairs, stood in corners, lounged on the floor, and talked loudly amongst themselves. People crowded the kitchen and looked through the wooden spiral dividers that bordered the dining room. Loons and mallards lined the wall shelves. The house had a strong smell of ammonia mixed with the smell of wet dog. Paul hoped his allergies wouldn't bother him.

Bert stood in front of the stone fireplace and motioned for quiet. "Come on, we're ready now to get started." He hesitated and cleared his throat. "I just want to welcome you to our home and let you know once and for all that we have word that the post office will be closing in, what is it, Paul, three weeks?"

"Less than three weeks now, on Friday, April 30," Paul said.

A loud murmur passed through the room as people heard confirmation of the closure. Paul sat quietly and nervously twitched his tongue against lower teeth.

Bert continued to talk. "So, I have Paul Wilson with me here tonight. He's the one who first made the discovery and who spoke to DeWitt a few days ago. I'd like everyone to hear Paul speak. For those of you who don't yet know Paul, he's lived with us for over a year now, and knows we need our office."

"Thanks for the introduction Bert." Paul stood and stared at people, many of whom felt like family, and lost his concentration. "Uh, a coup, uh," he stuttered, "a couple of days ago I was in the post office." He felt a loud buzzing in his ears and found it difficult to speak. "Uh, I scanned the bulletin board as I was waiting for counter service." He shuffled his feet and tugged at his pockets. "I was surprised to see a small written notice that said the office will be closing." Paul talked slowly and caught himself looking down at the floor. Look out at everyone, he quickly coached himself, and scanned the crowd. "When I asked Charlie about the closure he said the office is definitely closing and he had the same amount of time to get out—less than three weeks," Paul concluded, somewhat more relaxed with finally having stated the real problem

People groaned and murmured in unison, "But why weren't we told directly?"

"Good question," Paul said. He felt exhilarated with the opportunity to provide information. "Charlie refused to acknowledge there might have been a better way of communicating with us. Such as if he had small post-cards made to put in our boxes." Paul looked around the room and brushed hair from his eyes. "Charlie seemed adamant that everyone should read the bulletin board. He claimed there was enough information for us to set up our rural delivery boxes." Paul paused after the long presentation.

"Rural delivery boxes?" people questioned. "What's that?"

Paul shrugged. "I think he was referring to us putting up our own road mailboxes. He didn't provide any information on specs, such as set back or height." Paul quickly realized his neighbors needed the complete picture. "And Charlie said they can refuse to deliver mail if things aren't set up right."

"What do you mean?" Old Hawk demanded. "Refuse to deliver? Where will the mail be coming from anyway?"

"I'm still not sure about that. The next town over," Paul said and shrugged.

"The next town over?" Ethel stood and looked around the room. "That's fifteen miles down the road." Her voice was tinged with concern. "How will we be able to make any use of that? I think something is up here!"

"Yeah, what happens now?" The question echoed through the room.

Paul, suddenly caught in his year of indecisiveness about where to live, what type of profession to lead, and what type of relationship to have, lifted an arm to wipe sweat off his face, and said, "I don't know."

"Well, can't you and Bert do something about this?" Ethel asked.

"Whoa!" Bert said, "I gotta interrupt now and say I got the royal screw with what happened with the office before. First everythin' is fine, and then I'm layered with a ton of paperwork. So we find a solution and a year later we go bust. Nope," he sighed, "my turn is up. Paul, you're new to this. Time someone else finds a solution."

Paul hesitated, "I'm not really sure what I can do. When I moved here, within weeks the new office opened and then the modular came. It seems like only yesterday that I helped Bert move boxes out of the old of-fice. Why is it that within the year, and especially after an entire upgrade that probably cost bundles, is the office closing?" Paul felt increasingly angry with all the unanswered questions.

"And why can't we be better informed?" Bert yelled.

"Well, there seem to be lots of concerns," Paul said. "So what do you suggest we do now?"

"Letters," Ethel said. "We need to write to our representatives to let them know what is happening and to the Postmaster General in Washington. I'll help you with them, Paul."

"That's a great idea. I can even develop a petition and take it around to everyone." Paul felt thrilled with how the townspeople helped him to focus. "Then we'll write to folks in government and mail the petition along." He talked excitedly, certain that people in the room shared his enthusiasm.

"Do the petition," Mario called.

"Yeah, the petition," Alan said. "And to follow-up, this country is a democracy," he said slowly, clasping his hands together. "Those people work for us and if things fall down in one area, then we must reckon to let folks know. That's how things are supposed to happen. Let's not lose this opportunity."

"You said it best," Bert yelled. "Now, Paul, is it clear what we want done as a first step?"

"Couldn't be clearer." Paul smiled. He scribbled notes on a yellow pad.

"Good, well since everyone is here, let's have some of Carol's famous coffee cake. Anything else, Paul?"

"Yeah, if anything else comes up tonight let me know cause your support is important." He smiled openly. "Or give me a call or stop by." Paul stopped talking and headed toward the counter for coffee. He hoped Sarah would take the time to talk with him and wondered if he had made a favorable impression on her.

Chapter 36

Charlie knew the warmth of the spring night was a stark contrast to the snow from a few weeks previous. He stood in the kitchen and furiously spun a brillo pad over edges of a pan. "How could I burn my entire meal," he asked disgustedly as sweat beads surfaced on his face. The smell of smoke and charred meat permeated the room. How could there be so many distractions? Water splashed all over the pan, dripped from the sink and formed a puddle on the bright linoleum floor. "I'm coming, I'm coming," he muttered in response to a knock on the front door. Charlie walked toward the entrance and clasped a large dishcloth apron that covered his stomach. Made by his wife, Shirley, a year before she passed away, the soft material comforted him. He opened the door.

"Why, Henry! What brings you here?" Charlie extended a hand.

"Doin' here now. What doya mean?" Henry angrily asked. "Don't you realize there's a meetin' here in town? Everyone is getting into the act of investigation."

"I know. But, Henry, your timing is perfect. I was just about to call you to arrange a little get together." Charlie smiled innocently. "It does appear that the heat is turning up. Come in," he motioned. "Did you eat yet?"

"I'm fine," Henry muttered. "What's that funny smell in here?" Henry sniffed the air.

"Burned my dinner. I'm just going to take a minute and make a sandwich."

"You do that." Henry flopped into a cushioned chair and peered with hooded eyes at Charlie. His belly rested large and pliable, covered by a faded sweatshirt. "Well, I know we gotta do something. So I came over."

"You got any ideas?"

"Rumor has it that those nitpicks is going to fight the closure. You informed of the meeting tonight?"

"Yeah, Bert and Paul asked me to attend and I told them both to stuff it. I said I'm just following orders with the closure."

"Orders?" Henry laughed loudly with gusto. "Didn't you create the order?"

Charlie shifted uncomfortably and cut slices of tomato. "Well," he whined, "I did have to convince Rushton. And you know I have to be prepared."

"For what?"

"The complete investigation going on in Washington."

"So what do you suggest now?" Henry turned in the chair as his body rolled to the left.

"Suggest?" Charlie questioned just how much he wanted to tell Henry. Should he talk about the files, or about the need to get rid of any stockpiles of stuff? Stick with the basics, Charlie decided. "Take the stuff out of here tonight."

"What do ya mean?"

"I mean take the merchandise that is in this building to our connection at the border. You ready to drive tonight?"

"Didja talk to Hoofer or the others?" Henry asked.

"No. I'm not bringing them into it now." Was it him, or did Henry seem increasingly pushy? Charlie wondered.

"Well," Henry huffed, "I'm ready to drive anytime. My truck is outside and she's been runnin' good." He patted his fat stomach. "A few sputters that truck has, but they can be ignored cause it always happen when the weather changes like it did this week. Cold to warm and I'm sickka this stuff."

"Let me finish eating and we'll clear everything up." Charlie chewed loudly and repeatedly smacked his lips. "Want a beer?" He stood and reached into the refrigerator.

"Sure do," Henry said greedily. "Now that's the best thing you said."

Charlie handed a can of Budweiser to Henry. Henry popped the lid open, quickly guzzled the beer, and burped loudly. "Now this is nice," he commented loudly.

Charlie peered at Henry and thought, what a jerk! How did he ever let such an unruly character in on the operation? What about judgement? he questioned. And now he had to rely on this guy to get the evidence out of here? He should've listened to Hoofer who had said early on that Henry was disturbed.

"Okay, okay." Charlie shook his head as if to clear cobwebs from an old room. "We'll set everything up. You take the box and head out of town northwards."

"You don't have to explain the route. I've travelled it so many times I know it like the back of my hand. The only difference now is that it is a bit darker. I'll do fine." Henry finished the beer and burped again.

"I hope so." Charlie spoke cautiously. "A lot depends on this final connection."

"Yeah, especially my money. When do you plan on paying?"

"As soon as this is all completed." Geez! Don't let Henry start complaining about money at a time like this, Charlie thought. "Come on now," Charlie said. He headed outside and Henry followed him.

Charlie immediately noticed the evening's darkness provided a good cover. He watched as Henry lifted a small treasure chest. Locked with a metal lock, the box was covered with American eagle decals. Charlie feared the loss of an important part of his life and coached Henry in the details of "Operation Runoff."

"Remember, call me tomorrow and we'll review our options. Be careful," he cautioned.

"No problem," Henry said and waved goodbye. Charlie watched as the truck sputtered and rolled out of the driveway.

Depressed with the reality of handing pieces of his life over to Henry, Charlie walked back into the modular and headed toward the bathroom. He peered into the bathroom cabinet and lifted a vial of Valium. This will do it, he thought, and popped a handful of pills followed by a large swig of water.

Chapter 37

Paul watched as people milled around furtively examining Bert and Carol's possessions. He sipped coffee and thought about a logical pattern for writing letters. He tried to not be distracted by Sarah's presence. An hour ticked by quickly as darkness descended on the town.

"I know, I know! I got us a solution." Bert motioned excitedly with a can of beer in hand. "Let's see if we can all get slots on an afternoon talk show." Bert swayed happily. "You know? Rather than being forgotten by a boyfriend or girlfriend, we can be the people forgotten by our government. The people without a post office! The abandoned!" Bert shrieked hysterically and did a quick jig.

"I watch those talk shows all the time," Ethel said. "Do you want me to start calling? We could go as a group and probably even get all our expenses paid if they were interested in our story," she said, hopeful.

"Whoa!" Paul said excitedly. "First we have to get our representatives interested in this story before we go to the masses." Geez! he thought. How do we keep everyone focused? he wondered. "Washington and Albany have to take an interest in this, so let's get back on track. Now how do we get back into planning the letter campaign?" He worried people would be distracted if he didn't provide leadership and direction.

"I have a list of all our state and congress representatives posted on my bulletin board," Ethel offered.

"So, again, hey, is everyone listening?" Paul questioned, distracted by the number of conversations taking place at once. "Both letters and a petition?" he asked, intrigued by his community activist role.

"Yes!" Ethel and Mario yelled in unison.

"So, we'll meet tomorrow morning to write the letters," Paul suggested. Before Ethel responded, a screeching of tires and a loud crash distracted him. "Whoa! What's that?" he yelled to Bert.

"I don't know," Bert screamed. "Let's go look." Paul quickly followed Bert out of the house. He saw a rusted truck bent around a subcompact car.

"Quick, check the truck," Bert motioned. "Get the driver out."

Paul ran toward the vehicle, opened the door, and saw a body slumped behind the wheel. "Here, Bert, give me a hand."

Flames shot out of the truck. Paul reached down, and with Bert's help quickly lifted the man, and headed toward the house. Within minutes the fire curled around the truck and trailed along the ground. The smell of gasoline and fire permeated the air. Paul heard a loud murmur of, "It's going to explode," pass through the crowd.

"Did somebody call the fire department?" Bert bellowed as he and Paul entered the house. "Let's put him on the couch," Bert suggested.

"The fire department has been called," Carol said.

"We might have an explosion before they get here," Paul said and gestured toward the road. Whoa! he thought, and ran back outside. "Everybody—get back, back into the house; it's far enough away. Come on now, inside," he exclaimed.

He watched as some people ran into the house, while others headed away from the fire. The fire consumed the truck as a loud rumble resonated through the town, followed by loud tat, tat noises. Paul looked directly at the truck as it exploded against the spring sky. He was just far enough away to not be hit by the sprinkling of metal debris.

"My God!" Paul groaned. This is the end, he thought, and watched the fire form an ever-expanding circle. "It looks like there could be other explosions if the firemen don't get here soon," Paul shouted as Bert scrambled out of the house. Flames licked at the tires and steel edges of the vehicles which lined the road.

"There's a lot more we can lose than just some cars if this thing continues," Bert cautioned.

"Yeah, could you imagine?" Paul wiped sweat off his face. "Town lost to firestorm."

"It's one way to get rid of the post office. Get rid of everything else around it so the office ain't necessary. Here," Bert gestured, "come on. Let's see if we can set up a water line to stop this fire on the other cars." Bert ran inside and came out with various sized buckets and peanut butter containers. "We can use the water out of this hose but we got to use the lake water or we'll run me dry. Surprising enough for a spring, but my well is pretty low."

Paul joined residents who formed a line and began to slosh water from the lake while Bert filled containers directly from the hose. People chanted, "Where's that fire department!" For an interminable time water buckets sloshed from hand to hand as the fire licked at the stretch of cars. Paul could feel the heat of the flames. After about fifteen minutes, he saw a fire truck speed around the corner and come to a dead stop at the front of the line. A fireman in a vinyl coat jumped out of the driver's seat as other men climbed off the truck.

"Set up a pump off the lake," the driver called to the team. "We don't have much time, so start the hose off the truck." Within seconds a long stream of water showered over the flames that circled the cars. "Hey, what is it with you people? Wasn't I here last fall for a fire?"

"Ah!" Bert exclaimed. "It's just circumstance and proof of how we work together."

Paul waited until the fire was under control before venturing back into the house. "Does the driver need an ambulance?" Paul asked Carol who stood at the front of the door.

"He refuses one," Carol shrugged. "Nothing appears cut or broken."

"Who is he?"

"You don't know?" Carol asked and sighed. "It's Henry Ewing from up the road. We only see him around the store a few times a year."

"He lives down the road?" Paul shifted restlessly.

"Yeah, about five miles east and in another mile down a dirt road. Sarah ran into him last year doing the census work. He can be pretty nasty."

"Maybe I was introduced once by Bert, but why the rush through town?" Paul questioned. "Didn't he know there would be a meeting tonight?"

"I don't know, but I do know that I've seen him driving, usually once it gets dark, over to Charlie's post office. He rarely comes to town during the day. So I don't know what has been going on in the evening."

"To Charlie's place?" Paul asked. He sensed Carol's blue eyes bore into him. "So, he would've known there was a meeting then?"

"That's only if Charlie let him know," Bert interrupted loudly, walking through the door. "Where's our patient now?"

"In the front room resting." Paul offered. "He wants to leave."

"Leave? He ain't got no truck! And I doubt he's in any condition to walk." Bert wiped his hands on a towel. "With this mess outside no one can get away to drive anyway. Let's see what he's up to." Bert turned to Paul. "You've met Henry?" he questioned.

"Possibly," Paul said, vaguely remembering seeing the dirty, heavyset man on a previous occasion.

"Well, if he's no longer in shock, you're in for a treat of your life."

Paul followed Bert into the front room. "Henry, meet Paul Wilson," Bert said. "He helped me get you out of the truck."

Henry slowly pulled himself up. "Oh, a hero?" he asked. "Why'd you have all those cars parked there anyway, Bert? Where's my truck?"

"Your truck is a burning, crumbled mess." Bert spoke directly.

"Whatta you mean?" Henry attempted to stand as Paul reached out and provided a supporting arm.

"The truck is gone," Bert said bluntly.

"Who took her?" Henry asked, uncomprehendingly. He swayed in place.

"She blew up. Maybe you don't remember hitting that pile up of cars, but a fire started almost immediately after the crash. Paul and me got you out of the truck and within minutes she blew. There wasn't anything of value in it?" Bert asked, peering intently at Henry.

"Yeah," Paul said, "the firemen are here now. We were lucky that no other cars exploded out there."

Henry sat back on the couch and methodically moved his large hands up and down thighs covered in heavy wool. "I don't get it," he said, his brow furrowed with deep lines. He jumped up and rushed across the room. Paul and Bert followed him outside. "One small town visit and then I'm here without a truck!" Henry stood on the front lawn and flailed his arms. "This is the reason I stayed out of town for so long."

"Are you sure you're okay?" Bert asked. "Maybe you're in need of a rest? You had quite a bang up there."

"I'm fine." Henry swayed and in quick fashion slumped to the ground.

"Paul, here we go again." Bert sighed. The sound of sirens wailed against the night. "Let's bring him back inside."

Chapter 38

⊢⊷⊶⊙⊷⊶⊣

Flames burst behind the treeline as Charlie headed toward town. Hidden by shadows, he kept a low profile in what he knew was enemy territory. He still hoped to leave a victor and knew his cash stashes would be valuable. He strode furtively, expectant about the office closure. Could he try for early retirement? he wondered.

Flames raced along the paved road as Charlie walked past the International Airport. "What's all this mess?" he questioned loudly. "Why the fire?"

"Not sure," Mario offered and laughed softly. "A truck came through town and hit the edge of a parked car. The driver needed to be pulled from the cab."

"Yeah," Ethel jumped in quickly, "and before we knew it, there was the fire and explosion."

"Ethel, it's one of those side-saddle fuel tanks on the news for blowing up," Mario interjected enthusiastically. "That's right," Mario mused thoughtfully, "or why else would it have blown so quickly? Outside tanks that's for certain."

"Wouldn't you know? Henry would be one of those five million people who owned a defective truck," Ethel said.

"What do you mean? What about Henry?" Charlie demanded, suddenly very alert.

"It was Henry Ewing. That is his full name right?" Mario's voice sounded with a high pitch tone.

"What do you mean?" Charlie stammered.

"Bert and Paul had to bring him in the house. When he demanded to come outside he collapsed on the ground. So he's back inside." Mario gestured toward the building.

"What the fuck did he do getting into an accident?" Charlie screamed, knowing for certain that Henry was a good-for-nothing.

"Hey! You watch your language in front of my wife," Mario demanded. He stepped directly in front of Charlie, pointing an arthritic index finger. "Now, you listen here young man! Whatever happened—it's done. The fire trucks got here just in time to keep that entire line of cars from blowing. We could've lost the whole town tonight." Mario spoke forcefully.

"Okay! Don't get so excited," Charlie huffed. "What's left of the truck?" Charlie asked. He hoped his sudden panic was not visible.

"The truck?" Ethel questioned. "The truck is that heap of burned metal in flames on the road there."

"Oh no!" Charlie exclaimed and stumbled toward the fire. He was surprised to be held back by a line of firemen. "This is too much," he said, shaking his head in disbelief. He ran toward Bert's house and banged on the door. "I'm coming in now, in the name of freedom."

"You can come in for whatever damn reason you want," Bert muttered as Charlie rushed inside.

"Where the hell is Henry?"

"Where am I?" Henry yelled. He struggled to sit upright on the couch. "I'm right here," he said angrily.

"The truck!" Charlie called out and rushed toward Henry. "What the hell did you do?" Charlie grabbed Henry by the shirt, pulled and shook him. "Everything's gone!" How could one man be so intractable, Charlie wondered?

"Oh come on!" Bert said. "Let him go! He's been injured and he's in shock."

"Yeah," Paul continued, "the only thing that's lost is the truck."

"Ah, what do you know?" Charlie huffed. He stamped out of the room.

Once outside Charlie stood near a circle of firemen. How could he get the firemen to let him look in the truck? he pondered.

"Can't I look through to see what's here in the rubble?" he asked, hopeful.

"Come on, man! There's flames there," the fireman said. "What's so important that you want to risk being burned?"

"You're right," Charlie said, sulking. "Just a box of family heirlooms that I gave to the truck's driver. It meant a lot to me."

"Okay," the fireman said and shifted in place. "If we see it, we'll hold it for you."

"Well, I'll head home now and wait to hear from you guys. I live at the post office." Charlie gestured down the road and decided to introduce himself. "Charlie DeWitt." He extended his right hand.

"We know," the man said and turned back to the fire.

That idiot ignored his handshake, Charlie realized as he walked away. Well, the hell with them all. It was now obvious to him that old Henry was not to be trusted. Too stupid for the inner loop. The final recognizance mission blown into flames along a road that is usually empty of cars. Too, too much! Charlie thought, ever mindful that he was the true insurgent. He twisted the doorknob of the modular and knew it was time to leave.

Chapter 39

Paul slowly tracked Charlie back to the post office. Away from the fire and chaos, Paul was surrounded by the dark quiet. He listened as Charlie opened the door and entered. He watched as all the lights came on until the house was a beacon. Something is strange here, Paul thought. He saw Charlie, visible through the curtained windows, rushing around. Charlie appeared to be packing. Why is he so intent on getting things together tonight? Paul wondered.

How could Charlie leave now? Especially when everyone just learned the office would close within three weeks. Nothing made much sense to Paul as he saw Charlie rush through the front door with a pile of newspapers and magazines. Charlie moved toward the back of the building. From the corner, Paul watched as Charlie dumped the papers in a large metal barrel.

A loud snarl suddenly echoed through the inky night air. Charlie screamed, "Oh no! Get out of here! Scat!"

Within seconds of Charlie's yell and the noise of scuffling, Paul realized what had happened. He ran toward the back of the house. That's it all right, he thought. In front of him, the bear, newly awake from a restless winter sleep, towered on hind legs near Charlie.

"Whoa, Bear!" Paul screamed. "Stop!" He realized the bear, disoriented and hungry after a fitful hibernation, had come searching for food. The bear peered at Paul and rushed into the darkness. Charlie stood with a stunned expression. The ground was covered with magazines, newspapers and an old wooden box that lay open with an assortment of colored index cards.

"What the fuck was that bear doing here?" Charlie demanded.

'Uh, seemed she was hungry," Paul mused. "Came to search your burn can. Must've thought there was food in it."

"Ah, what are you doing here anyway?" Charlie questioned angrily. "Weren't you down at all the commotion waiting on Henry and listening to Bert's tales of woe about the town?"

"Come on, Charlie! Is that a nice way to say thank you for chasing Bear out of here?"

"Well, what do you expect? Welcoming arms? I was just going about my business of packing for my move in three weeks and look what happened."

"In three weeks?" Paul asked, suddenly interested.

"That's right. Now if you don't mind, I've got work to do. And I still can't figure out what you're doing in my yard."

"I was walking down the road when I heard the commotion. Be thankful! I maybe saved your life." Paul spoke excitedly. "Those bears can do some damage." He knew he spoke from experience.

"Yeah, yeah," Charlie muttered. "You know that bear?" Charlie demanded as he stumbled toward the building. The pile of magazines and cards remained on the ground.

"Yeah, her mother attacked me on my first day here in town. You got off a lot easier than I did. The mother chased me, and if it weren't for Bert I'm not sure what would've happened." Paul watched Charlie enter the house. He reached down, quickly pocketed some of the index cards that were scattered on the ground and took off toward the center of town.

Chapter 40

"Paul, where have you been?" Sarah raced toward Paul as he walked down the road. Nearby firemen stood idly observing the smoke which curled off the truck. Their coats rustled as they moved in the dark aftermath of the fire. "Bert's been asking about when you would be back."

"Bert? He was the one to tell me to keep an eye on Charlie."

"Well, we both were asking." Sarah smiled shyly. "Any news?" She hoped her curiosity about him wasn't too obvious.

"I've been watching Charlie, if that's news. He's busy packing and had a real close call with Bear. Lucky I was there to shoo her away."

"She's up, eh?"

"Yeah, her schedule is off, but she still scared the wits out of him." Paul spoke excitedly. "I, uh," Paul continued, "I found some pieces of paper that Charlie was throwing out. You interested in looking at them?"

Interested? Sarah wondered, somewhat taken back by Paul's question. She had been too absorbed in watching his excitement and how his cheeks were flushed and hadn't heard a word he said. "Okay," she said, distracted and overwhelmed by his closeness. She tugged at the pockets of her vest. "The police are talking to Henry," she said, happy to think of something to say. "They're trying real hard to get him to retrace the steps back to his visit with Charlie. That is where he was coming from, wasn't it?"

"Sure was. At least that's what Charlie complained about when he stopped by before."

"Let's look at these cards under this light," Paul suggested.

Sarah peered at Paul and felt suddenly energized, intrigued by the fact that he seemed a lot less nervous than usual. She still couldn't figure if he would be like her ex-boyfriend, Michael. Even though she was the one to head back east, she still believed Michael had abandoned her. The rejection had hurt and built on her fear that he had been having an affair with the red-haired neighbor. Just recently she had heard Michael married the woman who was supposedly five months pregnant. Sarah hoped Paul wasn't cut from the same mold as Michael.

"Huh?" Sarah questioned.

"Didn't you want to look at those cards?"

"Oh, yeah," Sarah said.

"Here, look at this." Paul pulled the pile of cards from his back pocket. "Let's see, each one is covered with names and descriptive words: routes through road, through air, through post office." Paul hesitated for a minute. "Sarah! Look at this one. It says, 'Move route from Washington to New York,' and is dated last spring."

"What do you think the routes mean?" Sarah asked.

"I'm not sure, but look at some of these names. Larva: code # 1; Lazy: Code # 2; Fidgety: Code # 3. What the hell do you think he was up to?"

"Who knows," Sarah said. "But he did move here last spring."

"Yeah, remember that first stop at the store with him covered with flour?" Paul laughed.

Sarah did her best to concentrate on the cards but felt both confused and rejuvenated by Paul's presence. "Well, what do you think if we go inside and show these to the police?" she suggested.

"Now there's an idea. But stand still a minute. You have a smudge of black under your eye."

"Here?" Sarah reached up and rubbed her face.

"No here." Paul's hand brushed the cheekbone under Sarah's left eye. "There—it's all gone."

"Thanks!" Sarah said. Her skin felt singed where Paul had touched her. She followed him toward the house. "The police think there is something much larger than an accident," she mumbled, finding it hard to think straight.

Once inside the house Sarah watched as Paul talked with Bert and Carol. She looked at the trio and was perplexed by her thoughts of wanting a relationship with Paul but being fearful about her own identity. That's why there seems to be such static, she thought sadly, fearful of losing her independence, or worse, being used again. She looked carefully at Paul, tried to shake herself free from anticipation, and headed in the direction of the living room.

"Don't go in there now," Bert said, motioning at Sarah. "Those troopers are drilling old Henry with questions. He claims he doesn't know nothing. In fact, he seems to have forgotten what he was doing in town tonight." Bert grinned broadly. Sarah thought he appeared amazed with the situation.

"That's what we have information on," Paul said. "Look at these. Charlie was going to his burn can when Bear frightened him. I was there and shooed her away. He went back inside before burning anything. I scooped these up."

Bert peered quizzically at the index cards. "What are all these code names?" he questioned.

"We're not sure." Sarah and Paul spoke in unison. She was secretly pleased to appear as a unit with Paul. "Paul found this stuff. We thought the police would like this information."

"I'll bet they would," Bert wagered. "Listen, I'll motion for Trooper Mike to come out here. You tell him the story."

Sarah listened as Paul confidently repeated the story of following Charlie. The bear attack and retrieval of the index cards only added to the excitement.

"And you found these tonight?" the trooper asked when Paul finished talking.

"Yeah, I think I picked up most of them. I don't know—there might be more, but because of that bear I don't think Charlie is going back to that burn can."

"Well, this is very helpful," the trooper said. "Any other questions or comments about Mr. DeWitt's activities?"

"Why yes, yes sirree!" Bert shrieked. "We've had questions about him for a long time now. What about the new modular? What about our reason for the meeting tonight so we could prepare for the closure of the office in three weeks?"

"To summarize, Bert is trying to say there have been more and more questions as time went by," Paul said. Sarah was proud of how at ease Paul seemed talking to the trooper.

"And the office was scheduled for closure?" the trooper asked, scribbling notes on a pad.

"That's right," Paul said.

"That guy in there has selective memory," the other trooper said, entering the kitchen. "Can't seem to put anything together about where he is or what he's been doing tonight."

"Ah, Henry was trained to be selective," Bert sighed. "So what do you do now?"

"We continue to investigate. Something will break." The trooper spoke confidently.

Sarah heard a cuckoo clock on the wall crow eleven times, followed by knocks on the door. Bert motioned a fireman inside who held a treasure chest box in his hands.

Sarah felt animated, thinking that maybe the fireman had some answers. She peered at the box.

"Here's a locked box," the fireman said, handing the unit over to the trooper. "Seems the postmaster was looking for it. Said something about a family heirloom being on the truck and would we bring it up to his house when we found it. It's yours for evidence."

That's what Charlie was after, Sarah thought. She wondered about its contents.

"Thanks for staying on top of things," the trooper said.

Sarah leaned forward and touched Paul's arm. "Henry's a snake," she whispered, "and not to be confused with the ones he shoots." Her hand felt tingley where it had rested on Paul's arm. She wondered if Paul felt the shock.

Bert looked at her and smiled. "So you fire guys will be here for a while?" he asked, turning back to the fireman.

"Yeah. The fire is under control. We've radioed a hauler to get the truck out of here, and then we'll have to hose the road down."

Sarah peered at the box covered with ships and American eagle decals. She wondered if the decals were to show Henry's patriotism and grimaced, filled with the fear she felt when she first encountered him over a year ago.

"Sarah are you okay? You look white," Paul said.

"I'm fine, but I really have to get going," she said, as fatigue overwhelmed her. "I'm parked in a place where I can pull out."

"We'll keep you posted. Thanks for your help tonight." Paul smiled and touched Sarah's shoulder. "If any news breaks, you'll be one of the first to know."

Deserted by the townspeople, the road was empty except for the few firemen and trucks that remained. The firemen motioned a hauler to back up to the wreck. Sarah walked toward her car and slowly drove past the entrance to the post office. Charlie was outside packing boxes in the trunk of his car. He shielded his face when her car passed. Once home, she quickly let the dog out of the house and wondered how she could feel so exhausted.

That night she dreamed about the weird treasure chest. Rain pelted the cabin's window and woke her. Darkness surrounded the room and resonated with the force of rain. It's the rain, Sarah thought, increasingly uncomfortable with the dream images. Sarah curled back under the covers and fell immediately back to sleep. By morning she felt overwhelmed with the vividness of the treasure box covered with American eagles.

Chapter 41

Oh the ignominy of it all! Charlie still couldn't believe his bad fortune. He rushed around the house and quickly packed. "How can it end like this!" he questioned, wiping his brow. He knew there was only one way out; only one choice to get away from that stupid Henry. He fondled a large stash of cash and could see his freedom.

Charlie rushed into the bathroom and dumped toiletries into a small carrying case. With a final glance around the house, he scooped up a suitcase and a filing unit. He ran out to the car and shoved his belongings into the trunk. He saw it was one o'clock in the morning. In the car's rear view mirror, the house lights shone brightly. Charlie accelerated, tore out of the driveway, and headed away from the town. Two miles down the road he passed a state trooper car headed north.

Charlie laughed hysterically. "They're headed in the wrong direction!" He drummed his fingers on the steering wheel. He was the one in charge, he thought. That was his point to Booker. He drove around a bend in the road and headed straight into the lights of a blockade.

He screeched to a stop. A trooper came toward the sedan. The window slid down easily when Charlie hit the electric button. "What's happening here?" Charlie asked as a flashlight shone in his face.

"License and registration," the trooper demanded, flicking the flashlight over the backseat of the car.

Charlie knew he had seen the trooper somewhere before. Was it when he first drove northward—was the trooper the man with the woman who had been nearby the abandoned hearse? Charlie wondered. He couldn't figure that he could remember such an insignificant event, particularly during his escape. Charlie rustled through the glove compartment and searched for his registration and insurance information.

"Get out of the car. Hands in the air. Now!" The trooper motioned as the light stalled on the various sized boxes. "Against the car, legs spread! Hey Dan, get over here. This is our man."

"What do you mean your man?" Charlie spun around.

"I said against the car!" The trooper twisted Charlie's elbow back and shoved him against the car. "Now stand still. Legs spread." The other trooper quickly frisked Charlie.

"This guy is clean," he said.

"Clean? That contradicts the search warrants our guys are going after."

"Search warrants?" Charlie whined. He suddenly recognized the extent of the entrapment.

"That's right. You're now under arrest for embezzlement, drug trafficking, and obstruction of a government office," the trooper said.

"Me?" Charlie groaned.

"Well, surprise, it's certainly not me!" the trooper exclaimed and snapped handcuffs on Charlie's wrist.

The trooper read Charlie his right to remain silent. Charlie thought about being reduced to silence, a jail cell and the right to make one phone call. Something mighty big happened, Charlie realized, furious about an evening that began with a town meeting which turned into a major firestorm and concluded with his arrest. A simple twist of destiny? Lightening crackled overhead as rain began to pour down.

Wet and sticky, Charlie knew the arrest was the center point for the closure of the post office. Charlie chuckled and thought of the movement of history. He knew the town had been wrapped around his finger. What would happen when the office, like the train, was gone? he wondered, and realized he couldn't care less.

The troopers forced Charlie into the back seat of the state sedan and drove through the black ink night.

Hauled off to jail, Charlie still could not believe the hand of fate. And to make matters worse Henry was already there! On the disgrace and tragedy of the fall. Charlie was shoved into a jail cell and fell on to a lumpy mattress. The metal door clanged shut.

Chapter 42

P aul sipped his morning coffee at the *STORE GENERAL* and looked over Bert's shoulder at the write up in the local newspaper.

"Hey, look at this," Bert said, pointing a bandaged finger at a full-page spread in the center of the paper. "Here's Carol and me."

Paul stared at the picture of Bert and Carol smiling and happy in front of the old post office. He felt strangely aware of how time and history had twisted in unalterable ways. How were the town's residents expected to understand the circumstances and crimes to which they had fallen prey? "What do you think Henry was up to?" Paul quizzically brushed a hand across his forehead. "There seems to be a gap in the details."

"Ah, who knows about Henry," Bert sighed. "That Ewing's been a nut from day one. Here, you can read the news yourself."

Paul reached over and grabbed the paper. "Whoa!" Paul pointed to a line in the paper. "Look! You missed this. It says the police have been investigating what they're calling a sting operation for the past four months." Paul sat on a log and sipped coffee. "It looks like they were probing into the post office and maybe figured there was a connection to Washington."

"There's lot of stuff unanswered here," Bert said. "And all that money spent and now we're without the office."

Through the window Paul saw a police car slide into a parking spot. Two state troopers entered the store.

"Hey, if it ain't Hank Stevens and Randy Stone," Bert called and stood and shook their hands. "We ain't seen you in a while. You guys missed all the action last night."

"Yeah, but we're here today," the first one said as his angular face relaxed into a quick smile."

"Last time you guys were here the young ones had been destroying our beachfront with parties and driving over private property," Bert yelled. "But even with that bit of destruction the town was in better shape," Bert said.

"Could be," Trooper Stone responded as he shifted uncomfortably in a uniform that appeared too tight around his wide girth.

"Well, of course it was better." Bert laughed heartily. "A piece of far-fetched heaven then. Here, meet our newest arrival, Paul Wilson," Bert motioned. "He lives in old Jim's cabin up the road."

"Good morning," Paul said. "But I'm not really the newest arrival. I was here before Charlie DeWitt."

In the background Otto squawked repeatedly, "Crime scene. Crime scene. Get the gangster."

"Which is probably the reason you guys are here today?" Bert asked. He turned toward the bird's cage and said, "Shssh, Otto, we have important talking to do."

Paul watched Trooper Stevens' reaction to Bert's exchange with the bird and felt more at ease when the man smiled. "You're very close," Stevens said. "You still got that damn bird?"

"Of course," Bert said, "gotta keep an eye on our occupants."

"Anyway," Stone said, "getting back to our visit. We need to hear from people in the community about what they think happened here. What have your impressions been of Mr. DeWitt's service and performance in your town?"

"Well," Bert said and grinned, "we nominated Paul as our spokesperson, so you'll have to listen to his telling of the story."

"That's fine."

Paul shed his earlier indecisiveness and shyness and began to retell the story of Charlie's arrival in town: the quick addition of the modular; the lights and traffic through the office from the likes of Henry Ewing; Bertha's mention of the continual meetings with Mr. Hoofer from the Down Fall Road. Paul talked about how late in the evening the lights would blaze from inside the office. "We never thought too much of his coming and goings. It was more of what he said and how he acted toward us. Nice, smiley and pleasant one minute, telling us that usage in the office was doubled, and then when he thought we weren't listening, snarley and negative." Paul stared at the troopers. "Charlie had a tendency to mutter to himself. Sometimes I would stand outside the office when I know he thought I was gone. He would sort mail and mutter about the stupidity of the town, the limitations of the people, and his failure in having to recommend this as a location to people in Washington." Paul looked directly at the men. "I don't know, this is really an intuition, but it was always my sense that he thought he had to get out of Washington for some reason or other. I don't know if it was a conflict with a superior or something he was doing. Then after last night, I had a strong feeling. Is Charlie DeWitt a man on the run?" Paul questioned.

"Your observations are very helpful," Trooper Stevens commented. "We're in the process of starting to investigate a long list of charges. DeWitt is now in jail."

"What are the charges?" Edith interjected as she walked through the doorway and blinked to adjust to the dark room. "Oh, I'm sorry," she squealed, "I didn't know Bert had company. I didn't mean to interrupt."

"It's okay Edith," Bert said. "You know these troopers—Hank Stevens and Randy Stone. Remember when they came out to talk to us when you and Mario had that car drive through your garden at two in the morning a couple of years back?"

"Oh, that's right," Edith said. She quickly shook hands with the two men.

"You said something about charges," Paul said, trying to continue the conversation.

"That's right. I was saying," Trooper Stevens spoke quickly, "the charges are lengthy: embezzlement, misuse of government property, fraud and drug trafficking through the mail."

"Whoa!" Paul, Bert and Edith exclaimed simultaneously.

"What have you got for evidence?" Paul asked.

"The F.B.I has been closing in on him for over four months based on leaks of higher ups in Washington. People busted on smaller drug charges released vital information. A lot of people were pointing fingers in this direction. Last night was all we needed. Troopers who were here after the fire said your neighbor, what his name? Henry Owon?"

"No, Henry Ewing," Bert said.

"Yeah, well, he was the one who tipped everything off."

"That's right?" Paul questioned. "He was the one who kept talking about some box or another."

"As you know," Stone continued, "we had him hauled into jail for harassment and abuse. Anyway, the firemen found Henry's so-called family heirloom last night and handed it over. Stock full of cocaine. Before last night we had threads of evidence and now we're secure."

"All right here in this town?" Paul said excitedly. "This is too much!"

"This town is in center news right now. You're going to see reporters crawl around here. I'll bet you can expect television too. So a word of caution," Randy Stone said, "be prepared."

Paul looked at Bert and Edith and saw their surprised, questioning looks. Wow! What a scandel. He couldn't figure out his own feelings about what happened. Crime was supposed to happen somewhere else, not in his new town.

Paul thought about how easily he adapted to not locking his door. He always shut it regardless of how hot it was outside. One bear experience was enough, he thought; he didn't need any stray animals breaking through the screen. But what about being in town with some common criminals? He thought of the circumstances he had encountered: a bear attack, followed by school and a permanent life in the north woods, and now rural crime. Was something expected of him? he wondered as the troopers left. The phone rang.

"Whoa!" Bert waved a hand in a stop signal and held the receiver. "You have a lot of questions there young lady. Hold just one minute and I'll give you our town's spokesperson. Paul Wilson is here and he's the first to have heard about the office closure and was the main organizer of the town meeting last night." Bert shook his head. "That's right. I've lived here my whole life and was quite dismayed with this turn of events. None of us are protected anymore. Here's Paul."

Paul took the receiver, thinking how he had been in town less than a year and here was a life-long resident making him the spokesperson. With no time to question Bert, Paul quickly responded to the reporter.

"The meeting was an attempt to review our options prior to the scheduled closing of the office in three weeks. The fact that there are arrests means we are without the office immediately." Paul listened patiently to the reporter's comments and responded. "Of course we have lost something. A scandal of drug trafficking in our home community is real bad, but it's also the changing face of rural America that concerns all of us. Many things will be lost: the flag waving above the office, the postmark from a vacation hideaway, the ability for vacationers to accept general delivery, and most importantly our connection to a larger world." Paul sensed that he was picking up speed and spoke quickly. "The saddest thing is that last night proved we are not insulated from larger problems in the cities. I'm not sure what they'll find in the court case now: drugs, connections to Canada, people who were involved in the operation..." He paused for a breath.

"Were drugs involved at the community level?" the reporter asked.

"Are you asking if there were any direct drug sales to our community?" Paul looked intently at the ceiling and held the receiver. He was concerned with the question. "You have to realize that we never thought there was drug trafficking when our postmaster, Charlie DeWitt, was arrested last night." Did he sound defensive? he wondered, hesitating.

"You know?" he continued talking, "up to that point we were only struggling with questions about why our office had to close in three weeks." Bert handed Paul a mug of coffee as Paul concluded, "Why, thank you. We'll look forward to seeing your story."

After he replaced the phone, Paul smiled at Bert. "That was interesting. I don't think I've ever had the chance to talk to a news reporter before."

"That's good," Bert laughed. "It's important now that you're connected to us."

"Connected?" Paul asked.

"Yes sirree! You're our man now." Bert excitedly shook Paul's hand. "You speak for us."

The morning passed quickly as Paul stayed with Bert in the store and talked with townspeople amazed with the previous night's events. Paul fielded questions from the various media staff who called throughout the day.

In late afternoon, there was a loud commotion outside.

"This is it!" Bert exclaimed. "We're all going to be movie stars. You go first, Paul. The television people are here!" Bert pointed outside to the camera people who descended on the town. "Incredible!" Bert said, shaking his head. "Could you imagine the level of interest in this story? Paul, let's go say hello to those two young reporters." Paul followed Bert outside.

"This is the biggest thing to happen and you're the one to go on camera and speak about it." Bert grinned wickedly.

"Uh," Paul stalled, "are you sure Bert? You've been this town's spokesperson for years."

"I told you before, Paul, you're in need of these connections. So now we're going to reinforce them for you throughout our area and wherever this station broadcasts. Be happy! You'll be our media star." Bert gestured toward the reporter. "Plus you're a lot better looking than me."

"Sure, Bert," Paul said uncomfortably. "Listen, I'll talk about all of us."

"That's fine. I knew you would," Bert said. Paul stood still as a reporter approached followed by a cameramen. "Remember," Bert whispered, "don't be nervous and you'll do good by us."

"Good morning, I'm Michael Keene here with Joe Palumbo from WALL Television." Paul watched as a dark haired man with a tight smile introduced himself. "I'd like to talk with people about last night's events while Joe gets some shots for us."

"That's great," Bert spoke quickly. "I'm Bert Gendron and this here is Paul Wilson." Bert shook hands and gestured toward Paul. "He speaks for all of us."

"Good morning," Paul said. He stepped forward and quickly shook hands with the strangers, feeling he had been typecast in a role that didn't totally fit.

"Well, like I said, we're going to ask some questions and put together some video of the town," the reporter said. "Everything will be edited for tomorrow's show."

Paul quickly calmed his initial nervousness and anxiety. He wondered should he look at the camera or the reporter asking questions? Soon surprised at how natural it felt to be interviewed, Paul talked easily about moving northward. He narrated the recent chain of events: the posted notice which announced the closure; the organization of the meeting; the night of the meeting combined with the accident; the sudden realization that the town had been a hub of crime.

"A little sleepy hamlet, almost on the edge of civilization, and now a simple twist of events that propels these people to center stage," the reporter commented.

"Edge of civilization is a little strong," Paul responded quickly as he watched the reporter's lips furl back to display little shark-like teeth. "The people here, many of whom have lived in this town for generations, have worked for decades to forest these woods and live in balance with the extremes of the seasons. And years ago, during the height of tuberculosis, before antibiotics, they provided care for the sick from around the world."

"So?" The reporter grimaced. "A town directly affected by forces outside of itself?"

"That's right," Paul said. "None of us knew there was any crime taking place. The thought was beyond our comprehension. We were interested in why was the post office closing. Why was Washington intent on abandoning our rural community?"

"Maybe with the evidence from last night it wasn't so much the federal post office that dictated the closure, but your current postmaster?" the reporter asked, pleased with his conclusion.

"We have no idea about what levels of government are involved in this type of cover-up. Maybe that isn't for us to know, but for investigators to discover. What we do know is that the office moved out of the *STORE GENERAL* less than a year ago." Paul pointed to a corner of the building that housed the old office. "Here you can even look at the room."

Paul led the reporter up the stairs and to the right of the entrance into a small room that had operated as the post office for over fifty years. "Why did this place close?" the newsman asked, pushing a cobweb away from his face. He reached up, swiped at his skin and looked disgusted.

"You okay?" Paul asked, amused with the reporter's reaction to the old office.

"Yeah."

"Well, uh, Bert Gendron had been the postmaster and got fed up with all the paperwork and requirements. So rather than staying on as an institution he decided to contact Washington about a transfer of duties to a government worker."

"And what happened after the request?" the reporter inquired.

"Well, I was new to the town when everything changed hands. In fact I even helped Bert pack everything up. Bert always mentioned how surprised he was with the speed of the government's response. Within two months we had the new office. They found a site and when Charlie arrived he quickly decided to move the old mobile home out and get a new modular. Must of cost tons with all the excavation, foundation work and new modular. You know where that is right?"

"Yeah." The reporter pointed down the road. "In that direction?"

"That's it," Paul said.

"We'll head down there for some shots. You say that modular was brought in new?"

"That's right." Paul smiled

"And taxpayers paid for it?" the reporter commented, as the cameramen wrapped up the various cords.

"We don't know," Paul said.

"We're going to walk down there now. Thanks for your comments." The two men walked away from the center of town.

"You sure you won't be needing anything else from us?" Bert called.

"Not for now."

"Real friendly type, huh Paul? How did you like those little beady eyes digesting our circumstances?"

Paul shrugged his shoulders. "What can I say?"

"You did your best. He talked with you for over twenty minutes and it'll all be reduced to about two seconds of coverage."

"You're kidding me!"

"It's true, Paul, but you looked great!" Edith smiled. "Look, they're getting a close up of the International Airport."

"Wow!" Bert said. "Just think of the potential for new signs! Town on the edge of civilization fights the future of corruption! Be a part—join our civil force."

"Yeah," Paul laughed. "We can become a patrol for our community."

"No, you be the Neighborhood Watch. I'm getting too old for all this commotion," Bert said.

"That's right," Edith said, tugging at Paul's flannel shirt sleeve. "This town's future is with the young."

Chapter 43

⊢⊷⊶⊙⊷⊶⊣

Paul munched on peanuts that Carol had passed around the room. He intently watched the television screen.

"A town in transition, caught in the changes of a century that has rapidly seen corruption within the highest levels of government office, and now, most recently, within the smallest communities where the thought of drug trafficking, embezzlement, and government corruption is alien to the people." The twelve o'clock news blasted over the television. The camera panned the center of town and rested at the American flag which floated above the *STORE GENERAL*.

Bert yelled, "Hey look at our flag! This is that second reporter that talked with Paul."

The old post office was contrasted against a shot of the new office. Paul felt lightheaded with anticipation when he saw the camera stop at the modular. "This is the sight of what has come to be recognized as one of the biggest crimes to hit this sleepy hamlet," the newsman gestured toward the building and spoke rapidly. "People in the town are surprised by the new postmaster, Charlie DeWitt, who moved here to take over the office less than a year ago. Mr. DeWitt was arrested, along with another town resident, Henry Ewing, this past Thursday evening. It has been a surprising turn of events that began with a town meeting to discuss the closure of the office, and ended with a truck accident, a firestorm and arrests before the night was over. Local comments are varied."

The camera moved to Paul, as Bert and Carol cheered. "There's our hero!"

Paul fidgeted and scrutinized his appearance—yee gods—hair out of place; afternoon stubble, did he really look like that? Paul looked at the words on his t-shirt. Did he really wear that shirt? The words *I THINK I CAN—I THINK I CAN* were highlighted over a picture of a cog train creeping up Mt. Washington in New Hampshire. But look at that—direct eye contact with the reporter. And clear responses to the reporter's questions. Not too bad, Paul thought and he shifted nervously on the couch.

"You live in town?" the reporter questioned.

"Yes, I moved here about a year ago from downstate to go to school and decided to stay. There's something about this town that got inside of me and gave me hope."

"Is that hope still alive in spite of last night's events?"

"Even more so. Our vulnerability demands our courage and certainty. We've come together as a town now."

"Good luck," the reporter concluded. The camera moved back to the old post office attached to the *STORE GENERAL.*

"You did great Paul," Bert said, as an advertisement for deodorant came on the television. "You were one man in control." Carol, Mario and Ethel teetered in agreement.

"Well, thanks for the opportunity to speak for all of you!" Paul gloated. "You were right about the two seconds though. I was edited down to a sound bite!" Paul grinned happily. He unfurled from the couch and stood upright.

"Yeah, your moment in the sun," Bert said. "There's still that other reporter, though. The one with the tight lips."

"Did we miss seeing that coverage?" Paul inquired. "That's the guy who implied we're lost on the edge of civilization."

"Yeah, was he ever wrong!" Bert said. "When this many people are involved in any one thing—in a right way, that is—there's no way they can be lost."

"You said that well, dear," Carol said. "And Paul, you've helped us a lot."

"Thanks, but you've also helped me."

Carol sighed, "We're all in this together. You know, Paul," she said, "I don't think I could've talked on television. I would've stood there stone dead with no words coming out. I would've been a stone fixture." Carol turned toward the window and exclaimed, "Look, there are more cars. Maybe they're reporters."

"Does this attention end?" Paul laughed, and followed Bert and Mario outside. A rusted station wagon stopped in front of the *STORE GENERAL.* Oh no! he thought, and watched as a woman with teased hair scrambled out of the back seat with a small suitcase. Paul squinted as she leaned into the car's window. It can't be! The woman stood upright and flailed her skinny arms.

"That's impossible. What kind of place is this anyway?" she carried on. "Thirteen miles and you're charging twenty dollars? Why didn't you tell me that before I got into this rusted heap?" She gestured wildly, thrust her hand into a purse, and threw a bill at the driver.

The blond, heavyset driver stuck in a Buddha trance smiled broadly, mouthed "Thank you," and drove slowly away.

"It can't be," Paul mumbled and walked toward the center of town. Francine patted her hair, took out a small pocket mirror and began to apply lipstick.

"Francine?" He waved despondently. "Is that you?"

She looked up with pinched lips newly stained with red lipstick. "Of course it's me," she said.

"Well, what are you doing up here?" The "you" was short and blunt. "I, uh, I had no idea," Paul stammered.

"Well, I had no idea I'd see you on my news last night acting like some savior for this town," Francine exclaimed. "I decided to come see for my-self."

"Last night?" Paul questioned, and he realized that one of the reporters he spoke to the day before must have been from his home area.

"It appears you've really helped out," she said smugly.

"If you know the story, it certainly has been an interesting couple of days." Paul shrugged nervously. "How did you get up here?"

"I took the bus. And then waited in town for an hour for the taxi."

"You should've called," Paul said. Talk about feeling trapped!

"I did but you weren't home," Francine whimpered.

Paul shifted uncomfortably as he tried to adjust to the sight of Francine and his new experience of being the town's spokesperson. "Uh, can I help you with your things?"

"That would be wonderful." Francine smiled bitingly.

"Are you planning on staying at my house?" Paul knew he sounded less than enthused.

"Sure, if I'm invited."

After a moment of hesitation, Paul said, "Sure. How long are you here for?"

"That's open ended."

Paul groaned inwardly as he tried to fully digest the sight of Francine. He tried desperately to ignore his memories of what they once had and deal with the fact that they had nothing in common anymore. "Wait a minute, Francine," he said, drawing on reserves of confidence and strength. "I'm a little surprised you came."

"Well, Paul I've come to be interested in the A-di-roan-diacks through you."

"Like I've said many times before, it's Adirondacks. Can't you get the pronunciation right?"

"Okay. A-ron-diacks." She shrugged as a deer fly descended on her head.

"Listen," Paul said, "I'm a little uncomfortable with all of this. You arrived uninvited. We haven't even had one decent conversation in the last four months. Every time we talk you ask about when I'm moving south-ward again." He let himself feel angry, and he looked hard at Francine. "You know what?" He hesitated momentarily. "You know? I'm not leaving here. I'm not." He kicked his heel into the dust. His face felt warm.

"But, Paul!" Francine whined. "I'm here because I'm so interested in what's been happening."

"Francine!" Paul exclaimed. "I'm not too sure that you've ever been interested in anything that happens to me." This time he wasn't going to give in. "You've only been interested in what happens to you. I've been peripheral to you. And you know what? I get the feeling you're here now, uninvited, planning to stay at my house, all with the intent purpose of getting me downstate."

Francine began to cry and he wanted to quickly end the conversation. "Listen, Francine. Think about it. This has been coming for a long time. Maybe being in home territory makes it easier for me to do this so quickly. We're finished. We've been finished for a long time."

"You mean, right here? Right in the middle of the road?" she questioned. "The middle of the town?" Francine sobbed and gulped air. A swarm of black flies buzzed around her head and she swatted hopelessly at them. "These bugs are miserable," she wailed.

Paul felt a pang of guilt. "My life is here now," he said defensively, and then realized there was nothing to be afraid of. "There's no better place," he said with certainty and began to gather Francine's belongings. "Listen, I'll drive you back. You can check on a bus out and stay at a motel if the bus doesn't leave until tomorrow."

"But!" Francine stuttered.

"Okay, let's go." Paul looked back at Bert's house. "Hang on a second." He ran toward the house. "Bert, I'm heading into town for a bit to take Francine back to the bus station. She arrived unexpectantly and is leaving a bit unexpectantly." Paul hesitated and realized he was really getting into the changes taking place in his life.

"You okay with all this?" Bert picked at a toothpick that hung from the corner of his mouth.

"I'm great!" Paul said excitedly. "I made a decision!" He spoke with relief.

"Well, well. A decision! Now that's something to speak of." Bert flicked the toothpick on the ground. "You mind if I tell Carol?" Bert laughed softly.

"Come on, Bert! You'll tell her whatever I say. But this is important. Some people could say I'm being ruthless. But unfortunately I've been unable to make decisions about this before, and now that I have, I'm exhilarated."

"Be careful," Bert said. "Francine seems to pull things over on you," he chuckled.

"I'll be fine. See you later today." Paul ran past Francine. He jumped into his truck and drove back to her. She stood waiting with her hands on her hips. Her few tears had dried and except for two raccoon eyes she appeared humbled by his resolve.

Paul threw her belongings into his truck. "We can go now. You ready?"

"Did I have a choice?" Francine asked and climbed into the vehicle.

Paul turned the radio on and heard his voice being broadcast about the fire and arrests in the town. He couldn't imagine any of this had any real affect on Francine. At the close of the broadcast, the weather man said there would be days of above normal temperatures.

They drove for miles in silence. Paul finally turned toward Francine and said quietly, "I'm sorry you came so quickly. It's been increasingly clear for a long time that we weren't meant to work."

"You changed Paul," Francine said, and stared out the window.

"Changed?"

"You're not the same anymore."

"Is that bad Francine? Is it bad to know where I want to live and what I want to do? Or are these changes a problem because they excluded you in the end?"

"I just don't like you anymore," Francine whimpered.

"Is that new? Or is it any different from what you thought you initially liked?" The truck screeched into the parking lot near the bus station. "Here, wait a minute. I'll go check on the bus." Paul hurried into the small gift store that housed the bus station.

"You're in luck. The return bus will be leaving in a little less than an hour. It's the only return today. Come on, I'll help you bring your stuff inside," he said. "You do have a return ticket?"

"Uh, of course," Francine stammered.

"Okay, well I'm going to leave you now." Paul could feel Francine's accusatory anger and knew the best thing was to get away as quickly as possible. "Listen, I'm sorry about all this."

"Yeah, Paul, you've always been sorry," Francine said. She sat down on a plastic chair.

"You take care now." Paul reached out, touched her shoulder lightly with his hand, turned and left the station. There was no response from Francine.

We're on our way, on our way... he chanted methodically and walked toward the truck. The sense of freedom and rightness was intoxicating. Why did it take so long? he questioned. Over a year to end a relationship that was dissatisfying? Paul marveled at how his weakness kept him stuck. But decisiveness permitted change! The feeling of renewal filled him with certainty and happiness.

Paul drove down the road and stopped at a new bakery for some bread. He walked in the direction of the bakery, saw Sarah inside the nearby laundromat window and sidestepped toward her.

"Paul? Is that you?" Sarah asked, as Paul's frame filled the doorway. Sarah squinted in the bright light that poured through the window. "And a hero at that," she said.

Paul saw that her hair was pulled back into a long braid that twisted down the back of her head. She wore a pair of shorts and a t-shirt.

"Hi, Sarah. How are you?" Paul smiled. Suddenly conscious of his clothes, he wondered about his overall appearance.

"Pretty good for a laundry day. One can never expect too much to happen on this kind of day." Sarah laughed and gestured toward a table piled high with old magazines. "But then again, there are a lot of magazines and papers here, so I manage to catch up on everything. Why I can even become up-to-date on events from six years ago! Anyway, I heard all about you and the town," she said.

"You never came back after the meeting to hear about what happened. The arrests and all." Paul felt the intensity of her blue eyes being fixed on him.

"Things got pretty hectic yesterday and I wasn't able to make it back," Sarah said with a guilty expression. She peered at a toddler who ran through the laundromat.

Paul looked at the little boy and smiled. "Your instincts about Charlie were real close to the mark."

In the distance the boy's mother yelled, "Johnny, don't go near that ashtray again."

"Two creeps in a town: Charlie and Henry. Henry was involved too, huh?" Sarah asked, shuddering.

"Sure was," Paul said. "The accident was the final tip-off in the sting operation. Especially with those two yuks yelling about some box that was some family heirloom or something. Turned out the box was filled with cocaine."

"All in Bert's town?"

"Yeah. We've all been surprised. Listen," Paul said with resolve, "I have to get back now. Would you be interested in going hiking with me? You know sometime in the future."

"Hiking?"

"Yeah, I pick you up at your house and we go somewhere to climb a mountain, possibly with a picnic lunch and all."

"A hike?" Sarah asked and laughed. "I know just the mountain. The peak is a rocky summit."

"Great. This Saturday?" Paul asked, hopeful.

"Sounds good." Sarah smiled.

"Okay. I'll pick you up at around ten in the morning. Would that be okay?" Paul questioned.

"See you then, Paul. I'll look forward to it. And thanks!" Sarah exclaimed.

"No, thank you!" Paul said happily and walked into the bakery. Did Sarah sense something was different? She certainly seemed surprised by the offer of a date.

"Two bagels and a loaf of whole wheat bread," Paul ordered. He watched the woman clerk whose red hair was gelled in sharp peaks. She wore a sweatshirt that said *I LIVE TO FISH*.

"Thank you," Paul said, reaching for the bag.

"That will be one eighty."

"Here you go." Paul passed the money to the woman. His hand brushed against the woman's long fingernails painted as miniature flags.

"I like your nails."

"Why thank you," she said. "I figured with Memorial Day coming, it was time to be patriotic."

"Good idea." Paul smiled. "The bread here is really good."

"That's so nice to hear. Thank you."

Paul walked outside toward the truck. The drive back home went quickly on a road that he knew had once been an old stagecoach path. Swept with wonder, he looked at the cathedral of surrounding trees. Within minutes he turned on the main road which led to the center of his town. Paul drove past the *STORE GENERAL* and looked at the *INTERNATIONAL AIRPORT* as if he saw it for the first time. The wind picked up and the little wooden bird flew round and round. He saw the American flag floated high above. Paul quickly saluted Bert, who stood on the porch of the store. He laughed and headed down the dirt road to his cabin.

Chapter 44

▸┄◆┄○┄◆┄◂

T he date with Sarah consumed Paul. He still couldn't believe he was finally going somewhere with her. What luck, he thought, and drove his
truck out of the dirt driveway. The day was perfect, captured in the fresh
leaves that had sprouted on trees.

Surprised by the brilliant cobalt sky, he remembered how the trees appeared in the previous fall.

"I'll bet you'll never see nothing like this," Bert had said, coughing as
he sipped an Old Milwaukee and maneuvered the truck through the fall
woods. "The sugar maple is the most spectacular with its fire-engine, red
glow."

The mountains that then had been covered with bright golds and or-
anges, had slipped into the browns and stark white of winter. All gone now,
Paul thought happily, somewhat dazzled with the new leaves that had
sprouted on trees. Winter was a distant memory, as remote as the break-up
with Francine, the firestorm in the town, and the arrest of Charlie. The full
drama of change made him somewhat uneasy. He drummed his fingers on
the steering wheel and thought about Sarah. He hoped for something new,
something so different from his normal life, something so unique with her
that he could forget himself for one brief moment. Somewhat nervous about
his lack of experience in climbing, he worried that Sarah would notice.

By the time he turned into her driveway, his lips twitched nervously and
he could feel the beginning of an allergy attack. Oh, just great, he thought.
She's probably an experienced climber who has scaled rock walls, and I'm
going to be a sneezing mess. He parked the truck and walked toward the
cabin.

Sarah immediately opened the door. She hugged him quickly, stepped
back and looked at him. "There's the stove," she said, and pointed to the
corner of the room. "It's not burning anymore, but survived the winter
beautifully."

"That's great," Paul said, happy with his ability to impress her. He felt
shy and tried real hard to not twitch his tongue against his bottom lip.

"I've got the water," Sarah said, holding up two plastic bottles.

"And I brought the lunch so we can go."

Paul followed Sarah from the cabin and was somewhat dazed at how
her boots, shorts and t-shirt all seemed to shout that she was an experienced hiker. Her hair was styled in one long braid that hung down her
back. He looked at his hightop sneakers and knew he was in trouble.

Paul drove down a road that followed a river. At a dam site Sarah told
him to turn left.

"That's the mountain," she said, pointing toward a rocky peak which rose out of the surrounding flatland of dry grasses.

He felt eager as he parked the truck. Together they scrambled toward the trailhead and were immediately surrounded by a swarm of blackflies.

"Uh, oh," Sarah said, swatting at her face, "this is the height of bug season. I should've remembered, and I forgot any bug spray."

"We'll do fine," Paul said, and walked behind Sarah through a hardwood forest dominated by sugar maples and yellow birches. Bugs attacked and he wondered if he had spoken too soon and too confidently. Except for the relentless buzzing, he was surprised by the sudden quietness, and followed Sarah up a steep grade. Within minutes he struggled to breathe and could feel his heart racing from the exertion. He was sweaty and his jeans stuck to his skin. The sneakers offered limited support and slipped on the wet, muddy areas of the trail. They ascended into a boreal forest, and the sweet smells of spruce and balsam firs reminded Paul of a Christmas tree yard he visited annually at home.

"You doing okay?" Sarah asked from where she stopped high above, sipping from the water bottle. "This hill isn't too bad? Is it?"

"I'll be okay," Paul gasped, pausing for breath. Within seconds a swarm of bugs descended and began to bite his neck, face and hands. Increasingly annoyed, he tried to take an interest in his surroundings, but found it easier to be angry at the bugs. He couldn't admit to her that his heart felt like it was going to explode. He was frustrated that the bugs seemed to not bother her.

Starting back uphill, he tried to pace himself, but soon realized the ascent offered no respite to restore his strength. His breathing was strained and he felt dizzy. The stench of his body odor dominated and muscles ached. He mentally chanted, this can't be done, this climb can't be done. How much longer? he wondered. Could Sarah see the extent of his struggle? he questioned. He looked in the direction of the summit and saw nothing but trees. Increasingly angry with himself and the mountain, he felt like screaming and desperately hoped Sarah couldn't see his discomfort. If she did, she'd know for sure he was an out-of-shape wimp.

My attitude is bad, he thought and realized he could die on the mountain. He couldn't imagine if Sarah would be upset. With Francine out of the picture, he didn't have her to be concerned about. But who would care? How many others would consider it a waste of taxpayer dollars to have him airlifted off the mountain? He tried to be comforted by the memory of his neighbors. They certainly had been pleased with his ability to take direct action with the post office closure. He too had been pleased, but that joy felt short-lived in comparison to the total alienation that began to consume him as he stood astride the mountain.

Discomfort, fear and bugs nipped away at him as he climbed higher and higher. What did the mountain want from him, and wasn't his sweat and fear enough? He wondered. Where the hell was the top anyway? Paul looked toward the summit and felt panicked by the dense forest.

Paul couldn't figure if his entire life had passed when a view of the rock summit became visible from the trail. He followed Sarah through a grouping of charred trees and saw a ledge of impenetrable granite.

"There was a fire here years back," Sarah said. "These dwarfed trees are the result".

Paul saw blackened and charred pines that appeared gloomy against the backdrop of granite walls. The landscape mirrored his inward entrapment and he felt depressed by the grey darkness.

"That's why this top is so rocky actually. What between cuttings and fires, this mountain was stripped over the last century." Sarah tugged at her braid and pushed wisps of hair behind her ears.

Paul imagined early loggers stripping the mountain of its trees, leaving scarred remnants of their long-ago efforts. He felt somewhat heartened by the comparison of the clearing of the mountain and his own inward stuff, and concluded that maybe he could really complete the ascent.

"You know we're at about thirty-one hundred feet in elevation. Four hundred straight up verticle feet to go. You ready?"

"Sure," Paul spoke thickly and picked a blackfly out of the corner of his eye. Yuk, he thought, realizing he had probably swallowed a few of the bugs.

"The stone piles will be our trail markers from now on. You keep a good eye out for them cause we don't want to lose the path," Sarah cautioned, looking experienced and sweat-free.

Dense shrub, verticle rock and granite slopes bordered the final ascent. Paul trudged behind Sarah, somewhat fixated on how her calf muscles appeared as she climbed higher and higher. He bumped into her when she stopped abruptly in front of a vertical rock ledge.

"Look at this," Sarah said, looking up. "Soft rock erosion. When I was last here this was like a staircase; now its straight up for eight feet." Sarah approached the wall and held her arm up. The wall extended for more than two feet beyond her outstreched hand.

Paul was fearful about his ability to climb and remembered he was never able to climb the rope to the top of the gymnasium in gym class. "Let me try it first," he said, trying to hide his hesitation. Paul ventured forward, grabbed at crevices of the rock that formed handholds and hoisted himself up. At one point, he clung midway from the top, unable to find any ledge from which to push forward. He had the immediate feeling of hanging suspended and vulnerable in space. It's either up or down, he thought. He tried not to think about falling, pulled upward and continued to climb. At the top, his arms tingled and he felt giddy and awake. He had done it.

"This is the worst of it, as long as we don't lose the trail," Sarah said and pulled herself up next to Paul. "Everything about this mountain seems steeper and more angled," Sarah commented. "It certainly seemed rounder years ago." Sarah walked to a rocky ledge, began to move, stopped and said, "Look how the path falls off into those trees. It's too steep. Let's turn around, we lost the trail."

"There's a rockpile," Paul said and followed Sarah in the opposite direction. Within minutes they were at the bottom of a sheer granite wall that was skirted by a narrow trail that brushed against dwarfed brush pine. The trail continued up through a crevice in the wall.

"I'll bet this will be sheer rock years from now," Sarah said. "Here, follow me up this cut in the stone."

Paul climbed behind Sarah, hopeful that the summit was finally near. They passed through a wooded area and entered a clearing. Within two-hundred feet he followed Sarah up another ledge of rock. The last stretch of rock exhausted Paul, but he felt exhilarated and thrilled by the pile of boulders and rock trail. When he finally stood still atop his first Adirondack mountain the bugs descended with a vengeance as he peered at Sarah through a black cloud of bugs. He felt strong and fit.

"We did it," Sarah exclaimed. "Now wasn't it worth it?" she questioned.

"Yeah," Paul said, "seems that the rocky section was the easiest." He flailed his arms and shook his legs in a futile attempt to thwart the bugs.

"Seeing the summit is the lure," Sarah said. "I guess the old adrenalin kicks in, or fierce competition." Sarah laughed. "It's only then that the mountain has beaten any of us up enough. When we finally see the top within reach, something takes over, and zap we're there," she said and smacked her hands together. "Is this your first Adirondack peak?"

"That's a fact," Paul said, still somewhat embarrassed by his climbing performance. His sinuses were congested and he hoped he wouldn't start having a sneezing fit. He began to jog and move back and forth to keep the bugs away.

"Well, you're due a mighty congratulations," Sarah said, leaning over and hugging him. "I started climbing when I first moved here. I've always liked the personal encounter—basically just me and the mountain. And now you," she said suggestively, and she smiled warm-hearted and open. "Would you like some water?"

"Sure," Paul said, taking the water bottle. He sipped the water and wondered if Sarah felt his presence added anything to her mountain experience. "Geez, it's like the mountain takes hold," he said, hesitating to talk about how the climb intensified his confusion, and how he longed for a relationship with her. He thought of himself as being fixated and stuck in a long-standing ability to review alternatives without taking action. He realized his self-defeating thoughts were the true definition of neurosis.

"That's what this mountain is about—a new self," Sarah said, fingering a blue prism of glass that hung off her neck. "Look, that's your town over there." Sarah pointed toward the east. "I like the fact everything looks a little different from this angle. Potato fields over that way. We're mighty close to having all our leaves, but there's still some brown areas."

The wind picked up suddenly and the bugs dispersed as clouds began to move in. Paul was thrilled by an overwhelming sense of peace. He shared a wonderful picnic of crackers, cheese and fruit with Sarah.

"When I first returned to the area," she said, throwing an apple core in the scrub pine, "I used to do a lot of climbing—every weekend. In fact, it got to the point where the minute I stepped into the woods, I would feel relaxed. Like some godliness or relaxation would come over me." Her fingers brushed hair off her face. "That's when I learned about how it feels to have mental chatter gone. It was very meditative."

Paul listened thoughtfully, and wondered what it would be like to not always be talking to himself about some alternative or other. He tried to imagine the state of mind Sarah had experienced, yet was distracted by her closeness and her woodsy smell. He wondered if he could ever find peace within, without trying to find it through someone else, or some thing. A rush of conflicting thoughts consumed him as he tried to remain focused on what Sarah was saying.

"People pay lots of money at retreats and with some guru or another," she said, "and it's all free here." She popped a grape in her mouth and chewed. She stood, brushed crumbs off her shorts, and pulled the elastic from her braid, shaking her hair free. She began to slowly and skillfully thread her long blond hair together in another braid.

Paul stared at her, unable to avert his eyes, and was convinced she was a goddess. His whole body tingled as he watched her hair blow free and then be captured in the braid. He didn't know if he felt love or desire, but knew his emotional landmine felt very different than his early encounters with Francine. Sarah finished with her hair, ran to a grass field, and returned with two stalks of grass.

"Here," she said, handing Paul an offering, "something to chew on."

Paul reached toward her, grabbed the timothy, and stuck it in his mouth. They sat together, thoughtfully chewing on the dried stalks. Paul felt ancient; he felt newborn. He felt different and the same. Together they sat side by side and watched a hawk do skydives in the open sky. Who would've thought, Paul realized, still consumed by the possibilities of him and Sarah being together.

While walking off the mountain, he experienced a sudden feeling of renewal. A calmness came over him and lasted for the briefest of time. He experienced a supersonic sense: footsteps on the trail, bird movement in the bushes, the rustle of leaves. In a flash he saw the obvious—his life was in the present moment of each foot slipping down the steep trail. His calf and hamstring muscles ached from the tension of holding himself upright on the descent.

Within minutes mental chatter rushed forward. He tried to understand what Sarah meant when she portrayed the mountain experience as a teacher and learning exercise. Relentless thought and hopes cluttered Paul's inner landscape. Over and over again he saw his mother, hopeful and unhappy in a marriage that lasted twenty years too long, and his dad, precise and English at their summer home along the Jersey shore; mad about the radish seeds costing too much; mad about the radish rows not being straight enough. Paul sensed that his dad never fully accepted the northward move. He saw his twin brothers and sister, expecting he would fail, and possibly even betting on it. He saw a family competition that rather than being supportive was undermining; Paul saw his own defeat and his potential to win something for himself. He realized he was conditioned to think his life was somewhere else—in some purchase, or trip, or relationship. He longed to see himself in the present moment.

Much as he wanted to be alone and separated from family, he wanted something else: a quiet life, in a small community, with real connections. Bert and Sarah lined up as links to his present life. He tried to picture Francine; could only envision tangled hair, and sensed the severity of their separation. He looked at Sarah and felt an intense longing. Do we ever really know the outcome? he questioned, glancing around. He followed Sarah into an open meadow.

It was in the open field that Sarah turned playfully toward him, grabbed his hand and said, "Look at that fresh grass. Let's go look at it."

Paul paused and saw what appeared to be a green, carpeted area surrounded by wild violets. He followed Sarah and watched as she sat down and gestured for him to sit next to her.

"I just have to feel this against my face," she said lowering her head and twisting to feel the spring grass. "Try it," she suggested, "it's like a feather massage."

Why not? Paul thought and lowered his face. He could just picture how the two of them appeared with their backsides in the air, their arms twisted on the grass, and their faces inches from each other. Paul was at a loss of words as Sarah looked at him, into him and through him. Her hand reached out and touched his forehead and he felt a miraculous clearing of his sinuses. For the first time since he arrived in the north, he could breathe freely.

Seconds ticked by slowly as Paul felt reborn. The dimensions of space and time collided within him as he and Sarah simultaneously collapsed on the grass. Lying on his back next to Sarah, Paul looked at the sketch of sky overhead and felt a new contentment. "This is awfully nice," he said, trying to feel, talk and be in the warmth of her presence.

"Yeah," she whispered, reaching for his hand.

Paul moved their entwined hands close to his face. He looked at Sarah and felt an overwhelming sensation. He leaned down and kissed her for a brief moment. His brain cells exploded from the taste of her skin. He pulled back and peered at her. They both began to laugh nervously. He reached down, wrapped her in his arms and kissed her with the hope that the kiss would last an eternity. Green moss tickled at his arms and face. He saw her clearly for the first time in his home, in his town.